MW01516635

Detective Jackson Mysteries

The Sex Club

Secrets to Die For

Thrilled to Death

Passions of the Dead

Dying for Justice

Liars, Cheaters & Thieves

Rules of Crime

Crimes of Memory

Deadly Bonds

Agent Dallas Thrillers

The Trigger

The Target

Standalone Thrillers

The Baby Thief

The Gauntlet Assassin

The Lethal Effect

THE TRIGGER

Cover art by Gwen Thomsen Rhoads
Copyedit by Jodie Renner

ISBN (ebook): 978-0-9840086-4-3
ISBN (print): 978-0-9840086-5-0
Published in the USA by Spellbinder Press

The Trigger

An Agent Dallas Thriller
By L.J. Sellers

This book is dedicated to my editor, Jodie Renner, who helped the story reach a new level of excitement.

Chapter 1

Saturday, April 27, 1:30 p.m.
Agent Jamie Dallas charged across the opening and dove behind a barricade. A shot flew over her head as she lunged, missing her by an inch, and landed with a thunk in the wall behind her. *Damn!* That was close! Heart hammering, she crawled to the end of the short wooden structure. The bastard was close now, firing nonstop. But where the hell was he? She peeked around the edge, hoping to spot him in the dim light. Another shot nearly hit her cheek, and the whistling noise made her heart skip a beat.

But now she had his location. He was in the burned-out church, shooting from a high window to her left. How to lure him out into the open? Playing dead might work. Dallas pulled in a deep breath and tried to feel calm, but adrenaline made her heart ring in her ears. She counted to sixty, the wait nearly unbearable. The faint sound of footsteps on stairs signaled that her ploy had worked. He was coming to her. Another twenty seconds passed while he stood in the doorway, assessing the situation. Or so she assumed. From her squat behind the barricade, she couldn't see him, only feel his presence.

It was time. Dallas ripped off her mask with one hand and

shoved it into the air. As the mask drew fire, she lurched out from behind the wall, blasting at the figure in the doorway with her other hand. She nailed the assailant with three shots in row.

"I'm hit," he called out, sounding squeaky and disappointed.

Dallas pumped her arm in the air, grinning. She crossed the dirt-and-straw floor and shook Nick's hand. He was only fourteen, but he was a paintball champ and she'd beaten him and his companions three games in a row.

"That was sneaky," he complained.

"I know, but it's survival." She glanced at his sweet young face and paint-splattered clothes and felt a pang of guilt. It wasn't fair to take her frustrations out on the kids. "Good game." She offered him a high five, set her long hair loose, and headed for the front counter. She felt the boys watching her as she walked. Even at twice their age, she was still young and fit enough to garner their attention.

But paintball—and occasional skydiving—on weekends wasn't enough to satisfy her need for excitement. She'd been cooped up in the Phoenix FBI office with white-collar crime for a couple of months and it was making her crazy. Her last undercover assignment had sent her to Oregon, where she'd infiltrated an eco-terrorist group and prevented a bombing. That was the kind of work she was meant to do. If she didn't land another field assignment soon, she might have to take a black-ops freelance gig just to stay sane.

Dallas paid her account and stepped outside. Time to move on.

Chapter 2

Wednesday, May 1, 3:30 p.m.

"What the hell are you doing?" Randall Clayton stared at his wife across the bedroom. A stuffed suitcase sat on the carpet, and Emma tossed more clothes into an overnight bag on the bed.

"My mother's sick, and I'm going to stay with her for a while." His wife turned and glared. "We talked about this."

"And I said no." Randall crossed his arms, still blocking the doorway. *The timing couldn't be worse!* He had a flash of hatred for her mother. "The meltdown could happen any moment! What if we have to blow the bridge and you can't get back to Destiny?"

Emma rolled her eyes, distorting her pretty face. "You've been predicting it for ten years, including the five I've been here. Nothing's going to happen while I'm gone."

"You don't know that! The financial system is on the brink of collapse, and an asteroid hit the Earth just last week. And they expect more." Randall strode forward, grabbed her arm, and forced her to look at him. "I know your mother. She'll guilt-trip you into staying for a long time. She never liked me."

Emma jerked free. "Her heart is failing, and I'm going. Get out of my way."

Her anger excited him, as it always did. But even if they had crazy-rage sex like they often did, it wouldn't change anything. Randall fought to control himself. "You're not taking Tate." Their four-month-old baby watched from a car seat on the floor.

"You know I am."

Damn! The birth of their son had changed Emma, made her more defiant. Randall's heart hammered in full panic. He couldn't let this happen! They were so close to being ready, and Emma knew too much to let her go. But how to stop her? A dark thought crossed his mind. Could he get rid of her for the greater good? Randall hated the idea. There had to be another way.

Spencer would help him. His older brother had been there through all of his troubles, and they'd built this community together, starting with their side-by-side houses. Randall strode from the room. As soon as he was outside, he broke into a run, knocked once on Spencer's door, then barged in.

He found him sitting by Lisa's bed, as usual. His brother's wife had been dying of cancer for years, and she seemed down to her last few days.

"I think it's time." Randall tried to sound calm and reasoned.

"What do you mean?" Spencer kissed his wife's gaunt face and stood. Lisa appeared to be sleeping.

Randall explained briefly about Emma's mother, then added. "What if she takes a long time to die, like Lisa has?"

His brother cringed, but Randall knew he understood. They needed wives to produce the next generation.

"Do you want me to talk to her?" Spencer headed for the living room.

"It's too late," Randall said, following him. "Emma's packing and planning to take Tate. We have to stop her, and there's only one way."

Spencer spun around, eyes wide. "What are you saying?"

Randall worked up his courage. "It's time to quit waiting and make the meltdown happen."

Spencer paused, blinking rapidly. Finally, he said, "We're not ready. We haven't sold the business yet, and the generator isn't performing as well as it should. Most important, I don't have a new wife."

Randall reached for his brother's shoulder, the way Spencer had always done with him. "We can delay the trigger for a few weeks, but we need to deal with Emma tonight before she leaves." For a decade, they'd been stockpiling everything they would need, waiting for a social collapse or earth-changing storm that hadn't happened yet. It was time to take charge.

"Are we sure we want to do this?" Spencer asked, his voice trembling a little.

"What choice do we have?" Randall filled with passion for their cause. "Global climate change is out of control. You know that if we don't shut down the major polluters and vehicle emissions now, the planet will become uninhabitable and our species will die. Everything we've talked about over the years is still true—only worse than ever."

Spencer's face grew pale and his eyes troubled. "It will be chaos out there, and eventually millions of people will die."

"They're going to die anyway." Randall didn't let himself think about it. "This way will be faster and less painful. Like euthanasia for a diseased society."

Spencer nodded. "The waiting is getting to all of us. We can't afford to lose anyone else from the community, and we can't live in limbo forever."

Randall's nerves jangled with excitement and dread. This was the moment. He and his brother stood at the edge of a bottomless cliff, about to step off, hoping the hang glider they'd built themselves took them down safely.

"What about Emma?" Spencer asked.

Randall was ready. "I think I have a plan."

Chapter 3

Monday, May 6, 8:47 a.m.

Dallas entered the Phoenix bureau, pulled on her business jacket to survive the air conditioning, and headed for her office. Before she sat down, her desk phone rang—an internal call. She snatched it up, hoping like hell it would be an interesting assignment. Another day at the desk might break her. "Agent Dallas."

"It's Gossimer. I need to talk to you about an undercover assignment."

Hallelujah! Dallas hustled down the hall to the corner office and didn't bother knocking. "Good morning, sir." She sat, e-tablet in hand, and grinned. "What's the assignment?"

"Don't look so happy." Special Agent Gossimer, a handsome man in his early sixties, had a crease in his brow. "This one would put you in a rural area in Northern California with a group of people preparing for the end of civilization."

"Preppers, huh?" Dallas was intrigued. The movement had been gaining steam in recent years. "What's the bureau's interest?"

"The community is led by two brothers, Spencer and Randall Clayton. Randall's wife, Emma Clayton, disappeared last Wednesday, along with their four-month-old son. She left on the evening of May first to go see her sick mother in San

Francisco, but never arrived. Her mother called Emma's father to see if he'd heard from her. Luke Caldwell contacted the bureau because he's convinced Randall is holding his daughter somewhere on the Claytons' property."

"Why can't local agents get a warrant and go in?"

Gossimer took off his glasses and rubbed his eyes. His voice had a note of weariness. "Witnesses saw Emma drive away. More important, Randall voluntarily let an FBI agent search his home. But they're survivalists, and the brothers own fifty acres with barns, greenhouses, and storage sheds, so she could be anywhere."

A dark thought crossed Dallas' mind. "Emma and the baby could be dead."

"Maybe. But her father doesn't think so. He says they're preparing for end times and they need young women and children."

Dallas had a flash of apprehension. "My assignment would be to infiltrate the group by joining? Then try to locate the missing woman?"

"Yes." Gossimer met her eyes. He didn't have to spell out the risks.

"Let me guess. They're heavily armed too."

"Of course." Her boss glanced at the file on his desk. "They've been buying weapons, mostly handguns and hunting rifles, since they bought the property in early 2002."

"Any history of violence?" Not that it mattered. Dallas knew she would take the assignment.

"None. That's the good news. The brothers are college educated and had successful careers before they built the community, which they call Destiny. If I thought they were trigger-happy nutjobs who were plotting something, I wouldn't send you in alone. We just want to locate Emma

Clayton."

"Why me?" Dallas thought she knew.

"You did an excellent job of infiltrating the eco-terrorists in Oregon. So when the request for a young female undercover agent was posted late Friday, I knew you were right for it."

Dallas couldn't help but smile. Her instincts had put her in the right place at the right time on that case. "Thanks. Anything else I should know?"

Gossimer grinned back. "To sweeten the deal, you look a bit like Spencer Clayton's dying wife."

Creepy. But it could work. "So I target the older brother."

"That's the strategy, for now." Her boss leaned back. "But you don't have to take the assignment. An agent in the 'Frisco bureau wants the case, but the field man in Redding thinks she's too old."

"You know I'm in." Just the thought of getting on a plane made Dallas' body hum. "What's my cover story?"

"I think you need to have money in your background. A trust-fund gal who works when she wants to as a social media consultant."

"I like it. Who are my clients? Small companies and artistic individuals?"

"Exactly. One of our tech people is putting up a website, and we'll have business cards for you by the time your ID is ready."

"What inspired me to fly out to California and join the Destiny community? The recent shootings in my hometown? Fear of the national debt and financial collapse?"

"The latter. More important, your fiancé recently died. Spencer will sympathize with that."

"Who's my local contact?"

"Agent Caleb McCullen." Her boss pushed a thick stack of paper at her. "Here's the background information on the Clayton brothers and the community. But I'll send you PDFs if you prefer."

"Thanks for the assignment. I was going a little stir-crazy." Dallas picked up the paperwork, knowing she'd read it on her e-tablet. "How long do you think I'll be gone?"

"That depends on how quickly you can get close to Spencer and be invited to join. You should plan for a month or two, but I expect you'll work faster than that. You always do."

This could turn out to be her longest—and most challenging—undercover job yet. "It'll take a few days to wrap up some personal business here."

"Sorry, but we need you on a plane tomorrow. Agent McCullen thinks Emma's father might do something stupid if we don't move on this immediately. The undercover unit will have your new paperwork ready and shipped to you shortly, but you'll need to visit the DMV today."

She already had a name picked out. "I want to be Sonja Olivia Barnes."

"SOB?" Gossimer laughed, but it was a hollow sound.

After answering emails and changing her voicemail message, Dallas left the bureau. Her main priority was to pack her clothing, but even before that, she had to take a box of personal items to FedEx. She kept a collection of photos, books, and emergency duct tape in a box that went with her on every out-of-town assignment. The knick-knacks made her temporary place look lived-in and personal if someone dropped by. The Redding office had sent the address of a long-stay motel where they'd booked her a suite. With any luck, she'd move out to the Destiny community within a week.

In the meantime, she had to notify her condo manager, call her friend Stacie, and say good-bye to her current boyfriend. She and Trevor had been dating about five weeks, and she suspected he would be more upset about the breakup than she was. Trevor had a good sense of humor and was an energetic lover—her top priorities—but she'd quit looking for a long-term relationship. Her specialty as an undercover agent kept her moving around, and sometimes her assignments took months.

Dallas drove to her condo on the edge of Scottsdale, pleased by the sight of Camelback Mountain, which wasn't really a mountain at all. But in a city that stretched forever into the desert, the view of the hill made her happy, even though it wasn't anything like the mountains around Flagstaff where she'd grown up.

Dallas called Stacie while she prepared the box for shipping. Her friend owned a beauty shop, and Dallas would get two things off her list at the same time. Stacie picked up after five rings. "I'm with a client, Jamie. Can I call you back in ten?" Stacie was one of the only people who still called her Jamie, but they'd known each other since high school.

"I'm leaving town on assignment tomorrow, and I need a cut and color."

"Can you come right now? I'll take an early lunch and squeeze you in."

"Of course. Thanks for making time for me."

"How long will you be gone this round?"

"Maybe several months."

"Crap. Do you have time for dinner?"

"Sorry, I have an early flight."

"See you in a few."

Dallas took another look at the photo of Lisa Clayton. Spencer's wife had shoulder-length hair that, in a bottle, might be called light amber brown. Mrs. Clayton also had more natural curl than Dallas did, so she considered getting a perm too. Dallas slipped the photo into her shoulder bag, hoping it wasn't a breach of protocol to show it to Stacie, one of the few people who also knew she worked for the FBI. Dallas had never told her parents, but they'd never been particularly involved with her life, and now that she was an adult, that was fine with her.

Her Aunt Lynn knew, because Dallas stayed in touch with her. Aunt Lynn had given her the only normal, happy parts of her childhood. Whenever her parents' drinking, fighting, and instability had spiraled out of control, she would call her aunt or grandmother, then pack her overnight bag and wait for one of them to pick her up. Often her parents would leave her with a cranky uncle while they partied, and later, as a teenager, she'd done a lot of sleepovers with friends. Her whole childhood had been spent on the move and now she couldn't stop. Packing to go somewhere gave her a rush, a sense that things were about to get significantly better. On top of that, becoming another person for a while was the ultimate high.

On the way downtown, Dallas picked up two prepaid phones. Her personal cell would go with her so she would have all her contact information, but she would keep it hidden and unused most of the time. Her FBI work phone would also stay out of sight when she wasn't using it to contact her UC team. In the car, she keyed her new ID into one of the burner phones. The second prepaid was just for backup. Dallas made a quick stop at the bank for cash, most of which would be stashed in hidden compartments. Her monthly bills were paid automatically, so she had no worries about finances while she was on assignment.

Stacie's Glamourama, a name Dallas hated, was in a strip mall off Indian School Road. She pulled in and parked in the last available space. She would miss her RAV4 while she was gone, but at least this time her background ID was that of a wealthy person, so the bureau would have to lease her something decent, unlike the time her cover had required her to drive an old piece-of-crap Volkswagen bug.

Stacie was with a client, so Dallas sat and read more about Spencer and Randall Clayton. Before he was thirty, Randall had been elected mayor of Santa Carmichael, a small mid-California city, then had run for Congress and lost. He and his brother had started building the community outside of Redding two years later. The 9/11 attacks had happened in between, and that could have been the driving influence. Dallas also wondered if the political defeat had undermined the younger brother's confidence and sent him into hiding.

After a few minutes, Stacie called her over, gave her a fleshy, perfumed hug, then stroked Dallas' long blond hair. "I can't believe you want to cut this off. Most women would kill for your hair."

"It'll be a nice break from the maintenance." Dallas took a seat in the beauty chair, feeling a flutter of apprehension. She'd been thinking about making the change for a while, but it would still be an adjustment. "I get more respect when I go brunette, and I think less hair will have the same effect. So what the hell."

Stacie, who changed her hair color every month, laughed. "With your cheekbones and luminescent blue eyes, you'd still be gorgeous if you shaved your head." Her friend grabbed a plastic drape and tied it around Dallas' neck. "How short and what color?"

She pulled out the picture of Lisa Clayton. "Like this."

Stacie's eyes widened. "She looks like you, only older. Are you going to impersonate her?"

"No. And if I was, I couldn't tell you. Let's do this. I still have a lot of packing."

While Stacie cut and colored her hair, they talked about the recent mass shooting in Glendale, and Dallas hoped her friend wouldn't ask if her new assignment was dangerous. She didn't. They both knew Dallas would lie anyway.

When her hair was finally blow-dried, Dallas decided she liked it. Not as sexy but more trustworthy. Stacie made a whistling noise. "Very nice. Trevor will be quite surprised."

"Thanks. I love it." Dallas stood and reached for her purse.

Stacie shook her head. "You *are* going to see Trevor and tell him you're leaving, right?"

"I thought I would text him."

Her friend rolled her eyes. "You're ending it?"

"I have to. I'll be gone for at least a month, probably more, and we're not that serious."

"Whatever." Stacie knew better than to argue. They'd had this conversation before. She hugged her tightly. "Be safe."

Dallas stopped at the Motor Vehicle Division, bypassed the long line, and went straight back to the FBI liaison. She'd been through the process a few times, so twenty minutes later she had a new driver's license issued to Sonja Barnes.

When she returned to Phoenix, she would trade it in and get her original back. Time to head home and pack.

The process was both an art and a science, and Dallas had perfected it. While she carefully crammed her life into two large suitcases and a carry-on bag, she called the property manager of her condo complex, then composed a text to Trevor in her head. When she was packed, she keyed in: *I'm leaving town for a month or so and won't be able to contact you. I can't expect you to wait, so feel free to start dating someone new. It's been fun. JD*

She hoped Trevor would take it well.

Feeling logistically ready, Dallas reached for her laptop, prepared to make contact. She opened the Clayton brothers' blog/website, called Uncertain Future. It covered subjects from how to grow vegetables in the winter to how to put on a gas mask in case of sarin poisoning. Dallas read Spencer's latest post about buying gold and silver and keeping it in a safe at home as a protection against the coming economic collapse when bank accounts and credit cards would be worthless. After registering as Sonja Barnes, she left a comment about how she'd been using her trust fund to buy gold for years and was pleased to find likeminded thinking on the subject. She perused a few more posts, then found the link labeled Destiny. She started to scoff at the name again, then caught herself. It was time to become Sonja, a pampered young woman who didn't trust the future...and was looking for a more natural life.

The website was a work of art: uncluttered, bold fonts, clear subcategories, and compelling photos. Its creator was an experienced designer, and she wondered about the tech level of the community, and the brothers in particular. Dallas clicked another link called *Joining Destiny*. The page outlined the process, which involved filling out an application, writing an essay, and meeting with the founders. The essay part irritated her, so she filled out the application first, referring to the background dossier the bureau had sent her.

A section near the top asked her to list her skills, and Dallas realized they might be critical to admission. To survive after the apocalypse, the community would need a diverse group of people with high-demand expertise. After ten years, Dallas assumed they'd found the basics such as doctors and scientists, so she listed marksmanship, outdoor survival, herbal knowledge, and multilingual. Most of it was true, and she could learn enough about herbs to fake that part. She spoke Spanish and could read and write simple French. Speaking the damn language was not something she'd ever mastered. She was slowly learning Arabic too, with the idea that she might someday work for the CIA.

Halfway through writing the essay, her doorbell rang. Dallas hurried to answer it, thinking it was an FBI courier with her new paperwork. She checked the peephole. Trevor stood there, looking blond, handsome, and worried. *Shit.* Dallas pressed the intercom to tell him she was busy, then changed her mind and let him in. He was a sweet man and— what the hell?—she could use some breakup sex.

"Whoa." Trevor stared at her hair.

Dallas' reflexively reached for it and regretted letting him see her new look. "That's why I texted instead of meeting you to say good-bye. I didn't think you'd like it."

He pulled her in and held her tightly. "I don't care about your hair. I care about you. Where are you going and why?"

"I can't tell you."

"Is this about your government job?"

"Yes." She'd been vague, as usual, knowing the relationship wouldn't last. "I'm sorry, but it has to be this way." Dallas wondered if she'd ever have a long-term partner she could confide in.

"You're going undercover, aren't you? Is it dangerous?"

"I can't talk about it."

"When will you be back?" Brow crinkled, eyes misty, Trevor had never looked sexier.

"Maybe a month or so. But we can't contact each other, so let's just say it's over."

"No." Trevor grabbed her shoulders and kissed her deeply. "I think I love you, and you'd better call me the minute you get back."

Love? Stunned, Dallas pulled away, no longer aroused. Even after years of therapy, she still had a central issue: She enjoyed sex with strangers and with men she'd dated briefly. But as soon as she felt emotionally connected, the sex lost its zing and the relationship fizzled. Apparently that applied if men felt overly attached too.

"We barely know each other and you have to go." She pushed him toward the door. "Find someone else. You deserve a good relationship."

Trevor tried to kiss her again, but she turned away.

"I'm not letting you go." He stood near the door and locked eyes with her, but Dallas waved him off.

He finally left, but instead of feeling relieved, Dallas felt lonely. She'd miss him and their art gallery visits, breakfasts at Chorios, and Jason Statham movie nights. She shook it off and went back to her laptop, where she clicked open a photo of the Clayton brothers. Spencer was in his early forties, lean and attractive with wide-spaced brown eyes, a classic nose, and perfect teeth. His brother, Randall, looked much like him, but was shorter and thinner-faced, with lighter hair. Something about the younger man's smile seemed off, then Dallas remembered he'd been a politician.

Around nine, a courier arrived with her packet of new ID. Dallas set her alarm and took a sleeping pill. When she woke in the morning, Sonja Barnes would take a cab to the airport and start a new life.

Chapter 4

Monday, May 6, 9:34 a.m.

Spencer Clayton called the hacker he'd hired over the weekend, but the young man didn't answer. Greg Rafferty, who liked to be called Raff, had arrived late the night before, but Spencer didn't care. He'd sent him a ten thousand dollar advance to get him here and would pay him an additional ten grand when he completed the job. Spencer had tried and failed to breech Morgan Bank's security, so he'd gone into the IRCs—the 90s chat rooms where hackers still hung out—and asked around for the best gray-hat hacker he could recruit. Rafferty had been recommended by several people and had contacted him within six hours.

After a Google chat session, they'd finally spoken on the phone, with Raff calling him from a blocked number. With the promise of cash, Spencer had persuaded the hacker to come to Destiny and help "test the banking system." Raff's *gray-hat* status made Spencer a little nervous. White-hat hackers were the good guys, supposedly, who tried to keep the malicious attacks launched by the black hats from doing severe damage. Gray hats swung both ways, but they typically liked to test companies' security by launching a benign assault, then telling the management how they'd taken advantage of their vulnerabilities. Raff was known for finding and testing security weaknesses and seemed perfect for the job. Spencer wouldn't tell him what he really had in mind until the last moment, then Raff would have a choice to either stay in Destiny or take his chances out in the crashing world.

Feeling wound up, Spencer pulled on running shoes, checked the temperature, and changed into a tank top. On his way out, he stopped in Lisa's room. His wife was sleeping, her breath labored. She'd become so gaunt he hardly recognized her, and the high doses of morphine would soon kill her if the cancer didn't. He'd been watching her die for so long, he'd learned to be in the room and not cry. But knowing she was only days away now made his heart ache. Still, her passing would be a relief—for both of them.

Outside, the morning sun warmed the wet grass, and the smell of spring blossoms filled the air. Spencer jogged around the community, as he did every morning, just for the pleasure of seeing his creation. Seventeen homes, a new four-unit apartment complex, a community center that also served as a school and library, and a small medical clinic made up Destiny's core at the end of Clayton Lane, a private drive off Bear Mountain Road. The residences were at the edge of the property and all that could be seen from the main road. Beyond the homes lay the fields and storage lockers that would sustain the members in the future.

A car started and he waved at Marissa, their nurse, as she headed into town for a part-time shift at a clinic. About half the members still had jobs in nearby Redding, about twenty-three miles away. Others made money online or had telecommuter jobs. He'd been lucky and had earned a small fortune as a software engineer, investing it wisely. In 2002, after the earlier attack on America, he and Randall had purchased the fifty acres together and built homes with help from local contractors. Over time, they'd invited others to join them, and the community had grown. They also owned a restaurant/bar in Redding—which would become worthless after the meltdown—and they earned a steady income from a website business that sold survival kits and prepper gear. He didn't like the term *prepper* and thought of himself and his members as futurists. Everyone in Destiny accepted that current environmental and financial practices were not sustainable and would eventually crumble, but only he and Randall knew of their plan to trigger the reset.

After circling the housing area, Spencer jogged down a dirt road that cut through their property and led toward Honey Creek. The waterway curved around their acreage and had to be crossed a few miles outside of Destiny. That bridge provided the only public access to the community. The dirt road he jogged on had a well-hidden entry on the back side of the property. Spencer passed greenhouses, barns, giant gasoline tanks, and storage buildings. The previous owner had cleared the land long ago for farming, but the back half gave way to a gentle uphill slope dotted with oak, fir, and madrone trees. Beyond the acreage were miles and miles of forested land, and the dirt road he ran along eventually connected to Old Oregon Trail Road. Both routes to the property crossed waterways, and they had contingency plans to blow the bridges after the collapse—if they had to keep marauders from taking their supplies.

At the three-mile point, Spencer turned and headed home. His thoughts drifted toward Emma. Now that the FBI had questioned everyone about her disappearance—and hopefully moved on—he was acting quickly to implement their plans. He'd been a law-abiding software engineer for most of his life, and all of this was out of his comfort zone.

After his run, Spencer fed Lisa chocolate pudding and hung a fresh IV. She tried to tell him something, but he couldn't understand. The morphine made her incoherent sometimes, but without it, her pain was excruciating. The cancer had started in her liver, but after a round of radiation it had metastasized to her spine and lungs. A doctor had encouraged Lisa to enter a clinical trial in San Diego, but his wife had decided to stay in Destiny and die in her own bed. They both regretted that they'd ignored the pain in her side for too long, but neither had ever considered cancer until the radiologist said the word *biopsy*.

Another regret overwhelmed him, and Spencer didn't have the will to push it away. If only he'd gone to medical school like he'd wanted to. He should have borrowed the money and ignored his parents. He could have become a researcher and found a cure for cancer. Instead, he'd studied computer science and spent his career creating technology that would destroy the social fabric. He couldn't go back and change that, so he was doing everything he could to correct it.

Lisa drifted off, so Spencer left the house and hurried down the long cul-de-sac to the apartment complex near the gate. He pounded on the door of unit one, knowing Raff was likely still asleep. "It's Spencer. I want to get started."

He could have called Raff —he had intermittent cell phone service—or sent an email through their satellite internet, but the only landline was in the community center and Spencer chose to live without electronic devices as much as possible. In the future they were preparing for, those luxuries might disappear, and in Destiny, they had little use for them.

After a long wait, Raff came to the door. Pudgy, with shoulder-length hair and an ugly black neck tattoo, the hacker looked older than his twenty-three years.

"What's the deal? It's not even ten yet." Raff glanced off to the side, not making eye contact.

Spencer had to step back from his lethal morning breath. "I thought I explained that I wanted to get this project done in the next few days. I need you to work 'round the clock until we've breeched Morgan Bank."

"You never mentioned working 24/7."

"I described it as an intensive short-term job. Get dressed and come over." Spencer noticed the defiant look on his face. "Please."

"I don't want to work that hard. That's why I'm a hacker."

"I'll give you a five-thousand-dollar bonus if you get everything done before Friday." Money was always a great motivator. Spencer pointed back at his house. "The data center room is the green door on the side."

"I'll be there in a few minutes." The hacker closed the door in his face.

Spencer resisted the urge to push it open and remind Raff who owned the apartment and paid his salary. For now, he needed the kid's talent, but he hoped the hacker would leave after he'd accomplished his mission. Raff was the first person to stay in the community who had not come out of concern for the future, and Spencer hated the thought of him stuck there after the collapse.

He headed back to his own home, a ranch-style house bright with natural daylight, and entered the tech room. A few years ago, he'd built the addition, which could be accessed from the outside by others. The computers and hard drives didn't take up much space, but this was where he, Randall, and their engineer brainstormed ideas, so the room also held a small fridge, a table and comfortable chairs. Spencer made a pot of coffee, opened the file list on his external hard drive, and savored his collection. Millions of email addresses, bank account numbers, and other personal data. He'd never used, let alone abused, any of it.

Yet.

He'd been collecting the data since his job at CyberSecure. The first batch had come from a security breech at an investment bank, and he'd accessed it inadvertently while trying to patch the flaw in their system. Once he'd realized he could download and keep the account information, the temptation had been overwhelming. It was never about money. He had plenty and wasn't a thief. But the potential power of all that data had been intoxicating, and he'd downloaded it to a portable hard drive and taken it home. For years, Spencer hadn't told anyone, but possessing the data had given him such pleasure—and peace of mind— that it had changed him. Everyday anxiety and job pressure had become inconsequential. He'd stopped working so hard and had started studying medicine on his own. He'd become a better husband and had finally agreed to have a child, but they hadn't been blessed with one.

And he'd collected more data. The second batch came from a breech in one of the early social networking sites. A hacker had accessed the data and offered it for sale. In the tech world, everyone knew someone who knew the most active hackers, and word got around. Spencer had bought the list anonymously, for a cheap ten bucks a profile, knowing the hacker had probably sold the profiles many times over. After that, he began his own campaign of hacking into customer databases and downloading information. The financial account data was harder to break open, but worth the effort. Only in the last year had he decided what to do with the millions of files, and Randall was the only person he'd discussed it with. Still, Spencer hadn't been able to penetrate any major banks, and without at least one, he worried his main plan wouldn't work.

A few minutes later, Raff moseyed into the computer room. All he had done was change out of his pajama bottoms into a pair of jeans. "Where's the coffee?" he grumbled.

Spencer suppressed his irritation with the man's lack of social skills. "On the counter. Help yourself."

"What's the rush on this project?" Raff found an oversize mug and filled it.

"Congress' failure to raise the debt limit puts the economy in jeopardy. We need to send out warning tests before things get ugly."

Raff plopped down in front of a giant monitor. "Aren't you worried we'll trigger a run on the banks?"

That was, in fact, the plan. "It could be the jolt the banking world needs."

After the financial meltdown started, Raff would fully understand what he'd participated in. But by then it would be too late to stop it, and Spencer suspected the hacker wouldn't care. Not at first anyway. Once the financial institutions collapsed, taking everything down with them, Raff would no longer have anything interesting or challenging to hack into. They would all have to adjust to the new world, and in the long run, they'd be better off.

"Are you gonna tell me what you're really doing?" The hacker looked alert for the first time.

"It's simple. We're sending a wakeup call to the banking

institutions so they'll tighten their security." Spencer couldn't help but add, "More important, world governments need to realize they can't run on credit. We need to get back to the gold standard."

For a long moment, Raff just stared. It was obvious he didn't believe Spencer's motives. Finally, the hacker said, "Tell me your plan again."

Relieved, Spencer outlined the basics. "We use social engineering to access the log-in information and password for a key employee in each major bank. Then we find a fraud alert the bank has sent out, copy it, and embed our virus." He took a sip of coffee, suddenly worried that his plan would sound amateurish to someone like Raff. "We send the warning email with the virus to millions of customers. When they access their bank accounts to check their balances, the virus uploads to their account and starts manipulating it. Millions of customers panic and withdraw their money." Spencer also planned to scare millions of other recipients in his database with an email that looked like it came from the FDIC, the Federal Deposit Insurance Corporation. And that was just phase one.

Raff nodded. "It's simple and devious, and in theory, it could work. But the reason no one has done it yet is because banks have the best security in the world."

"Have you tried hacking any?"

Raff shrugged. "I've taken a shot at it, but banks aren't my main interest."

"I want you to access Morgan Bank. If it works there, we'll do the other main financial centers." Morgan was international, the biggest bank in the world, and it had pissed him off one too many times.

"First we have to take control of zombie computers in

another country and do everything from those desktops so nothing can be traced here."

"Of course. How can I help?"

"You can write chunks of code for the account balance manipulation once I get the patterns worked out."

"All right." Spencer hated writing code, which was why he'd hired Raff, but he wanted to make this happen fast—before he got cold feet and changed his mind. "Thanks for getting on this." Spencer finished his coffee and stood to leave. "I have to go see our engineer, but I'll be back soon."

"Bring me some pizza." Raff winked and clicked on a monitor.

Spencer found Grace in the community center. He'd never seen her in anything but camouflage pants, but she seemed to have an endless collection of bright T-shirts. Today's was hot pink. He stood near the door and watched her teach a small group of students about electricity. Only twelve kids lived in Destiny, but three were too young for school, and two others attended high school in Redding. Their mother worked in town and drove them in every day. The rest were all home-schooled by Tina Blackwell, a thirty-something certified teacher, but all the members did their part by instructing in specific subjects.

After a few minutes, Grace gave the kids a hands-on assignment, turned them back over to Tina, and walked toward him. The engineer moved with muscular smoothness. A striking, mocha-toned woman of forty, she had served two tours in Iraq, was an electrical and mechanical genius, and had deadly combat skills. Spencer admired everything about her. He wished they had sexual chemistry. Grace would have been a terrific partner, but she seemed content to be single.

While she'd served in the Middle East, her husband had left her and moved with their son to Texas. Coming home had been a nightmare for her. After two years of medicated, zombie-like days and terror-filled nights, Grace had joined Destiny and soon found peace in their community.

At the moment, she looked a little worried. "This must be important."

"It is. I'm sorry to interrupt your class."

Spencer stepped outside and Grace followed. The bright May sun heated the air, and he moved toward the shade of a tree. Keeping his voice low, he said, "We need the generator at full capacity as soon as possible." He'd wanted to get her going on it days ago, but he'd thought it best to wait until Emma's disappearance wasn't at the top of everyone's mind.

"Has something happened?"

"Not specifically. But yesterday, a power grid in Indiana went down, and scientists are tracking another asteroid that could hit the Earth next week." So far, everything he'd said was true—reinforcing his belief that he was doing the right thing. The next part would be a variation of the truth. "More important, cyber rumors are flying about Morgan Bank being hit by hackers. If one of the major banks has a run on cash withdrawals at the same time an asteroid does damage, people are going to panic. It's time to get ready to be on our own."

"I'm still having trouble with the lithium batteries overheating." Her eyes sparked, and he could tell she was already thinking ahead. She'd built the generator at the edge of the creek, which supplied the energy. They also had smaller gas-powered units attached to every home, but the gasoline supply was finite, so the micro-hydro generator was essential for the long term.

He grabbed one of Grace's hands. "I need you to find a solution. It doesn't have to be perfect. It just has to be fast."

"Give me a deadline and I'll make it happen."

"Friday."

Chapter 5

Tuesday, May 7, 9:45 a.m.

Randall Clayton rounded the curve where Emma's car had gone off the road and nearly hit the sheriff's cruiser parked along the edge. *Shit!* They'd found it—despite the steep drop-off and camouflage. He and Spencer had covered it with shrubs and dirt, hoping to buy time, but it hadn't been enough.

Slowing, Randall glanced over like anyone would and kept driving. A second, empty sheriff's patrol car sat on a nearby turnout. Randall expected the FBI would soon be at the scene as well. Would they question him again? He didn't want the distraction, but the last interrogation had challenged and invigorated him in a way he hadn't experienced since he'd left politics.

Ten minutes later, he pulled into the community and spotted a dark sedan near his house. McCullen sat behind the wheel, facing him. Randall had no choice but to park and acknowledge his presence. The agent was out of the car and standing in the driveway by the time Randall shut off his engine. The man moved like a running back and was built like one too. McCullen's height and rugged good looks intimidated Randall, who'd always felt more effeminate than he cared for. His own face was too narrow and too pretty.

Women liked it, but men often thought he was gay. Taking testosterone for a year had only made him more short-tempered. And now, knowing that jerk McCullen had dated Emma first enraged him.

Randall climbed from his car and glanced over to see if Spencer was coming out to back him up. The house had no movement.

"I have more questions." McCullen's face was impassive. "Let's go inside."

That meant the agent intended it to be a long session. Randall didn't have time "We can talk here."

McCullen hesitated for a long moment. Randall assumed the agent was considering taking him into the Redding FBI office.

"Have you heard from your wife?" McCullen asked.

"No, why? Have *you*?"

McCullen scowled and squared his shoulders. "We found her car this morning."

"Where? Is she okay?" Randall expressed the correct amount of alarm, then realized he had to take it farther. "Is that why I saw the officers on the road near the curve?"

"Her car went off the embankment and landed in some shrubs at the bottom."

Randall brought his hands to his face. "Emma? Is she all right? And the baby?"

"They weren't in the car." McCullen's eyes narrowed. "But I think you knew that. Where are they?"

Randall slumped back against his truck, the picture of concern. "Stop accusing me and tell me what you know. This is my family!"

"Her luggage is still in the car, but her purse is gone. And if she had a diaper bag with her, it's gone too."

"She must have gotten out after the wreck and climbed up to the road." Randall allowed himself to look hopeful. "Maybe someone gave her and Tate a ride. Maybe she's in a hospital somewhere."

McCullen cocked his head. "You said you called hospitals."

"Of course I did. I'm just trying not to think the worst."

"What was the last thing she said to you when she left?"

Randall blinked, thinking fast. "She said, 'I love you. I'll miss you.' Why do you ask?"

McCullen jotted something in a small notebook, then looked up. "Emma's mother says your relationship was volatile and that Emma planned to stay with her for a while. She thinks Emma was leaving you."

"Typical mother-in-law bullshit." *The bitch!* "Nadine has heart disease, or so she told us, and asked Emma to come take care of her. I told you that. Emma didn't want to go, but she thought she had to." Close enough to the truth.

"Did you fight about her leaving?"

"We discussed it."

"Your neighbor described it as an argument."

The bitch! Grace had never warmed to Randall, but he expected Destiny members to support each other. "I didn't want my wife to leave. Can you blame me? But I understood that she had to." Randall forced himself to think about his father's funeral, hoping to produce mist in his eyes. "I love my wife and I'm worried sick. Please stop harassing me and go find her."

"Who is Timothy Gains?"

Randall was taken aback. "I have no idea. Why?"

"Emma called him the afternoon she disappeared."

What the...? "How do you know that?"

"We have her phone records. She texted Gains the day before too. They planned to meet in San Francisco."

Rage, fear, and confusion collided in Randall's chest. Had Emma been cheating on him? *No!* The agent was trying to provoke him. Randall forced himself to shrug and be casual. "I'm sure he's an old friend. Emma grew up in 'Frisco." Randall leaned toward the agent. "Have you asked Mr. Gains if he's seen Emma? Are you doing your job? Because this, right now, is a waste of time."

McCullen stepped toward him, and their faces were only a foot apart. "I will find Emma and bring to justice the bastard who made her disappear."

Randall ignored the threat. No one would ever locate his wife. "Good. Go do it." He walked away.

Inside his house, he resisted the urge to watch out the window and make sure the agent drove away. He heard the sedan leave and felt his shoulders relax. Moments later he thought about Timothy Gains, and his tension returned. Randall hurried to his computer and googled him. He found several men with that name in SF, but none seemed connected to Emma. He remembered he had her phone and hurried to the safe in their bedroom closet. Along with ten thousand in cash, he kept two gold bars, the deeds to their properties, and now his wife's cell phone. He was about to turn it on to read her texts and emails but hesitated. The feds would quickly pinpoint the phone's location and know he had it.

Why had he kept it? It was better not to think about what he'd done to his wife.

He closed the safe and forced himself to put Emma out of his mind. He still had too many arrangements to make before they set everything in motion. Another trigger of his own was in development, and he had to connect with his non-local followers to finalize their plans. He hadn't messaged them recently because he thought the FBI was watching him and monitoring his email and phone. This morning he'd gone into town and bought a prepaid cell phone with cash, so he could make calls without worry. He and his followers needed to be able to communicate instantly when it was time.

Randall changed into grubby clothes and headed for the locker where they kept the explosives they would use on the bridges. He needed to reassure himself that they were ready. One thought kept playing in his mind. *How long would the collapse take?* That was a question they'd never had a good answer for. Randall didn't trust Spencer's financial and power-station cyber assaults to be destructive enough, so he was planning a supplemental *physical* attack on communication centers, such as internet hubs and tech companies in Silicon Valley. Keeping the plan from his brother had been stressful. Spencer was the one person he rarely lied to, and Randall wished he could tell him, but he worried that his brother would freak out and try to stop him. Spencer thought a financial collapse would be enough to cripple the industries that were doing the most environmental damage. But Randall wanted to ensure a global reset, so his followers around the world were on board and waiting for final instructions.

He glanced out his bedroom window at the fields and storage buildings and wondered if it would be enough. Or would they run out of everything in five years and end up living like squatters and cavemen? Sometimes the alternate future scared him, but the idea of a fresh start always drew him back. He wanted to live in a society where he was a leader, a man sought for his knowledge and guidance. Where his political failures were long forgotten and the future always looked brighter than the present.

As he left the house, he spotted Grace crossing her backyard. They had no fences, not around their yards or around the community. Openness was a key philosophy. He jogged over and said hello as she entered her workshop crammed with tools and electrical components.

"Hey, Randall." Grace turned and their eyes met on the same level. She was bigger and stronger and it bothered him. He had also failed to charm her like he did most other women.

"Was that the FBI again?" she asked.

"Yes. They found Emma's car near the junction. It went off the road, but Emma and Tate weren't in it." He managed a sad, concerned look.

"That means she's probably alive. Maybe she's in a hospital somewhere with amnesia."

"I keep telling myself she'll turn up." Randall was glad for the opportunity to confront her. "Why did you tell Agent McCullen that Emma and I argued?"

Grace flinched. "I didn't say you'd argued. I said I could tell by the conversation that you didn't want her to leave."

"I didn't! But now she's missing, and the FBI is treating me like a suspect. I could use your support." His tone was harsh and he didn't care. This was serious shit.

"I'm doing the best I can."

For a moment, they stared at each other in silence.

Randall suppressed his anger and asked, "What are you working on today?"

"The lithium batteries for the main generator. Spencer wants it running at full capacity by Friday." Worry flashed in her eyes.

"He's concerned about hackers forcing a run on Morgan Bank. The value of the euro has been falling for months, so we think the financial crack is coming soon."

Grace gave him a tight smile. "We'll be ready."

"Damn right we will."

Chapter 6

Tuesday, May 7, 7:30 p.m.

Dallas spotted McCullen near the baggage claim. Even if she had never seen his photo, she would have known he was a federal agent. Dark gray suit, short hair, stiff posture, like someone expecting the worst. They all had that stance, and she'd had to unlearn it for undercover work. McCullen saw her, and they nodded to each other across the nearly empty terminal. The Redding airport would have fit inside a small shopping mall, and most of the passengers on the flight had not stopped to pick up luggage. Dallas braced herself for a tedious stay in a rural community. As long as she had the internet, she'd survive.

A couple of strides and he was there, holding out his hand. "Caleb McCullen."

"Jamie Dallas. But call me Dallas." Out of occupational habit, she noted his details: Six-three, two hundred and thirty pounds or so, dark blue eyes, and a square boyish face with prematurely gray hair at the temples. She noted his shoulders were broad, his torso was lean, and his thighs were as thick as utility poles. A football player turned cyclist, she guessed.

"Good to have you here." He turned to the luggage carousel. "I'll bet you have a few bags."

"Just two." Dallas smiled. "I mailed boxes as well." She

was eager to talk about the assignment but not in public. "Thanks for picking me up. I could have taken a taxi."

"No problem. A trip to the airport is not a big deal in Redding." He grinned. "Plus, I have the key to your new place."

Dallas couldn't help but wonder if he had a family at home. Most likely. The Redding office only had three agents, and they probably got bored, unlike the high-pressure bureaus where agents' spouses walked away after years of neglect.

McCullen made small talk about the weather and local points of interest while they gathered her luggage and headed to his vehicle. As they drove out of the parking lot, he updated her. "We found Emma Clayton's car this morning where it went off an embankment about ten miles from the compound. There was luggage in the back seat, but no purse and no diaper bag."

Dallas had almost forgotten about the baby. "How old is the child?"

"Four months."

The thought of someone kidnapping or killing an infant enraged her. What kind of people would she be dealing with? "I hope they're both still alive."

"Emma's father, Luke Caldwell, is convinced that Emma and Tate are being held on the Destiny property. He thinks his daughter planned to leave Randall and their little utopia, and Randall refused to accept it. One of the community members admitted that Emma and Randall argued before she took off." McCullen got up to speed on the main road as he talked.

In the twilight, Dallas caught her first glimpses of the tree-studded landscape. Green, but not as lush as Oregon. She wanted to see the vehicle Emma had been driving, but she couldn't do that and keep her cover. "How much damage to the car? Was it traveling fast when it went off the road?"

"We think another car slammed into her Nissan and knocked it down the slope."

"Maybe Randall rear-ended her."

McCullen's jaw clenched. "Witnesses saw Emma leave, and they claim Randall was at home afterward."

"But they could be protecting him. Is the group like a cult? Do they view the Clayton brothers as revered leaders?"

"Good question. I've been looking at their backgrounds, and most are educated professionals. And there's no religious component." McCullen signaled to exit. "We'll be at your motel soon and can finish the update tomorrow. You must be tired."

"Not really." Dallas was enjoying his company, and once she made contact with Spencer Clayton, she'd have to stay away from McCullen. "Let's unload my stuff and get a drink while you tell me everything. I want to hit the ground running tomorrow."

He seemed surprised. "I suppose we could."

"Do you need to get home to your family?"

He laughed. "I've got a big dog that gets lonely if I'm gone too long, but McGoo will survive."

No wife. She couldn't help but grin. "McCullen and McGoo?"

"I know, it's corny. But it wasn't my idea."

A familiar longing fluttered in her torso. She loved big cute guys who loved big cuddly dogs. *No*, she told herself. *He's an agent.* "We won't keep McGoo waiting long. I just need to unwind and get up to speed."

"Sounds good. I know just the place."

Dallas had second thoughts. "We can't be seen together in town."

"You're right. Let's pick up some beer or wine, and we'll confer at your place."

Even better. "It's a plan."

McCullen bought a six-pack of Pliny the Elder and a can of cashews at a local market, and they drove to the Shasta View Motel, which catered to outdoor enthusiasts who came to the area to ski or hike. Dallas knew the mountain was out there in the dark somewhere, but she wouldn't have time to enjoy it, unless she hung around for a while after finding the missing woman. But that wasn't her style.

McCullen insisted on carrying her bags, then handed her the key. "Welcome to your temporary home."

"Everything is temporary." Not wanting to seem jaded, she gave him a charming smile.

The motel suite had a large living area, a little kitchenette, and a separate bedroom. The furniture was tacky, but Dallas didn't care. If things went according to plan, she wouldn't spend many nights here. They left her luggage near the door, settled on the couch with their beers, and Dallas clicked on her tablet to take notes. "What else did you find at the scene of the accident?"

"We scraped a paint sample from the damage in the back of the car, and we'll have it analyzed." He rubbed his chin. "I also got a call from the sheriff this afternoon, and he says there are tire marks at a turnout near the accident, as if a car sat there for a while."

"You think someone waited there, flagged Emma to pull over, abducted her and the baby, then ran her car off the road?"

McCullen looked sheepish. "Sounds a little far-fetched

hearing it out loud."

"But it's possible." Dallas visualized the scenario. "He would have had to render her unconscious with a drug or chloroform, then put her and the baby in his car while he disposed of hers."

"Several witnesses saw Randall at home after Emma left, so we think his brother might have done the dirty work. And they might have had help from another member."

"But if Spencer rammed her car, his would be damaged too."

"It's not. I didn't see any damaged vehicles in Destiny."

Dallas thought about how she would have pulled it off. "Did you check Emma's gas tank?"

"Not yet. Why?"

"Maybe they drained her gas tank and waited for her to run out of fuel. Then Spencer picked her up to give her a ride and drugged her instead."

McCullen looked intrigued. "And the car?"

"They left it for someone else to smash into."

"Interesting. I'll check the tank first thing in the morning."

"Wouldn't it have been easier to kill her?" Dallas speculated. "What makes Emma's father think she's alive?"

"He says Randall is a hot head and a control freak but maybe not a killer. A doomsday nut who really believes a cataclysmic event is imminent."

Dallas laughed. "Like what? The North Koreans nuking us? Another asteroid hitting the earth?" There had been two in the last year, and scientists were tracking a third.

"Luke Caldwell says last Christmas when she visited him, Emma talked about global storms coming. The kind that could wipe out most of the population."

"So the group is preparing to survive an ice-age type

thing?"

McCullen gave her a tiny wink. "I guess that's your job to find out."

Dallas' email icon on her new account beeped. "Hey, someone just contacted Sonja." She grinned. "That's me." Dallas clicked open the message. "It's from Spencer Clayton." She scanned the text: *Hey Sonja. I love your enthusiasm. When are you thinking of visiting Destiny? Sooner is better. We've got a lot going on later this month.*

Dallas turned the tablet to McCullen so he could read it. When he finished, he nodded. "You work fast."

"I started posting comments on his prepper blog right after I got the assignment. Spencer commented back and asked me to email him, so I did." Dallas turned the tablet and clicked reply. She talked as she keyed in a response. "I set up a Facebook page too and sent him the link so he could see my picture."

"That's all it would take. You *are* gorgeous." McCullen blushed a little.

Nice. He was as attracted to her as she was to him. "Thanks, but my understanding is that I look like Spencer's dying wife."

"That could also be effective."

"I just told him I was here in Redding and would love to see the community."

"Wow. I thought it might take weeks for you to get inside."

"It still might." Dallas finished her beer and got up to fetch two more. She was still wound up from a day of building her background and making connections. Undercover work was like plugging into an exotic energy source. She handed McCullen a beer and sat a little closer to him on the couch. A subtle mix of scents wafted off him: wood smoke, Ivory soap, and dog hair. Oddly intoxicating. No agent in Phoenix ever smelled like that.

"Spencer mentioned having a lot going on later this month," McCullen noted. "I wonder what that's about."

"I'll find out."

While they drank their second round, Dallas asked about his life in Redding and what it was like at a small rural bureau.

McCullen laughed. "It's nothing like your work. Our biggest case lately was a drug-smuggling operation involving a tourist-guide service for hikers at Mount Shasta. We do a lot of community outreach just to keep busy."

"Who's in charge?"

"My boss, Special Agent Ezra Gibson. He was out of the office when the San Francisco bureau called and asked for our help. I think he's a little irritated that I caught the case and will be your contact person."

"I'm glad it's you." Dallas patted his leg, regretted it, and reached for the tablet. "Let's see if Spencer responded."

The email came in as she tapped the icon: *You're already here? That was strangely fast.*

"Shit. He sounds suspicious." Dallas keyed in a response: *I was packed and ready to go stay with my sister in Ashland. Then I found your website and realized I was meant to be here instead. I hate to sound sentimental, but it feels like fate.* She pushed send.

McCullen had read over her shoulder. "You're good."

Lying effectively was an art, and she had perfected it as a kid. Her mother—who was just mentally ill enough to be unpredictable but not bonkers enough to get treatment—was the Queen Liar, and Dallas had adopted the habit at an early age. She'd been making shit up for as long as she could remember. Her Aunt Lynn had tried to correct the unpleasant habit, and out of respect, Dallas had tried to be honest with her. She had also focused on getting better at misdirection and obfuscation. Mixing in a bit of the truth was essential. She glanced at McCullen. "Spencer will buy it. Civilians want to believe that others are essentially good and truthful. Only criminals and law enforcement personnel assume the worst."

"You're too young to be jaded."

"You haven't met my parents." Dallas glanced at her tablet. Spencer had responded: *Maybe it is fate. Let's meet for lunch tomorrow at the Cornerstone Cafe. Noon?*

Yes! She keyed in her agreement, and a tingle of excitement played in her chest. She would soon contact her target. She loved the challenge of extracting people's secrets. "Maybe he'll take me out to Destiny for a tour."

"Don't go anywhere without contacting me or one of the team. We've named this undercover project Eden."

"As in Garden of Eden?"

"More like East of Eden."

McCullen wrote down two email addresses and phone numbers, tore the paper from his notebook, and handed it to her. "These are for Gibson and our tech guy, who can help you with anything computer related."

"The support team is the best part of undercover work." Flirting was in her DNA, as natural as breathing.

"I'll be there for you 24/7." McCullen was cute even when he was serious.

"I'm very attracted to you."

His eyes widened in surprise. Before she could stop herself, Dallas leaned in and kissed him.

He grabbed the back of her head and met her mouth with passion. For a long moment, she was lost in the pleasure. Then a phone rang in her shoulder bag, and they both pulled back.

"Sorry." Dallas stood and moved away. "I shouldn't have done that."

"No. We shouldn't have." McCullen looked a little stunned.

Dallas dug for her personal phone, which she hadn't hidden away yet. The caller ID said *Trevor*. What the hell? She'd only been gone twelve hours. She hit reject and turned to McCullen. "We'd better call it a night."

He stood. "You'll keep me updated? I want to know when you head for the compound. I'm worried for your safety."

"I'll stay in touch, but worrying is pointless. I plan to move out to the community as soon as Spencer will let me."

His eyes tightened. "Are you going to seduce Spencer?"

Was he jealous? "Spencer Clayton is my assigned target for intel gathering. But my goal is to find Emma Clayton...and her baby. I'll do what needs to be done." She hoped he could see the regret in her eyes.

"Just remember that Spencer probably kidnapped Emma, so he's dangerous, no matter what he seems like on the surface. And everyone in the community is tight. You can't trust any of them."

"I'll keep that in mind." Dallas kissed his cheek and sent him on his way before she changed her mind again.

Chapter 7

Wednesday, May 8, 10:17 a.m.

Caleb McCullen forced himself to stop thinking about Agent Dallas and how she'd kissed him. She was so pretty—and confident. He loved women who showed no fear. Even though he would communicate with her every day while she was undercover, he wouldn't see her again until she released her UC role, and then she would fly out of here. It was probably for the best.

Meanwhile, he was on Dallas' team and she needed him to dig into the Claytons' past. He'd already checked the gas tank of Emma's car and found it empty. Now he had county records open on his desktop and was looking at the building permits the Claytons had been granted over the years to see if any structures had a basement.

A moment later, his boss stepped into McCullen's cubicle, a small bright space in a big office they shared with other professional firms—only their chunk of the building was harder to get into. Gibson was starting to look a little gray and soft, but McCullen knew he lifted weights and boxed for fun, so he'd want Gibson on his side in a street fight any day.

"What's the update on Agent Dallas?" His boss took a seat.

"She has a lunch date scheduled with Spencer Clayton today, and she expects to be living in Destiny by the end of the week."

"She's moving fast." Gibson shifted in his seat. "Once she's in place, she probably won't need much help, so I have another assignment for you."

Surprised, McCullen said, "Dallas still needs a contact person. Is the case something minor?"

"I need you to investigate a dead body that turned up this morning." Gibson handed him a thin file folder. "I'll take the lead on the Eden project, and Dallas will report directly to me."

McCullen was too stunned to respond for a moment. "A homicide? Why isn't the police department taking it?"

"They asked for help. Their only homicide detective is on leave after back surgery, and no one else in the department has the time or experience to investigate a cold case. And it may not be murder."

Cold case? "How old is the body?"

"She's been in the water, so it's hard to tell."

A floater!

Gibson chuckled. "Don't look so glum. This is an opportunity to get out of the office and use your skills. Do something besides fraud cases."

"You're right. Thank you." McCullen was torn. Homicide investigations were rare and if he solved it, the case could earn him a promotion to the Sacramento Field Office. But he hated losing contact with Dallas, and he hated being bumped from the Eden case. Randall Clayton had stolen Emma from him five years ago, and McCullen had never trusted or liked him since. He wanted to be the one to cuff Randall and escort him to the federal holding cell in Sacramento. "What about our end of the missing persons investigation? Emma Clayton may not be in Destiny."

"I'll keep working it, but you know there's not much more we can do." Gibson took a gulp of the coffee he always had with him. "She's probably either dead or out there with the preppers." Gibson's tone held scorn. He assumed every isolationist was anti-government.

A shapeless worry started to take hold. "Did the victim have ID?"

"No. Start with the missing persons database."

Could it be Emma? The thought made his stomach clench. He tried not to visualize her corpse. Just as he had tried for a week not to imagine Emma held captive or hurt in any way. He couldn't let this investigation get personal. He and Emma were long past. "Where is the victim?"

Gibson pointed at the report. "The Four Corners Motel. They pulled back the winter cover over the pool this morning and found a body in the water." His boss stood to leave. "I'll let Agent Dallas know to contact me."

McCullen drove south on Victor Avenue, looking for the cheap motel near the outskirts of the city. The bright sun and vast blue sky took the edge off his foul mood. Planting season was finally in swing, and he couldn't wait to get some basil and cilantro growing. He'd missed cooking with fresh herbs.

The dirty-white building came into view on his left. Long and low, it stretched out along the road, welcoming weary travelers with bright orange doors and a huge sign that lit up at night. McCullen had been inside just once—a night that had been both glorious and regretful.

He'd lived in Redding for six years, moving from Sacramento after his bureau training. Part of him wanted to go back to the bigger city with its higher crime rate and faster pace. The other half liked leaving work at five with most weekends free to bicycle, hunt, and garden.

He pulled into the parking lot just as the Shasta County coroner and a crime scene tech loaded the sheet-draped body into a van. A patrol officer stood nearby. McCullen walked over to the van, smelling the rotting corpse from a distance. "Dan Michelson? I'm Agent McCullen with the FBI."

"Yes, we met in court once." The coroner was too old to even guess his age, but he refused to retire.

"The Turnbull case. I remember." McCullen nodded toward the body. "What have we got?"

"Female, probably between twenty-five and thirty-five—based on the condition of her teeth—and dead for at least a week. Maybe longer. She also has quite a dent in her skull, so it looks like someone clobbered her." The coroner moved toward the driver's side. "I'll do the autopsy tomorrow and send over my report, but don't get your hopes up. The forensic evidence is long gone."

"Thank you." *Please don't let it be Emma.* McCullen braced himself and started for the motel office.

Inside, the smell of cigarettes and burnt coffee was a welcome relief from the wet cadaver odor clinging to the inside of his nostrils. He showed his credentials to the young man at the counter and followed him into a small back office. A fifty-something man with a toupee looked up from his computer.

"Agent McCullen, FBI. Are you the manager or owner?"

"Bob Hamper, owner. I assume you're here about the body?"

"Yes." McCullen took a seat in a plastic chair that looked like it had been made in the sixties. "The victim could have been a guest here. Any idea who she is?" He wondered—even hoped— she was a prostitute who worked out of the motel.

"Yes and no." Hamper took a pull from a silver flask that came out of nowhere. "I've been thinking about it since I found her, and she might be connected to the rental car that was left in the parking lot two weeks ago."

Two weeks ago Emma had been fine. McCullen pulled out his notepad, thinking more clearly now. "What date was that?"

"I've been trying to pinpoint it. I think I noticed the car on Thursday, April 25th, so it was probably there before that."

"What happened?"

"Like I said, the car had been sitting for a couple days, but the license plate didn't match any guests. So I opened the vehicle and found papers from Shasta Rentals." Hamper took another pull. "The name Charlotte Archer was on the contract. She'd been a guest here on that Sunday and Monday night and left without turning in her key."

McCullen jotted down the name but had a sinking feeling it was as fake as the license plate number she'd given the motel. A woman with something to hide. "Did you report any of this to the police?"

"I didn't have a reason to. She paid for the room in advance, and there was no indication anything had happened to her." A bead of sweat formed on Hamper's upper lip. "Shasta Rentals was happy to send someone over to retrieve the car. She may have owed them for a couple more days, but that wasn't my problem."

Jackass. McCullen resisted the urge to correct the man's thinking. He might need the leverage later. "How did she pay?"

"With cash."

Of course. "Describe the woman."

"Early thirties, short blond hair." He paused, as if

searching for the right word. "Curvaceous."

That sounded like Emma. *Just a coincidence*, he told himself. "Did she say where she was from?"

"She listed Sacramento."

That could be phony too, but it was a place to start. "What about the room she stayed in? Did she leave any luggage? Or anything unusual?"

"The maid didn't report a thing, but you can ask her yourself. She's cleaning in that area now." Hamper glanced at his monitor. "Charlotte Archer stayed in room eight. It's right next to the pool."

An image of a man dragging her body in the dark popped into his brain. "I need copies of anything she filled out or signed, and I want to see the room."

Hamper stood. "You're lucky it's empty this morning. But we've had guests in there since the Archer woman."

McCullen knew he probably wouldn't find anything, but if she had been murdered, he needed to see the crime scene. He tried to visualize the scenario: An assailant killing the woman and dragging her to the pool. Then what? Back to the room to get rid of her luggage and anything incriminating. "How often do your dumpsters get emptied?"

"Once a week. They came on Monday."

Shit. He hoped he didn't have to search the damn landfill.

Down the walkway, he found the maid in room nine. The tiny Latino woman remembered nothing unusual about room eight on any recent morning. Charlotte Archer, the mystery woman, had left nothing behind—except a rental car.

An inspection of the room turned up nothing obvious: no blood stains in the patterned carpet that he could see, no broken or scratched furniture. He didn't even know for sure that the dead woman had stayed in this room or if Charlotte was her real name. He took one last look around to visualize the crime. What would he use for a weapon if he hadn't brought one with him?

A lamp on the nightstand caught his eye. The heavy ceramic base could do a lot of damage to someone's skull. It looked clean, but trace evidence was hard to completely eliminate. With gloved hands, he carried the lamp to his car and placed it in an evidence bag. He would overnight it to the crime lab at Quantico. Maybe they'd find a fingerprint, blood, or scalp tissue.

If not, the case looked impossible. Still, he had to give it his best effort. A woman had been killed and dumped, and her family, if she had one, needed to know what had happened. McCullen gathered up the orange-floral bedspread, thinking it might not have been washed and could possibly contain DNA. As he stuffed it into a plastic bag from the trunk of his car, the maid hurried out from next door.

"I think I remember something," she said, sounding a little winded. "The worried lady from room eight asked me where she could buy a sledge hammer."

What the hell?

Chapter 8

Wednesday, May 8, 6:45 a.m.

Spencer woke feeling upbeat for a change. For the first time in two years, his thoughts were not about his sick wife or the uncertain future. Instead, Sonja Barnes was on his mind. The young woman had commented on his blog a few days ago, then engaged him in a lively conversation about water-purification tablets versus portable purifiers. Yesterday, after she'd applied to join their community, he'd checked out her Facebook page. Her photo had pulled him in like a magnet. She was more than pretty—she was intensely compelling, with bright blue eyes that dared anyone to tell her no.

Now she was here in Redding and wanted to meet for lunch! The thought gave him a rush of pleasure. He headed for the bathroom, catching sight of himself in the mirror. Not bad for forty-two, he thought. No stomach fat, no gray hair. He could still attract a younger woman.

Lisa's feeble voice called to him from the next bedroom, and a stab of guilt sliced through his heart. He was still a married man who loved his wife. Spencer pulled on a robe and rushed to see what she needed.

"I'm thirsty, hon." Her cracked lips had dried blood on them.

Had he forgotten to apply lip balm the night before? He'd given her a gentle rubdown with lotion. "Your water bottle is right here." Spencer grabbed the container and handed it to her. Had she been unable to reach it or did she just need attention? Others in the community helped care for her, but Lisa was still alone for periods of time.

He worried she no longer had the strength to even stay hydrated. How many days did she have? Would she die before he set off the financial trigger? That could be a problem. He would need to report her death to the county coroner—who would want to come out. Spencer shook off the worry. They had made it through rounds of FBI questioning about Emma, and they would get through this.

After a workout on the weight machine, which he hadn't used in a while, Spencer headed for the data center. Raff was already at work, and he'd been there at midnight when Spencer finally called it quits. The hacker looked up. "You're late, buddy."

Spencer laughed. "How's the progress?"

"Slow. Morgan's key employees change their passwords twice a day, and they don't open unsolicited email."

"Keep at it for now." Spencer wondered if they could go ahead without Morgan Bank and still achieve the same effect. "We need to start thinking about a plan B." He had a second assault lined up that would cause power outages in ten major cities, but it would be more effective if the financial collapse was already happening.

Raff turned to him. "As a prepper, what is your biggest fear?"

"I'm a futurist."

"Same question. What are you most worried about?"

"Global climate change caused by cars and companies that pump massive carbons into the atmosphere. And by climate change, I mean major storms, droughts, and temperature shifts that make our planet uninhabitable for humans."

"That's some serious shit, man." The hacker cocked his head. "You think you're going to save the species, don't you?"

Spencer squared his shoulders. "Yes."

"Cool." Raff went back to work.

After an hour of grouping emails into sendable chunks, Spencer's mind drifted back to Sonja and her sudden appearance in his life. An unpleasant thought gave him pause. Was she a scammer? An opportunist? He would be careful until he knew more, but he really wanted her in Destiny. They needed young people, especially women. He didn't care that her skills had little to offer in the way of technology or medicine.

"Oh, shit." Raff bolted upright in his chair.

"What is it?"

"They've made me. We've got a pingback coming."

A cold fear seized Spencer's chest. "I thought we had proxy computers."

"We do." Raff's voice was tight, and he didn't look up as he madly worked the keyboard. "I'm just deleting all my files over there before anyone sees them and figures out what we're up to."

"Can I help?"

"Just let me focus."

Spencer moved toward the window, too nervous to sit and wait. If Morgan's security pieced together their attack plans, it would warn its customers, and their assault would likely fail. Would they be able to trace control of the proxy computers to Destiny? If they did, Spencer would go to jail, and the community might fall apart. Raff had assured him a trace was impossible, but Spencer knew that in the tech world, nothing stayed impossible. Should he move the computers to an office in town? He could rent a heated storage unit as an immediate backup, then look at available office rentals after his lunch with Sonja.

For five long minutes, the only sound in the room was Raff clicking the keyboard like a transcriptionist on speed, with only an occasional soft grunt. Spencer tried not to pace.

Finally, the clicking slowed and Raff let out a small whoop. "I think I cleared it all in time."

Relief washed over Spencer. "Thank goodness." He strode over and stood near the hacker. "We need new proxy computers."

Raff got up and stretched. "That's the easy part. I think we need to forget the banks and try an asset management firm. They have less security."

"But what can we accomplish?"

Raff laughed, almost scornfully. "Bentley & Eastman is an international firm that controls the money of Standford Oil, Conner's Electric, and the governments of Lebanon and Syria. Just to name a few entities with mad cash. We could cause a major shutdown if we started making their money disappear."

* * *

Raff was totally charged. He'd been hacking since he was twelve, but compared to this new gig, everything he'd done up to now seemed like goofing off, including hacking into a casino and shutting it down for a few hours. The Palm Royal had lost a lot of money that day, but none of it had gone into his pocket. He was proud that he'd never stolen anything, no matter how easy it would have been. That was important, because until now his life had been a wasteland with little to be proud of. But hacking was an addiction—kind of like gambling, he figured, but with a different kind of payoff. It gave him the only sense of power he'd ever had.

The Claytons were a different kind of power hungry. Maybe a little insane. They wanted to take down society and send everyone back to an agrarian culture. Raff respected the balls it took to launch such a project, but he had to be skeptical. World commerce would likely rebound. Still, with his help, they could do some serious damage, and in the long run, maybe some good too.

He got back to work, scanning Bentley & Eastman's website. This would be a major coup. If only he had more time... But Spencer was in a hurry and wanted everything done by Friday. Why was May 10th so important? *Oh crap.* If Friday was May 10th, this was May 8th, his mother's birthday. Raff jumped up, excused himself, and went outside. He'd better be able to make a call. The service out here was shit.

The call went through and his mother answered right away. "Good morning, Gabriel. How wonderful to hear from you."

"Happy birthday, Mom." Only his family called him that. He'd adopted a pseudonym for hacking long ago. "What have you got planned?" He knew what she would say, but he had to ask.

"Just a quiet dinner with Alima."

His sister, the lawyer, who made their parents proud. "What's new? How are you doing?"

"I don't see you enough, but my health is fine, and the business is finally starting to pick up."

"It's all good." His parents owned a bakery in New York,

where he'd grown up. They'd immigrated to the city as young, Middle Eastern refugees, a Jewish man and a Palestinian woman who'd run from the violence and condemnation. His grandmother was still in Gaza. "How's Noni?"

"Her eyes are very bad now, but she's found a family to live with."

"Good. I didn't like that she was alone." Raff had only met her once, and he'd hated everything about his trip to Israel— except his grandmother. Her life was poor and tragic, but she'd kept her sense of humor.

"Still, I'm worried about the trouble with Syria," his mother said. "It could become a regional war."

In the Middle East, that was always the case. Raff didn't respond.

"How are you, Gabe? Are you tired of the desert? And the stripper girls? We want you to come home."

This was how it always ended. "Not yet, Mom. I like Vegas. But when I move again, I'm heading to Hollywood."

"What about a girlfriend? Have you met anyone?"

"I know lots of girls. I just haven't settled down yet. I'm still young."

"But we're not and we want grandchildren."

They must have given up on his sister. "Some day. I've got to get back to work now. Happy Birthday."

"You have a job?"

He was already hanging up. Raff stared at the phone, visualizing his mother's face, her mixed emotions. He wished he hadn't mentioned work, but if it gave her a little peace of mind, what the hell. She had no idea he was a hacker. She thought he made money online buying and selling things. Close enough. He went back inside to see if he could Trojan-horse his way into a firm that controlled billions of dollars—and cause a little chaos while he was in there.

Chapter 9

Wednesday, May 8, 7:15 a.m.
Dallas drank a cup of coffee and thought about swimming laps in the motel pool, then decided it wasn't warm enough. Maybe by midafternoon. She changed into workout clothes and headed for the small gym at the end of the building, relieved to find an elliptical machine. The glider faced out the window, and the view of the snow-covered Mount Shasta was stunning. She wondered for the hundredth time why she didn't leave Phoenix. Would she still be compelled to do undercover work if she lived somewhere aesthetically pleasing?

After a shower, she slipped into a black skirt and low-cut, sky-blue blouse for her lunch with Spencer, then applied more makeup than her usual foundation and mascara. Time to try the pheromones she'd purchased for this assignment. Strictly her own idea, but the bureau rewarded creativity and success. Dallas applied the liquid to her wrists and neck, curious to see if the potion would work and if she would notice the difference. The goal was to win Spencer Clayton's affection as quickly as possible. She hoped the pheromones didn't backfire and attract the wrong person.

With time to kill, she opened her laptop and checked her various email accounts. In her work folder, McCullen had sent her a message saying Emma's gas tank was empty, reinforcing her theory that the Claytons had engineered the abduction. Their motivation was still a mystery though. In her personal file, Dallas found a sad little note from Trevor, which she ignored. In Sonja's email, there was a message from Spencer: *Thanks for applying to join us at Destiny. You can meet the other members for an informal interview this evening at our monthly gathering.*

Yes! She wondered if he had run background checks on her. The undercover unit at Quantico could create a whole life of details in a matter of hours, so she was good either way, but she'd expected more paranoia from a prepper. Their website clearly stated that only those with some college education were welcome, so that limited the applicants to the small group of people who were smart but a little crazy. Dallas responded to his email, then read more of Spencer's blogs, hoping to get to know him better. Thanks to FBI analysts, she already knew where he'd attended college, what music he liked, and every job he'd had since high school. All of it could be used to establish a connection.

Her Skype icon pinged, startling her. Then she remembered her bi-monthly therapy session with Doctor Harper. *Oh crap.* She really wasn't in the mood, but she clicked the answer button anyway.

The therapist's wrinkled face quickly came into view. Doctor Harper was almost seventy, which had made Dallas uncomfortable at first, but she'd come to trust and respect the shrink. Still, their progress was slow, and Dallas' patience was growing thin.

"Hey." She never quite knew what to call her.

"Good morning." Doctor Harper wasn't smiling. "I see that you're not at home. Where are you?"

"Redding, California. It's a new assignment."

"I thought you were going to take longer breaks between out-of-town work."

Dallas didn't remember the conversation quite that way. "This case is critical. A woman is missing, and I'm the only agent who can get into the community quickly."

"Why is that?"

"I look like the wife of the man who kidnapped her."

Her therapist scowled. "You're supposed to charm a kidnapper? Maybe seduce him?"

"You know the bureau forbids hooking up with the target."

"And I know you do it anyway." Doctor Harper paused for a long moment, then glanced at her notes. "How is your relationship with Trevor progressing?"

Dallas felt like a kid who'd failed an assignment. "I broke up with him before I left." She grinned. "But the sex was still good."

"You'd only been dating a few weeks."

"Five or six."

"That relationship was shorter than most. Why?"

Dallas squirmed. Why did she put herself through this? "Because I was leaving, and I might be gone for months. It wasn't fair to make him wait, especially since..." She trailed off. There were so many reasons.

"Since what? I want to hear this."

Dallas used her fingers to count them off. "One, I was going to end it eventually anyway. Two, I need to feel free to be intimate with my target and not have any guilt. Three, I'm too young to get serious."

"But you came to me because you wanted to develop a long-term relationship and not have the sex go stale. Because you were tired of hookups with strangers." Doctor Harper softened her tone. "Those are your words."

"That was before I developed a specialty for undercover work. I like it too much now to let a relationship get in the way." Even though that was true, there was more to the story. She'd actually started counseling long ago. Her Aunt Lynn had taken her to a shrink when she was twelve, after her parents had become homeless meth addicts for a while. Dallas had sometimes fantasized about her parents dying in a car crash so she could go live permanently in the big house with her sweet, sane aunt. The psychologist had told her that was normal, and Dallas had decided that therapy could be a good thing.

Dr. Harper gave her a look. "Maybe you like the undercover work because it supports your pattern of enjoying sex with strangers and moving on."

Dallas knew it was partly true. "It's also exciting and meaningful work—and I'm good at it." She shrugged. "I'm happy."

"Except when you're not."

"Those episodes are rare now."

The therapist raised an eyebrow. "Because you're doing more and more undercover work that lets you become someone else?"

Dallas laughed. "Probably."

"I want to talk about your abandonment issue. Do you still carry your security cloth?"

"Yes, but it's only about three inches now." Dr. Harper was the only person who knew that she'd kept a security blanket from her early childhood and liked to sniff it when she was stressed or lonely. It had a musty blend of her mother's shampoo, her own baby sweat, and a sweet kitty named Pickle—and the smell took her back to a time when she felt secure. Over the years, her shrink had encouraged her to cut the dirty blanket in half and throw away a chunk at a time. Dallas was pleased with her progress, but she still liked to keep a tiny piece in her pocket, like a good-luck charm. "I don't have time to talk about this today. I have a lunch date with my target."

"Are you going to sleep with him?"

"I doubt it." But she might hook up with Agent McCullen if the opportunity came up again. "I'll call you when I get back to Phoenix."

"I want to see you again in two weeks."

"That's not gonna happen. I'm joining an isolated community that may not have internet access."

"That sounds dangerous." Doctor Harper looked worried.

"I'll be fine." Dallas reached for her mouse. "See you again soon." She clicked off Skype and shut down her computer. *Abandonment issue.* She hated that phrase. It made her sound weak and whiney. Her parents had never really walked away from her—but they'd never really been there either. She would have been better off if they had dumped her and let Aunt Lynn have custody. Dallas put all the bullshit out of her head. She had to get into Sonja mode and go meet Spencer Clayton.

Dallas googled the restaurant, checked the map for directions to get a visual layout, and took off in the white Audi. The Redding Bureau had taken care of the motel and the vehicle, and McCullen had probably handled both. She liked his taste. With only three agents, the Redding office was even smaller than the Eugene bureau where she'd conducted her last assignment. She wouldn't likely see the building or meet the other members of her team until she'd found Emma and/or made arrests.

The drive took only fifteen minutes, but she noted that Redding was clean and attractive, with an eclectic mix of historic buildings, modern malls with all the familiar retailers, and lots of stucco and red-tile roofs. The palm trees surprised her, as did the town's size. Redding was bigger and more bustling than she'd imagined. Under a bright blue sky, distant mountains surrounded the town, giving it a sense of place.

Still operating on Phoenix driving time, she arrived twenty minutes early, so Dallas sat in the car and read through her Sonja background again. She liked her character and her desire to reject her financially comfortable world and seek a more meaningful future. Especially after the death of her fiancé, who'd killed himself after he began to show signs of Huntington's disease.

Knowing it all by heart now, Dallas closed the password-protected file and shut off her tablet. She had studied the slim profile again on the plane and was as ready as she could be. Now she just needed to be charming and sincere and eventually express an interest in having children, despite the uncertain future. The thought made her chuckle. Would she be able to say it with a straight face? Of course she would. Aunt Lynn had paid for acting classes when Dallas was in high school—after piano lessons, tennis instruction, ballet, and she'd noticed anyway.

The parking lot started to fill up, so Dallas went inside, where she asked for a private booth and told the hostess she was expecting someone to join her. "His name is Spencer."

"Spencer Clayton? From Destiny?"

"Yes. Do you know him?"

"Of course. He comes in here all the time." The hostess

gave her a long appraising once-over. "How do you know him?"

"We met online." Dallas smiled warmly. "The internet is an amazing social tool for bringing likeminded people together." Spoken like a true social media consultant.

"You're joining his community?" The hostess' middle-aged face registered concern.

"I'm thinking about it." *Time to start digging.* "What do you think of Destiny? Should I be worried about anything?"

The hostess glanced around to see if anyone was within earshot, then leaned forward. "A month ago, I would have said 'Suit yourself. It's harmless.' But one of the main members disappeared last week, so we're all a little more skeptical now."

Dallas feigned surprise. "What do you mean *disappeared*?"

"Spencer's sister-in-law left Destiny to visit her mother and never arrived." The hostess' voice was a whisper. "They finally found Emma's car yesterday about ten miles from the community, but she and her baby were gone."

"That's weird. Do you suspect her husband of something?" Dallas kept her voice low too, hoping to keep her talking.

"I don't know." The hostess led her to a corner booth and spoke in a regular tone. "The older brother is nice and her husband seems okay."

"What about the other members?" Dallas wondered how the town folks viewed the community.

"The Destiny members are just regular folks. No wackos or crackpots. Just people who want to be ready for the worst." They both heard the front door open, and the hostess spun toward it. "I have to get back to work. Welcome to

Redding." She hustled to her podium and seated two women in casual business clothes.

Dallas was relieved to hear the preppers weren't viewed as crackpots. Still, they possessed a significant stash of weapons, and she would have to keep that in mind at all times. Anyone she encountered out there could be armed. Her backup weapon was in a hidden compartment in the bottom of her purse. The shoulder bag was a new department-issue item, but the zipper on her last one had stuck when she needed her gun, so she felt less secure than she should have. Her Glock was at home in Phoenix, because they hadn't had time to create the paperwork she needed to take it on the plane. That was the only part of undercover work she didn't like—not having her primary weapon at her fingertips.

She glanced at the menu, wondering what Sonja would eat. She wasn't a vegetarian. Maybe a foodie, with high-end tastes. A moment later, she sensed movement and looked up. An attractive, forty-something man was walking toward her. Spencer Clayton. Thank goodness he was physically fit and easy to look at. She had once faked an interest in a chubby, flat-faced drug dealer, and it had been challenging. Dallas gave her new target a bright smile. "Spencer?" She stood and shook his hand. "Sonja Barnes. Thanks for meeting me. I'm very pleased to be here."

"The pleasure is mine. We love when bright young people want to join our community." Spencer sat across from her in the booth, and Dallas looked him over. He seemed dressed for golf in a short-sleeve pullover and khaki pants.

No concealed weapon that she could perceive. "How many members do you have?"

"Just thirty-seven. We've had hundreds of applicants, but

we have high standards for admission. The essay portion disqualifies many, and the psychological evaluation eliminates half of those who come out here for it."

The psych test was news to her. "What are you screening for?" Dallas laughed. "We can all be a little obsessive about something."

"Obsession can be a good thing." Spencer's tone turned serious. "We're trying to keep out people with paranoia or conspiracy issues and antisocial attitudes. We're a close-knit community and personal interaction is essential."

"Whew!" Dallas joked. "I'm a social media consultant, so I've got that under control."

Spencer grinned. "I knew that. As long as you're not afraid the government is out to get you, I think you'll breeze through."

"Good government is essential, even in small communities. Does Destiny have a council of leaders or some kind of mechanism for democratic decision making?"

"We do. And the council will decide whether to accept you."

"When do I meet them?"

"Probably this evening. Let's order lunch, then tour the community this afternoon and see how it goes. You may reject us." Spencer signaled the food server, and a young man came over. Dallas ordered a specialty salad with pears and candied pecans. She wasn't crazy about pears, but gourmet chefs loved them, and she wanted to look like someone who had grown up with gourmet food instead of rice and beans.

"Good choice. I've had everything on the menu by now, and that's one of my favorites." Spencer ordered a patty melt, then sheepishly admitted, "It's my weakness, but I went for a long run this morning."

"Don't worry, I'm not a purist. I love free-range beef." This was almost too easy. "Do you raise livestock out there?"

"Some. We have a little bit of everything."

Another food server, a woman about her age, walked by, seeming familiar. After a moment of mental searching, Dallas' heart skittered. *Holy shit.* Ashley Townsend. They'd gone to high school together in Flagstaff. What the hell was she doing in Redding? More important, would she recognize Dallas with her new hair? Most likely. Not much else about her had changed in ten years. She couldn't sit here and let her cover get blown.

"Do you mind if we move to the patio? It's such a nice day." Dallas grabbed her purse and got up, not willing to take no for an answer.

Spencer looked surprised, but said, "Sure. I'll let the hostess know."

Dallas was tempted to make a break for the restroom so she could call McCullen, but she wasn't willing to cross the restaurant. What could her contact do, anyway? Detain Ashley? Force the owner to close the business because of a security threat? No. She just had to keep her face averted and move things along as quickly as possible.

Outside, she chose a table that wasn't visible through the windows. Spencer came along a moment later and sat down. "This is a nice idea. I love spring when the weather is perfect."

"Me too. Although spring in Phoenix comes a little earlier than this." The bureau had kept her real location because they'd had to move so quickly.

"I don't know how you live there. I hate the desert."

"Me too. That's part of why I'm here now."

"Why else?"

"I'm tired of living in uncertainty about the future, and I'm tired of grieving. I want a new life."

"You lost someone?"

Dallas nodded, mustering up a sad expression. "My fiancé. We were together five years, then he killed himself after he developed Huntington's disease."

"I'm sorry for your loss." Spencer reached over and held her hand. "Destiny is a good place to heal, but it's also where I hope to spend my last days."

The handholding irritated her, and she was relieved when their server hustled up with their food. Dallas pulled away and dug in. Ashley was still in the building, only fifty feet away. Dallas wondered again how the woman had ended up in Redding. The sight of Mount Shasta brought it into focus. Ashley was a skier, and Redding was a similar size and geography as Flagstaff. Ashley had probably moved here for the skiing—and better state politics. Had she brought her high school boyfriend along too? Dallas had to get out to the anonymity of the compound as soon as possible.

While they ate, she brought up the news she'd read that morning about a European banking scandal, and they discussed the financial system. She learned that Spencer believed globalization was contributing to the demise of the human race because it accelerated carbon emissions. He was also vehemently opposed to recreational air travel and the "superfluous" burning of jet fuel. Dallas nodded, asked polite questions, and didn't find anything too laughable.

Fortunately, Spencer didn't mind chewing while talking, so they finished their meals quickly. Dallas was jumpy to leave before Ashley spotted her. "I'd love to see Destiny. Can we head out?"

He looked at his watch. "I have an errand to run, but I'll

meet you there in an hour."

After a twenty-five minute drive through scrubby pines dotted with occasional homes and small farms, Dallas found the little community at the end of a narrow private road. Few people would ever stumble upon Destiny by accident.

Before she reached the cul-de-sac, Dallas noticed retractable gates on both sides. Did they close the entry every night? Or was the gate just part of preparing for the apocalypse? It wouldn't deter anyone on foot, but it would keep most vehicles from advancing. The trees along the road made the gate difficult to drive around...but not impossible. If she needed to escape the community with the gate closed, she would plow right across the last lawn and head through the thicket. The Audi was nice, but still only a rental.

Dallas eased past the gate stubs, noticing narrow side streets that led to a second layer of homes on both sides. She spotted Spencer's Jeep and parked in front of the largest house at the end. Beyond it were fields and at least one greenhouse she could see. Curiosity made her nerves hum. What else was out there? And where were they keeping Emma and her baby?

Spencer stepped out of the bright yellow house and waved for her to come in. Dallas took a deep breath and jogged up the path. This was the turning point. She was no longer sniffing around the edge of this scenario. Once she entered, she would be committed.

"This is my home," he explained as they stood in the vaulted living room. "But the annexed building is our data center and meeting room. We also have some informal gatherings here."

"It's bright and beautiful." Dallas didn't have her eyes on

the tall windows or teak floor. She noted instead a small handgun on the foyer table. What was he worried about?

Spencer noticed. "We have to protect our livestock from coyotes and wolves."

"We *are* out here in the boonies." She tried to sound casual. "Did you clear the land yourself?"

"Most of it was already farmland. We tore down an old homestead when we started building."

"You had quite a vision."

He beamed, obviously proud of his creation. "I'll show you the data center, then we'll walk around." He glanced down the hall. "I'd introduce you to my wife, but she's sleeping."

Spencer started toward a side door, then turned to her, his voice low. "The truth is, my wife is dying. She may only have a few days left." His expression didn't change, but his voice held a reverent tone.

"I'm so sorry to hear that. You must be devastated. Is this a bad time for me to be here?"

Spencer touched Dallas' shoulder, his fingers staying longer than she expected.

"I've had a long time to grieve for Lisa, and she's in a lot of pain. It will be a relief for both of us to move on." He started across the room again.

"Will you have a service for her here?"

"Of course. And I'll scatter her ashes in the lavender patch she planted."

They stepped into the data center, and a young man glanced over his shoulder. Catching sight of her, he popped to his feet. Dallas wasn't impressed: scraggly hair, sweat pants, and pudgy from lack of exercise.

Spencer gestured. "This is Greg Rafferty, but he likes to

be called Raff."

The techie didn't offer his hand or make eye contact. *Odd.* Men rarely ignored her. And he didn't look like a prepper. More like a slacker or, in this room, a hacker.

"Sonja Barnes." She nodded and glanced around. The data center held three main computers, a host of monitors, and a small server. How unusual. Why did a back-to-nature community with fewer than forty people need all that digital capacity? Raff was obviously a cyber geek, but why was he here and what was he up to? She turned to Spencer. "You have satellite internet?"

"Yes, and it's quite reliable unless we have really bad weather."

"What about cell phone service?" Questions any other applicant would ask, but the answers might be critical to her ability to relay information.

"It's intermittent. But some locations, like right outside the community center, seem to be better than others." Spencer chuckled. "You'll see members standing there talking on the phone."

Her personal smart phone would plug right into her laptop and, hopefully, connect to the community modem and satellite internet, so Dallas felt somewhat reassured that she could stay in contact with McCullen. But what if they monitored outgoing calls on the server? She'd be uncovered instantly. *Crap.* She would send emails or use her burner phone in front of the community center unless things got hinky.

She turned back to Raff. "You must be the tech guy."

"Yep. If you ever need any help with your personal computer, just ask."

"Since you're here in Destiny, you must be concerned

about the future. What happens when the internet goes down?"

Raff grinned, a man happy to show off his knowledge. "I belong to a group that's preparing for that. We have a patchwork of landlines in place and people inside the major cable companies that will keep some streams going even if their companies shut down."

"Good to know. I'm sure that in a post-collapse world, we'll all be too busy trying to survive to have time for social networking."

Both men laughed, and Spencer said, "That may be true for a while. But pockets of preppers all over the world will survive, and we'll need a way to communicate."

"It's reassuring to know you're prepared for everything." Dallas sort of meant that. She admired their willingness to see an alternative future and prepare for it. "I can't tell you how good it feels to be here."

"Great. Let's go see the rest of the community. Maybe meet a few people."

The afternoon went quickly. At first they walked around the homes, with Spencer talking about the members who lived in each. Behind the houses, paths crisscrossed the grass, leading to the community center and various storage buildings. She also met Grace, a fatigue-clad engineer who'd built a power station by the creek. Her tight smile didn't distract Dallas from noticing her physique. Unlike the Clayton brothers, Grace would be a worthy opponent in a physical confrontation.

Eventually, Spencer backed a golf cart out of his garage and said, "Let's tour the back property in comfort."

Dallas climbed in. "It's such a pretty day, I was prepared

to walk."

"I usually do, but I've got a lot going on right now and have to get back to it."

Dallas touched his arm. "Preparations for your wife's passing?"

"Yes, but that's only part of it." Spencer drove down a dirt road leading into the fields behind his house. "We think something major is coming, and we want to be ready."

A shiver shot up her spine. What were they planning? "It sounds like I came here just in time." Dallas had to press. "I heard buzz on the internet that the next asteroid could cause climate change if it hits us. Is that what you think it is?"

"Not really. We're seeing financial activity that indicates the banks are ready to panic."

The bureau kept abreast of those things, but she hadn't heard a word. Was he referring to hacker activity? "That's not good. I'm so glad I've been buying gold."

"Where do you keep it?"

"In a safe deposit box in Phoenix. If I'm accepted here, I can have the trustee transfer it here."

Spencer patted her leg. "You'll be accepted. I can tell you're a good fit for us."

They drove past barns, storage buildings, and a corn silo, with fields and pastures behind every structure. Spencer kept up a running inventory of everything they had stocked and planted. Corn crops would be processed into biofuel, which they would use to run tractors, chainsaws, and other gas-powered equipment. They also had five hundred gallons of gasoline stored, along with a supply of diesel and propane. Dallas was blown away by the extent of their preparations.

"You said there are other communities like this around the world?"

"I wish." He shook his head. "Other groups are out there, but none that I know of with this much land or bio fuel planted. I believe we also have the only large-capacity hydro-generator. But other futurists are prepared enough to survive."

Dallas took a risk. "What about a nuclear event or a major ice storm? Don't serious futurists have underground bunkers too?"

Spencer was quiet for a moment. "We have one planned, but it's hard to build something big enough for all our members. So it's politically sensitive."

Dallas interpreted that to mean Spencer and his brother had probably built a bunker but didn't want anyone else to know about it. "You've got enough land, but the excavation would be overwhelming."

They were traveling up a gradual incline, and Spencer glanced out to the right where the ground rose more sharply. A rush of adrenaline made Dallas almost giddy.

The bunker was in the hill.

Chapter 10

Wednesday, May 8, 6:35 p.m.

Randall showered and dressed for the gathering at the community center, annoyed with the intrusion. Why had his brother invited a new member into Destiny just as they were planning to trigger the collapse? Spencer needed a new partner, of course, so he could finally have children, but with Emma missing and the FBI still snooping around, it seemed damn risky. His brother was thinking with the wrong head at the wrong time.

Earlier, he'd watched Spencer take Sonja on a tour of the property, and he'd been hit with a pang of jealousy. She was so young and pretty, and he could tell by the way she looked at his brother that she was into him. Randall hoped she wasn't an idiot or a flake like so many of the women who found their website and wanted to join. Most of the female applicants were running from something or looking for someone to take care of them. The few men who applied were usually angry, immature, or trying to avoid paying taxes or child support.

Randall felt lucky to have had a sexy wife like Emma in his life for a few years. He'd first met her in a restaurant in Redding, and it had taken a while to convince her to marry him. But she'd come to love Destiny and see it as the perfect place to raise the kids they wanted. Randall's first wife had left him after a short time on the property. The other homes hadn't been built yet, and she'd grown bored, then angry at all the money they were spending on stockpiles and equipment. She'd had no vision, and they'd fought constantly. The crazy cunt had even called the police on him once for grabbing her. But they'd never had great makeup sex to hold them together.

Randall stopped in the kitchen and downed a beer to put him in the mood for socializing. Now that they were finally implementing their plans, he just wanted it to happen so they could be on the other side. He hated the uncertainty.

Randall crossed the patch of grass between his home and the data center, planning to check in with a couple of his conspirators, then head to the gathering. Just as he sat down at a keyboard, his cell phone rang. Randall glanced at the number. It didn't seem familiar but the area code was New York. Randall picked up. "Who is this?"

"Damon Estes. Sorry for the call, but I've hit a snag and wanted to discuss it." The man, whom he'd never spoken to in person, kept his voice low.

"What snag?" It was dangerous to discuss their plans on the phone. Until now, they'd used Google chat because the company didn't keep logs of IM conversations, so authorities couldn't wiretap or subpoena transcripts.

"They started changing the code on the ninth floor twice a day. I'm not sure I'll be able to get in and get the explosives close enough to do the job."

"You mean the candles?"

A heavy pause. "Right. That's what I should have said."

"Can you get close to the person who changes the code?"

"It's computer generated."

"Shit." Randall pounded his palm against the mouse pad.

If the network hub at 60 Hudson Street didn't go down, their operation wouldn't be as effective. That center was pivotal to most of the internet communication in the United States. They had other similar attacks planned, including one in the Google building in New York, several in Silicon Valley, and two in Europe. He'd done the best he could to recruit people who were close to important digital targets.

He remembered the tech guy Spencer had brought in. "We have someone here who may be able to hack into the building's security system and disable the lock or rig the codes. I'll get back to you."

"Are we still aiming for the thirteenth?"

"Yes. I'll be in touch." A new layer of tension wrapped around his chest. They had to pull this off soon.

"Hack into what system?"

The voice made him jump and he spun in his chair. Raff stood near the interior door with a beer and a peculiar grin. Randall tried to sound casual, despite his racing heart. "How much did you hear?"

"Enough to be curious about what you mean by candles."

"I can't talk about that."

"Am I the hacker who's supposed to help you get into the building's security system? What building?"

Randall's heart slowed a little. "I considered asking you."

"Your brother doesn't know about this part of the plan, does he?"

"No, but like his project, this is just a test of the system. We want to give this country a wakeup call."

Raff laughed, a nasty sound. "You're both full of shit. You aren't planning tests, you're planning a doomsday scenario. Only you're a couple of amateurs. You'll do some damage for sure, but you won't bring civilization to its knees."

A long silence made them both look around to see if anyone else had slipped into the room.

Randall's brain raced. The hacker didn't know everything they had planned, but would he go to the FBI? What would it take to stop him? Finally, he asked, "Will you help me?"

"Why should I?" Raff took a seat, as if negotiations had begun.

"Because it's the right thing to do. Human-caused global climate change will wipe out the species if we don't shut it down. The pace is accelerating at a rate no one predicted." Randall didn't understand why this wasn't obvious to everyone. "With our financial system running on borrowed money, it's just as vulnerable. We need a reset."

Raff chuckled again. Randall wanted to slap him.

The hacker held out his hands in a questioning gesture. "Who do you think I am?"

Randall started to respond, but Raff cut him off. "None of those issues concern me. Other than my family, I care about three things: money, pussy, and fun. And by fun, I mean hacking into electronic systems where I'm not wanted. If you're willing to pay me a nice chunk of change for doing something fun, I'm on board."

Randall tried to hide his relief. Of course the hacker wouldn't go to the authorities. He was probably on their cyber most-wanted list. Rafferty probably wasn't even his real name. "How much?"

"Fifty thousand."

Oh shit. They didn't have that kind of cash anymore. He remembered that Sonja claimed to have gold being transferred here. It was one of the reasons Spencer had decided to bring her in so quickly. "I can give you ten grand now and another ten in gold bars after you're successful."

"What the hell am I supposed to do with gold?"

"After the financial collapse, the value of gold will double." No reason to add that his paper money would become worthless.

"I want all cash. Transfer half to my bank account today."

"What if you can't get in?"

"Which building?"

"60 Hudson Street in New York. Where all the network hubs are."

"You want to take down the internet?" A wicked grin.

"Just long enough to cripple certain industries."

"You know why the internet is still running?" Raff smirked. "Because without it, hackers wouldn't have a playground. But I'll get you the codes. I want the money, and I don't think you'll pull it off."

Randall bristled with resentment. The dickhead didn't know how extensive his plans were. "I'll transfer the funds, but you can't tell Spencer. I will inform him, but not yet."

Raff shrugged. "Not my concern." He pointed at the nearby computer. "Send me the cash—I want to get back to the party. That new chick, Sonja, is hot."

Randall resisted the urge to laugh back. Sonja was light-years out of Raff's league. But not his. He could win her over if he wanted to. Hands trembling, he accessed both his personal account and their business account to pay Raff. Soon the money wouldn't matter.

* * *

Still wearing her black skirt from the lunch date, Dallas felt overdressed. Most of the members wore shorts, T-shirts, or casual sundresses. Everyone had a warm smile, but no one stopped her as she headed for the wine table. To jumpstart her social wheels, she drank half a glass of red, then filled it again before turning to find Spencer. He was with Grace and another couple, who were in their mid-thirties.

Spencer squeezed her hand briefly as she walked up, then introduced her. "This is Tina and David Blackwell."

Dallas shook their hands as Spencer kept talking. "Tina has a master's degree in education and runs our school program. David is a biologist who keeps our fields and greenhouses thriving. Their two teenagers are members as well."

"It's a pleasure to meet you." Dallas gave a sheepish grin. "I don't have your backgrounds, but I hope to make a meaningful contribution here too."

Tina laughed softly and patted the engineer's shoulder. "Grace is the brilliant one." She glanced back at Dallas. "But we're happy to have an educated and enlightened person want to join us."

"Where did you go to school?" David's tone was casual, but his eyes were serious.

"Arizona State. I majored in political science." The truth was easy but not as much fun.

"Have you worked on any campaigns?" Tina asked.

"No, I got distracted by social media and ended up as a consultant to small businesses."

Tina smiled. "Maybe you can use your skills to help us recruit others."

"Why not?" Dallas gave it some thought. "I'd probably start by using Facebook's new search filter to find specific postings about future scenarios."

Another woman walked up. Her gray shoulder-length hair didn't match her smooth, tanned face, and she wore a draped purple caftan with little underneath. "You must be Sonja. I'm Marissa Collins." She held out a hand covered with rings.

Dallas shook it. "Beautiful turquoise."

"Thanks. I love to wear my rings when I have the chance—most of the time I have to wear latex gloves."

Spencer put an arm around Marissa. "This wonderful woman helps me take care of Lisa, in addition to working at a health clinic."

Tina cut in. "We all help you take care of Lisa."

Dallas thought she detected resentment.

"So true." Spencer touched Tina's arm. "I'm grateful to live in such a supportive community."

David spoke up again. "And we appreciate the financial support you contributed to building our house."

Interesting. Dallas suspected the Claytons kept ownership of the land and homes. "How long have you been here?"

"Six years." Tina turned to her husband. "We wanted to raise our boys in a safe sustainable environment."

Dallas wasn't sure if she should ask the next question, but she couldn't stop herself. "Do people ever get disillusioned and leave?"

Tina started to speak, but Spencer cut her off. "Not really," he said. "Sometimes people have family situations that demand their attention, and one member left for a career opportunity she couldn't pass up."

Grace's eyes flashed and she shuddered. "Remember Bruni? We had to kick him out because he couldn't get along with anyone. That was our worst year."

Dallas smiled at everyone. "Don't worry. I play well with others. I promise."

* * *

Randall strode down the path to the community center, waving at Marissa, who was coming from another direction. He usually enjoyed these gatherings, but this one—with Emma missing and so much on his mind—would be awkward.

Inside the no-frills building, about twenty Destiny members stood around chatting, some with drinks in hand. The student desks had been pushed to the back wall and padded folding chairs formed a circle, but no one sat in them yet. Bottles of wine were open on a front table, along with appetizers, but Randall headed for the kitchen area to grab a cold beer.

The members were chatting in small clusters, and everyone kept glancing at Sonja, the point of the gathering. Admitting a new person was a rare and important occasion. Everyone thought they had a vote, but the truth was, he and Spencer always made the call. This time, his brother had already made up his mind and pressured him to go along. It was time to meet Sonja in person.

She stood with Grace and the Blackwells near the refreshment table. As Randall walked over, he heard children's voices in a side room that was stocked with toys and books. Randall experienced an unexpected longing for his baby son. He pushed it away.

Randall walked up, waited for an opening in the conversation, and introduced himself. He stuck out his hand and the young woman took it with a smile.

"Sonja Barnes."

Damn, she was pretty. And familiar. "Have we met before? I used to be in politics."

"I don't think so." She tilted her head. "Local or national?"

"I was mayor of Santa Carmichael, then ran for Congress. So a little of both." Randall had mixed feelings about his past career. He'd been proud of his accomplishments—right up to the day he lost the election because of a hot-headed moment caught on camera.

"I studied political science at Arizona State," Sonja said. "But I've become rather jaded about the effectiveness of our system."

"We all have." Then it hit him. Sonja looked like Spencer's wife. Or like Lisa had before her battle with cancer. He glanced at his brother. Had he noticed?

Tina Blackwell jumped into the conversation but Randall wasn't listening. The back of his neck prickled. Was it a coincidence that someone who looked like Spencer's wife showed up at the community two days after posting on their blog for the first time? Was she a scammer, looking for a sugar daddy? A darker thought hit him. Could she be a federal agent looking for Emma?

Randall excused himself and hurried to find his brother. Spencer was in the small kitchen, pulling more appetizers from the refrigerator. Randall whispered, "We need to talk privately."

"Now?" Spencer's face was mellow with alcohol.

"Yes." Randall stepped out a side door and Spencer followed. The sun was still bright on the horizon. "I know you like her, but I think we should hesitate before admitting Sonja."

"Why?"

"It's happening too fast. We've always taken more time and done a psychological evaluation." Randall didn't want to share his theory. Spencer would call him paranoid.

"We don't have more time." His brother lowered his voice even more. "Once the trigger happens, we'll end up cutting off access. And you know I need a lover, someone to have children with."

"But I'm not sure I trust Sonja."

Spencer scowled. "Why not?"

"She looks like Lisa."

"So?"

"Doesn't that seem like a coincidence?"

"What the hell are you saying?" Spencer squinted, a familiar sign of anger.

"I'm not sure. What if she's a plant? A federal agent looking for Emma or maybe to bust us for growing pot? Not to mention, all the illegal weapons."

"Oh christ." Disgust filled his brother's face. "You're being paranoid again. Everything about her checks out."

Old childhood irritations flared. Just because he'd taken mental health medication in his younger years didn't make him crazy. "I wish you wouldn't say that. It's good to be cautious."

"You're right, and I'm sorry. But Sonja is a good fit, and I deserve to be happy."

After a long moment, Randall said, "I hope it works out for you." Maybe he *was* just being paranoid. Being repeatedly questioned by the FBI could do that to a person.

Chapter 11

Thursday, May 9, 10:30 a.m.

Dallas stuffed her jeans into the dresser and wondered how long she would be in this lovely—but middle of nowhere—apartment that still had a new-carpet smell. Spencer said they'd built the fourplex the year before and that her unit had never been lived in. Raff lived next door, and the lower spaces were empty. If the bureau succeeded in arresting the Claytons for kidnapping, those apartments would probably stay empty, and Destiny might eventually become a ghost town.

Dallas finished unpacking, grabbed a breakfast bar she'd purchased on the way out—along with other basics like French bread, brie, and vodka—and opened her laptop. She logged into Google and keyed in her location. She still needed to study a topographical map of the acreage, particularly the hill, to see if she could spot anything that indicated an underground bunker. She'd stayed in Destiny until late the night before, meeting all the members at the gathering. She'd been charming and supportive of whatever they discussed, treating the event like an audition, in which she played a bright, concerned and slightly nutty debutante. Those high school acting lessons had paid off many times over.

Overall, the group seemed pleasant and thoughtful, yet passionately convinced that "life as we know it" was doomed.

Even though she considered herself a cynic, she at least gave political leaders and scientists credit with wanting to keep themselves alive. Therefore, they had to safeguard everyone else.

A knock interrupted her study. She pushed her laptop cover down and checked the peephole. Raff. *Damn.* He'd flirted with her mercilessly the night before, and she couldn't stand the arrogant slacker. From what she'd learned during the party, he was new to the community and had been recently hired as an IT guy. But how necessary could the job be for these few people? Even with their online prepper business?

Dallas stepped back to open the door. He wasn't her target, but everyone in Destiny was a potential source of information, and she might be able to charm some valuable intel out of him later, with alcohol as a lubricant for both of them.

"Good morning. What's up?"

"I thought you might want to have breakfast." His breath was sour from last night's beer, even though he'd tried to cover it with toothpaste. The booze smell came from his belly, and a toothbrush didn't reach that far.

"I've already eaten. But thank you. Maybe tomorrow?"

"What are you doing right now?"

"Getting ready to go out for a run." That should discourage him.

His face fell. "Stop by when you get back. We should get to know each other, being the only young single people in this—" He hesitated. "This odd little village."

Dallas was sure he'd been about to say something unpleasant. "You think Destiny is odd? Why are you here?"

"Easy money." He grinned. "Why are you here?"

"Peace of mind."

"Oh, come on. You're hiding from somebody or something, like everyone else here. Ex-boyfriend is my guess."

Dallas did her best to look sad rather than highly irritated. "My fiancé died, and I needed a change of pace. I have to go. We'll talk again later." She closed the door. What a prick. She decided to break into his apartment at her first opportunity and poke around in his computer files. Maybe he was the one who was hiding something. As a young male techie, he was probably a hacker, and the thought of busting him made her smile.

Dallas opened her laptop again and studied the terrain on the first hill beyond the cornfields. A few oak trees and some scrubby, unidentifiable bushes. Near the top of the front side was an outcropping of rock about ten feet across. Not easy to excavate. As she studied the back side, her computer pinged. An email landed in her FBI account. From Special Agent Gibson. Surprised, she read: *I'm now your contact on this assignment. Please report directly to me. McCullen is still on the team, but another investigation is taking his time. Do you have an update?*

Disappointed, but always professional, Dallas keyed in: *I checked out of the motel and moved to Destiny early this morning. I attended a social gathering last night and met most of the members. I'll begin a physical search this afternoon, if I can. The IT guy here is Greg Rafferty, but it's probably an alias. Will you run a check on him?*

Dallas was surprised that a town the size of Redding would have an investigation come up that took precedence over a missing persons case. Unless they'd had a murder or kidnapping. Crimes always seemed to occur in clusters.

Sometimes they were connected, and sometimes they were about opportunity, logistics, or weather.

She took a quick look at the Google Earth map of the back side of the hill. Several boulders showed as dark blobs near the bottom. She wished she could take a look in daylight, but that might be too obvious—and too soon. First she had to establish a pattern of going out for a daily run to the hill and back. Then she would make a night journey and explore the hillside. If she found anything that looked like an entry, she might request that the bureau send out a drone to detect for a heat source. They needed a specific location and credible intel before they could commit those resources.

Dressed in knee-length yoga pants and a T-shirt, Dallas left the apartment. She could feel Raff watching her from his window. *Creep.* Once she hit the asphalt, she decided to take another quick tour of the houses to familiarize herself with the layout. Who knew where Emma was? Just because Agent McCullen had searched Randall's place didn't mean Emma wasn't being held in another house a hundred yards away.

The homes were all new, single level, and well cared for. A few had kids' bikes and toys on the lawns, one yard had been planted with herbs and flowers, and another had several bizarre metal sculptures, most likely created by the owner. Nothing too out of the ordinary. Except the gas-powered generators connected to every home. These people were ready to go off the grid at any moment. She'd learned that the community also had a hydropower generator set up by the creek, but her tour yesterday hadn't included a look at it. She would jog out there tomorrow. Today she wanted a look at the hill where Spencer had cast his eyes when they talked about bunkers.

She waved at a woman pulling weeds in her yard. Beth. A

physicist who had once taught at Berkeley. Dallas had met her last night. So far, the members seemed normal, in fact, more intelligent and rational than the average civilian. The only two who bothered her were Raff, who seemed out of place and had joined the community after Emma disappeared. And Randall, a cold man with a smoldering intensity under the surface. He'd mentioned Spencer's wife soon after they'd met, so she assumed he was feeling protective of his brother. But maybe he was a borderline psychopath, who had his wife in an underground bunker like a caged pet.

Dallas headed for the dirt road behind Spencer's house and picked up her pace. It felt good to run outside. At home, she swam laps and used the elliptical machine at the gym. Nobody jogged in Phoenix.

As she passed his backyard, Spencer called from his deck, "Wait, Sonja. I'll join you."

Damn. So much for her plans. She stopped and worked up a smile. *Be patient*, she reminded herself. It was only her first day in the community. But it was Emma's eighth day missing. "Good morning. You're a runner too?"

"My whole life." He jogged up, his face glowing with a fresh tan, his body lean and sexy.

A surge of pleasure washed over her, and Dallas realized she was attracted to him. Could she get away with a hookup? Technically, Spencer wasn't really the target, Randall was. In her head, she heard her boss scoff.

"It's a gorgeous day," she finally commented. "I feel lucky to be here."

They started down the road at a good clip. Spencer asked, "How's the apartment? Will you be comfortable there?"

"It's very nice, but I'd love to grow an herb garden."

"I'll build you a raised bed in the space behind the fourplex."

"Thanks. I'd like to help with that."

"I think we have most of the supplies, but I may need to run into town for hinges."

"No rush."

Dallas sucked in air, loving the fresh purity of it. The blue sky, the fragrant fields with their new crop of corn, the snow-covered mountain—all of it pleased her senses, and she understood why the members loved this place. For a moment, she let herself forget why she was here and simply enjoy the experience.

"It's beautiful, isn't it?" Spencer echoed her thoughts.

"Incredible." Dallas glanced over. "I have to ask. What are the winters like?"

"They're not bad. Mostly in the forties with very little snow down here." Spencer paused to take a few quick breaths. "But the skiing on the mountain is terrific if you're into it."

"I used to ski, but I lost interest." Her work at the bureau consumed much of her life now, but she loved it.

"What does interest you?"

"I'd love to do some exploring and see what herbs grow naturally in this area. Maybe make some tinctures and start an online business." While she caught her breath, she decided to stimulate the discussion. "I'm tired of the pace of social marketing. I feel like I've developed ADD and forgot how to relax."

Spencer nodded his agreement. "I'm worried that our whole culture is moving at such a frantic pace that it's become unhealthy."

"I know what you mean. You have to wonder how much

the internet, instant communication, and digital games affect our escalating rates of mental health problems." Dallas had given some thought to the subject, but she was as hooked on digital stimulation as anyone. Without missing a stride, she turned to Spencer. "Do you think it contributes to autism and bipolar disorder?"

"Of course it does. But the toxins in our environment are as much to blame."

A long line of trees came into sight, and Dallas realized the growth ran along the creek. "I'd love to see the generator. Can we head that way?"

"Sure. The path is just up a ways."

As they made the turn off the main dirt road, Dallas asked, "What do you think is the solution? I mean, beyond what you're doing here for a small group. How does our society reverse the trend?"

"I don't think any of the traditional methods of education and/or regulation will work."

"You're probably right. Parents put digital toys into the hands of babies." An interesting thought occurred to her. She hoped it would help win Spencer's trust. "The only way to prove the effect is through a rigorous study. Comparing one group of people raised on digital technology with another group that grew up without it. Like the kids in Destiny for example." It took a moment to get it all out while breathing hard.

"I've thought of that," Spencer said. "But the research is such a long-term commitment. I don't think our way of life will last that long."

"What do you predict will hit us first? Global economic depression? Nuclear war?"

"The U.S. seems headed for a financial collapse that will

fundamentally alter our society." Spencer's tone was serious, despite his labored breath. "Global climate change will contribute to making it a permanent setback. Possibly even wipe out our species."

Dallas had never heard concern that extreme. "I've read reports that indicate the earth's population will dwindle to ten million or less in this century, but scientists seem to believe we'll survive."

"It's wishful thinking. I don't believe we'll last through the decade."

His conviction surprised her. A true doomsayer. "In that case, I'm glad we'll both be here in Destiny."

After a few minutes, they neared the line of spruce trees and jogged down a gentle bank. Anchored on a cement platform near the creek was a two-foot-wide turbine and a large generator, much like the ones she'd seen connected to the homes. This one, though, was powered by creek water pouring down from a pipeline.

The engineer stood from where she'd been squatting behind the generator.

"Hi Grace. How's it going?" Spencer jogged up to the power station.

Dallas took a detailed mental picture of the micro-hydropower setup under a carport-like structure. She noticed a series of batteries next to the generator.

"I'm making progress, but the batteries are still overheating." Stress tightened Grace's melodic voice.

Dallas noticed the circles under her eyes but didn't comment. "You're storing the power in the batteries?"

"Temporarily." Grace wiped sweat from her forehead. Her camouflage pants and lime-green shirt seemed overdressed for the weather. Probably an old military habit.

The engineer continued, "We also have an underground power line to a relay station near the community center." She pointed back toward the road. "But without the batteries, the power fluctuates too much."

Ambitious. Dallas realized just how serious these people were. "I'm impressed. Did you do all this yourself?"

"Mostly. One of Tina's boys helped me dig the line. We rented a trencher, of course."

Spencer cut in. "When do you think the batteries will be fully operational?" His tone was more like a boss now.

Grace started to say something, then stopped. She met Spencer's stare. "Tomorrow, as you requested."

Why the rush? Dallas wondered. The poor woman looked exhausted.

"Excellent." Spencer squeezed Grace's shoulder, then turned to Dallas. "Seen enough? I can explain how it works as we run. I want to keep moving."

"Sure." Dallas smiled at Grace. "Let me know if I can help."

The engineer nodded politely.

Spencer turned and jogged back up the slope. Dallas felt it was reasonable to ask, "Why tomorrow? Is Destiny going off the power grid?"

"It's been our goal for a long time." After a moment, he added, "Randall and I think it's time to be ready."

"Any word on his wife?" They hadn't talked about Emma's disappearance, but other members had mentioned it at the gathering. It seemed natural to inquire.

"No. That's part of what's driving us. It's just more proof that the world is a very uncertain place."

Dallas asked what seemed like another natural question for a doomsayer. "Do you get tired of waiting? Sometimes I wish that whatever is coming would just happen already. Uncertainty is almost harder to deal with than chaos."

Spencer let out a soft laugh. "I couldn't have said it better myself."

They reached the main road. Dallas felt charged, as if she could run for another hour. Spencer turned to her. "If you had a way to make the collapse happen, knowing your effort would ultimately save the human species, would you do it?"

A chill ran up her spine, even as the May sun beat down. What was he really asking? Was it connected to Emma's disappearance and the rush to improve the generator? Dallas didn't know what to say. "Maybe. If the circumstances demanded it."

Chapter 12

Thursday, May 9, 11:35 a.m.

McCullen pulled into the car rental, noting that the victim had chosen a small locally owned business rather than one of the national chains. Had she wanted to avoid registering in a database?

He parked in the shade and finished the venison sandwich he'd brought from home, washing it down with lukewarm coffee from a thermos. Before getting out, he pulled on his jacket and grabbed a notepad. The suit still didn't feel natural to him, but he liked the respect it commanded.

Inside the office, he pulled off his sunglasses, not wanting to appear cliché. The clerk, an older man with smooth skin and dark eyes, looked up from his little reading device. "Welcome. How can I help you?"

"I'm Agent McCullen with the FBI. I need to know about the rental car that was left at the Four Corners Motel a couple of weeks ago."

"That was a weird one."

"Can I see the file for the vehicle?"

"I'll print it for you. We scan all our signed documents, then shred the paper at the end of the month. The owner hates clutter."

So much for finding her fingerprints on the paperwork.

"What's your name?"

"Walter Wolf."

Native American. "Were you working when the woman, Charlotte Archer, rented the car?"

"Yep. The owner's son is here on weekends, but otherwise it's just me behind the counter." He clicked his keyboard, and a printer hummed in response.

"Describe her, please."

"She had hair that came to her shoulders, dyed blonde with dark roots starting to show. Probably thirty-five or so." The clerk paused. "If she had smiled she would have been pretty, but I remember thinking she seemed uptight."

Had Charlotte known she was in trouble? McCullen made a note. "Do you remember her height or weight?"

"She seemed average. I don't know, maybe five-five." He chuckled. "I have no idea what she weighed, but her bra size was a 34-D."

Not helpful. McCullen gave him a tight smile. "Had you ever seen her before?"

"She seemed vaguely familiar, but I didn't recognize her name."

"Any chance there's a picture of her driver's license in the file? Or an image of her on a security camera?"

"We scanned the license but there's no video in here." He chuckled again. "It would be boring, except when I do pushup breaks."

McCullen reached for the printed stack of papers. The license scan was on top, but the blurry one-inch photo wasn't much help. Still, tension melted from his shoulders. It was definitely not Emma. He would have to enlarge the image back at the office, but for the moment he stared. The woman was kind of pretty in a pixie-faced way, but her mouth seemed bitter. Charlotte Archer, born July 7, 1979, address: 3250 Linwood Street, Sacramento, California. A mid-quality fake. He could tell by the ink color.

"It's a forgery." He kept his disappointment to himself.

"Sorry." The clerk shrugged. "I don't know how to spot them."

McCullen guessed the man had been too busy looking at her 34-Ds. He knew the answer but he had to ask, "How did she pay?"

"With cash. Sorry."

"Did she say anything about why she was here? Or where she was going?"

"I don't remember."

"What about the rental she drove? What was it?"

"A Dodge Avenger."

"Did she leave anything in it?"

"Just a little trash, like everyone does."

"What exactly did she leave?" McCullen leaned in. "This is important. I need to know where she ate or what she bought."

Wolf looked amused. "What did she do? Kill someone?"

Close. "She'd dead. And I need to figure out who murdered her. But first, I need to know who Charlotte Archer really is."

"Sorry I can't be more help."

"Is the car here? I'd like to see it."

"Sure, but it seems like a waste of time." Wolfe pulled keys from a drawer. "We wipe down the vehicles after each customer, and this one has been rented a few times since."

"Who cleans the cars?"

"Jimmy Pearson. He's a high school kid who comes in at one-thirty."

"I'll wait."

McCullen sat in his sedan and glanced through Charlotte's rental contract. It told him nothing, so he studied the tiny driver's license photo. Why did she seem familiar? Was she a local? And why had she used a fake ID and cash? Clearly, she had something to hide. He would get her picture into the local paper as well as the Sacramento Bee to see if anyone recognized her.

The detailer showed up forty minutes later. McCullen recognized him by the blue jumpsuit he pulled on when he climbed out of his beat-up car. McCullen approached him before he reached the building. "Jimmy Pearson?"

The kid spun around, a worried look on his face.

McCullen introduced himself, and the young man's mouth tightened.

"I just want to ask about a rental a few weeks ago." They stood in front of the entrance, and he held out Archer's little photo. "A Dodge Avenger, driven by this woman. Do you remember her or the car?"

"Yeah, the banana lady."

"What do you mean?"

"She left two banana peels in the car."

"Anything else?"

Jimmy made his face look impassive. "Some gum wrappers. Stuff like that."

He was hiding something. McCullen could tell by the wary look in his eyes. "What did you find? I need to know. This woman was murdered."

"Nothing." The kid squeezed his hands into fists, then released them.

McCullen lost his patience. "Let's go into the bureau and

talk there."

"I can't, I'm working." Jimmy started to turn away.

McCullen grabbed his arm. "Just tell me what you found. You won't be in trouble."

"Nothing!" The high schooler looked scared.

What was he hiding? McCullen knew he had to take him in. "Don't make me cuff you. It'll look bad to your boss." He steered the young man toward his sedan, opened the passenger door, and urged him inside.

McCullen climbed in and locked the doors. Jimmy's shoulders hunched forward, and he mumbled something.

"What was that?"

"I'm just praying."

"You should talk to me instead." He pulled out of the lot.

Jimmy rocked back and forth, straining against the seat belt. "Did you mean it about not getting into trouble?"

"Unless you killed her." A little pressure to nudge him.

"No. I just found some things under the seat and kept them." His young voice squeaked in panic. "But you can't tell my boss. I can't afford to lose this job."

"What did you find?"

"A set of lock-picks, a sledge hammer, and a center-hole punch."

Burglary tools. "Do you still have them?"

"Not the sledge hammer."

"Why did you take the lock picks? Are you planning a break-in?"

"No! I just thought they were cool. I'm sorry. I know it was stupid."

McCullen turned on Churn Creek, then pulled into a parking lot. He didn't want to put this kid in the interrogation room if he didn't have to. "I need the tools. I might be able to pull a fingerprint."

"My mother can't know, and she's probably home."

"That's your problem." The kid could probably come up with some plausible lie to cover his tracks. McCullen had pulled his share of stupid stunts at the age of sixteen and had nearly gone to jail. A few months later, one of his classmates had shot up the school and killed four people, including his best friend. That horrible day had changed everything—and most likely led to his current career. "Where do you live?"

"Saginaw Street. Near the highway."

A low-rent neighborhood. But at least Jimmy had a job and he was still in school, so the kid might turn out all right. McCullen stared hard. "What else did you find in the car?" No harm in asking.

The young detailer licked his upper lip. "There was a gun under the seat too. I know I should have turned it in to the cops, but my mother needed the money, so I sold it."

McCullen wanted to curse. "That was such a bad idea. You're making my job impossible."

"My mother needed a prescription." Jimmy sounded defensive. "I didn't know the lady was dead. I just assumed she was long gone and not coming back for her stuff."

"What kind of gun? And who did you sell it to?"

"A small black handgun. And I don't know the name of the guy who bought it. But if you have two hundred dollars, I can probably buy it back."

A shakedown. This just got better and better. As evidence, the gun was practically worthless. Hearsay testimony at best. But if he could retrieve the weapon and track the owner through the serial number, it might help him ID the victim or the killer. "Let's go get it."

They wasted two hours looking for "the dude" Jimmy had

sold the gun to and didn't find him. McCullen drove Jimmy home and let him go in by himself. The young man came out with a black leather zipped pouch and handed it to him through the window.

"This isn't over," McCullen warned. He handed Jimmy a business card. "Find that gun and call me or I'll press charges for selling a weapon without a permit."

McCullen wasn't optimistic he would ever see the gun, and he wasn't likely to press charges either. The kid was a minor. Why ruin his life? If his own mother had needed money for medical help, he would have done the same thing. She'd died the year before of heart failure after a lifetime of diabetes. Her medical bills had kept them from having the money for high school sports. McCullen had resented not getting to play football—until the school shooting—but he'd loved his mother too much to be bitter about it.

He drove back to the bureau, enlarged and scanned the license photo, then sent the file to a reporter he'd dated at the *Searchlight* newspaper. Kaitlin had been a rebound girlfriend after Emma and it hadn't lasted long, but they'd remained friendly. He also called the *Sacramento Bee* and asked a managing editor to run the picture as soon as they could.

With any luck, someone would come forward. Even if they didn't recognize Charlotte, they might have spotted her and be able to shed light on her presence in Redding. The victim had come here with burglary tools and a weapon, under a false identity, then had been murdered.

What the hell had Charlotte been involved in?

Chapter 13

Thursday, May 9, 2:05 p.m.

Randall examined the dynamite-based explosives in storage and decided they were no longer adequate. Too crude, not powerful enough, and too limited by their fuses. When they'd made them, the meltdown—and the need to protect Destiny—had seemed surreal and faraway. But now it was happening, and it was time to get serious. His followers had crafted IEDs with compact materials and sophisticated timers to use on the communication centers. He needed to do more research and step up his game.

He left the storage locker, thinking he would go home, then changed his mind and headed for the generator. He wanted to check on Grace's progress. Producing electricity was critical if Destiny was going to do more than just survive in the new world. He'd also ask Grace a few questions about building a timer. He braced himself for the interaction. She'd been tense with him lately, but she was the only one in the community with that kind of knowledge and he was too paranoid to search online or discuss bomb-making details in digital conversations.

As he jogged down the path to the creek, the sun was hot on his back and a deep weariness made his legs feel heavy. He hadn't slept well in days, and tension had built up in his neck, giving him a constant mild headache. He would be glad when this was over.

He spotted Grace, in her usual camo pants, climbing up from the creek bed. Her shirt and hair dripped with water, as if she'd dunked her head in the creek, but even with a wet T-shirt, she didn't look feminine. "Hey, Grace. Cooling off?"

"Uh huh. What can I do for you?" Her tone was terse.

Boy, was he tired of her attitude. "I'm just checking on the generator. We need it functioning soon."

"I know! And I'm doing my best." She practically shouted, before turning toward the generator. The side panel was open where she'd been making adjustments.

What the hell was her problem? He strode toward her. "I'd like specifics. And I wanted to ask you about making a timer for the explosives."

She drew in a long breath but didn't look at him. "I'm busy right now, and I'll report my progress to Spencer, as I always have."

Arrogant! "Would you show a little more respect? Don't forget I pay your salary."

Slowly, she pivoted and met his eyes. Grace stood shoulder to shoulder with him, and her muscles flexed under the wet shirt. "Don't forget I can walk away from this community at any time. And if respecting you is a job requirement, then I just might."

Her threat gave him pause. Spencer would be outraged if Grace left. And they needed her more than ever. But still, she infuriated him with her aloofness and her physical superiority. In the last week, she'd been worse than ever, showing outright contempt.

"What's going on with you? First you tell the FBI that Emma and I were fighting. Now you're threatening to quit and leave?"

Grace shook her head, jaw twitching. "No, you tell me. What's going on here? First Emma and Tate disappear, then Spencer's suddenly in an all-fire hurry to have the generator ready, and now you're asking about detonators. What the fuck are you up to?"

He should have known better. Grace was too smart for her own good sometimes. He started to offer an explanation but she cut him off.

"I know we're all supposed to pretend that everything is fine, but I think you know what happened to Emma."

She suspected him. The accusation hit him like a blow to the chest. "What are you implying?"

Grace stepped toward him, unblinking. "I'm not implying, I'm saying. I think you killed Emma because she wanted to leave you, and you couldn't stand the idea. Under all that futuristic ideology, you're weak and insecure and controlling."

How dare she! Rage pulsed in his temples and he fought for control. "You're fired. Pack your stuff and get off my property. I won't let you destroy this community with your hatred and lies."

"You can't fire me! Spencer won't let you. Now leave me the hell alone or I'll tell Agent McCullen what I know about you and Emma."

What did she know? His heart thundered with fear and loathing. "There's nothing to tell!"

"I heard the fight. I saw you leave your house after dark. I saw—"

Randall couldn't take anymore. Blisters of heat exploded in his brain and he lashed out with both hands.

Chapter 14

Thursday, May 9, 1:05 p.m.
Still feeling upbeat after his run with Sonja, Spencer showered and checked on Lisa. Marissa was putting ointment on his wife's bedsores, but she looked up. "Lisa's restless this morning, but not in pain." The nurse rolled his wife to her back, kissed her forehead, and left.

Lisa gave him a weak smile. "Spencer."

"Hi, sweetheart. Can I get you anything?" He'd quit asking how she felt long ago.

"Maybe some juice."

Her voice was clear and strong, another surprise. He hurried to the kitchen, poured a small glass of orange juice, and brought it back. He started to transfer it into a cup with a lid and straw, but his wife's cool fingers touched his arm.

"I'd like to sit up more and drink it from the glass. I'm thirsty."

He raised the head of her bed and handed her the juice. "You look pretty in that blue gown." He had bathed and changed her that morning, and she'd barely noticed. He remembered reading that sometimes terminal patients rallied right before they passed on. Would this be their last conversation? Heaviness filled his heart.

"Thanks, honey." She took a long drink. "I know we've talked about this, but I don't want you to grieve for me anymore. Find a new wife while you can." Lisa was even more worried about a social collapse than he was.

"I'll be fine. We have some new young people here, and I think the wait is almost over."

"I know about Sonja." Lisa's voice was quiet. "Tina visited me this morning, and she's such a gossip."

A sharp stab of guilt. "Sonja is just a new member. My heart still belongs to you."

"I know." The loose skin on her forehead wrinkled into a frown. "What did you mean by the wait is almost over?"

Spencer wanted to tell her. He and Lisa had never kept anything from each other. But since the day he and Randall had started talking about the trigger, he'd known he couldn't share his plans with his wife. She would worry too much about the potential suffering of others. "I just meant that your pain, and our time together, is near the end."

"Sing to me. I love your voice."

He'd never understood why, but it didn't matter. He sang "Forever and Ever," a Randy Travis song that always made Lisa misty-eyed. She drifted off before he finished.

Feeling melancholy, Spencer headed for the data center. He'd heard Raff come in earlier and was relieved to find him still there. They'd been up past midnight again, working to set up new proxy computers in Puerto Rico, using remote desktop protocols and 3389 ports. He sat down at a monitor and asked, "How's it going?"

"I found an employee at Bentley & Eastman who telecommutes two days a week and accesses files through a remote portal." Raff glanced up from the monitor. "I posed as a customer and sent him an email embedded with a surprise. As soon as he opens it, I'll have access to his files and can upgrade his security status."

Spencer felt impatient. "Then what?"

"Once the employee, David, has the upgraded security clearance, we can move money around—or make it disappear. I'll start with Standford Oil. Without cash, the company will be paralyzed and will have to shut down refineries. A massive gas shortage will follow."

"How long will all that take?"

"I don't know." Raff shrugged. "Maybe a couple of weeks. Predicting the outcome is not my area of expertise."

Spencer felt a new charge of optimism. There was a Standford refinery near Houston, one of the cities where he planned to shut down the electricity, so the effect could be immediate. Their potential started to seem unlimited. "It's not enough. We need to target several companies at once."

"I can do that."

"For my part, I'll create a fake fraud warning, then I'll start cuing up recipients. I've got millions of addresses." Spencer felt another rush of adrenaline. "If even a third of those people go to their bank and pull out money, it'll cause a ripple. That will make the news, which will cause a bigger ripple."

Raff gave him a sly grin. "You like fucking with people as much as I do."

Offended, Spencer squared his shoulders. "You're wrong. I'm doing this to shut down our carbon output and reset our climate-change trajectory."

Raff rolled his eyes. "If you say so."

Spencer didn't bother to respond. The hacker was too shallow to understand their goals. He opened an email he'd been saving from the Federal Deposit Insurance Corporation. After copying the contents, he created a new email that looked identical—with a perfect blue and gold logo—and modified the text. The message was reassuring, yet contained an alert that customers should monitor their accounts for irregularities. Next he altered the sender's URL to look like it came from the FDIC, then embedded a chunk of code that would access the person's financial information when they logged into their banking information. Once he had access to all those port 443 accounts, he could manipulate the money, causing further panic.

The fun part over, he began the tedious task of duplicating the email and attaching thousands of address recipients to each communication. He had the files batched and ready to go, but with millions, it would still take all day.

The work kept his mind off phase two, which he tended to worry about. Months ago, he'd created a worm that he would soon send out, causing the office computers in major power companies to malfunction. But that was only part of the attack. He also had to hack into the software that controlled the flow of electricity so he could manipulate a shortage. He knew the security weaknesses of both Siemens' and ABB's power-grid equipment and had taken several dry runs, but the real-life scenario would still be challenging. Technicians would be working madly to correct the system, and he would have to keep overriding them for days—if he could. The financial collapse would work in tandem, and, in theory, business would quickly grind to a halt. Once the U.S. economy tanked, the rest of the world would follow like dominoes.

By six, his stomach was growling, his back was stiff, and he had to get away from the computer. He stood, knowing it would be polite to invite Raff to dinner, but he wanted to get away from the annoying and immature hacker. Spencer's thoughts shifted to Sonja. Was it too late to ask her to join him for a meal? Or was it too early in the whole scheme of things to begin to court her? Lisa's words echoed in his head. His wife had encouraged him to find someone else.

He realized he hadn't checked on Lisa all afternoon, so he hurried to her room. She was sleeping peacefully, and he was relieved to keep moving. He still had so much to do. Grace came to mind, and he wondered if she'd made progress. Did it really matter? They would be fine for a while even if the electricity from the generator was intermittent. Guilt hovered around his conscience. Grace had looked so tired and worried today, and he hadn't given her nearly enough support. Spencer decided to pack a picnic dinner for the two of them and take it down to the creek. He called Grace, but she didn't answer so he left a message.

As he made sandwiches, he wondered about future meals. They had chickens and turkeys in a pen near the greenhouse, and after the collapse, his meals would be made with recently slaughtered, fresh-roasted turkey. He could have already started eating exclusively from their land—as some members did—but he'd been too busy taking care of Lisa and everything else to home-prep food. Spencer looked forward to a healthier diet.

The sun was still bright but low in the sky as he drove the golf cart down the path to the creek. On another day, he would have gone on foot, but now that things were in motion, every hour was precious. When the terrain began to slope down, he parked the cart and walked the rest of the way. In the dusk, he spotted the structure over the generator. Something wasn't right. Where was Grace? Had she quit for the day?

He saw feet sticking out from behind the metal turbine housing. Spencer's pulse quickened and his throat closed up. Why was she lying down? He'd never seen her nap on the job. He ran toward her. "Grace? Are you okay?"

Rounding the generator, he kneeled down. The acrid smell of burned flesh assaulted his senses. Oh dear god. Grace lay motionless, and her face was angry red. Blood trickled from her eye sockets. "Grace!"

Spencer started to check her pulse, then remembered his first-aid training. He looked to see if she was still touching whatever had electrocuted her. *No.* Her hands were at her sides and burned nearly black. Oh shit, oh dear. What had happened? Spencer checked her pulse. Nothing. Life was gone from her body.

How had this happened? Grace was so professional, so careful. But she'd also suffered from PTSD and depression when she'd first joined them. Spencer had another ugly thought. Had Grace and Randall argued again? No, this must have been an accident.

Crushed by the loss, he wanted to weep. Grace had been his friend and a wonderful source of encouragement. But his brain was in panic mode. What now? He couldn't call the authorities and report her death. They'd want to investigate, and he couldn't risk having them on this area of the property. Even if federal agents didn't find anything, they might press charges for negligence or try to shut down their community. He couldn't let any of that happen. They were too close to setting the trigger.

Spencer grabbed his cell phone from his pocket and shakily dialed Randall. The damn call wouldn't go through. He pushed to his feet and cursed out loud. The connections out here were tenuous, so he charged up the path, hoping for better reception. He didn't get it.

Spencer ran to the motorized cart and gunned it toward the housing area. He and Randall had to talk this through. Grace was estranged from her family, so her people weren't likely to get worried, but another sudden disappearance would be alarming to community members. They could tell them Grace had an emergency and had to leave. After the meltdown, community members would understand if Grace didn't come back. Travel, especially commercial flights, would become impossible.

What other choice did he have?

Ten minutes later, he pounded on Randall's door, but his brother didn't respond. He tried calling again, and this time it went through, but Randall didn't pick up.

Spencer stopped at his garage and grabbed shovels, gloves, and a small lantern. He hoped no one was watching as he dropped everything in the back of the cart. It didn't matter. He used hand tools all the time, and this would look like just another outdoor project. Still, he glanced around. As the sun set, the cul-de-sac homes were quiet, as his friends and supporters cooked dinner and settled in for the night. He jumped back on the cart and raced back toward the generator. The thought of Grace lying alone on the ground as darkness descended made him ill. She deserved so much better. Was her death his fault? Had he pushed her too hard?

He refused to believe it. Accidents happened. People got sick and died. Lisa came to mind. How would he handle her death? There would be nothing suspicious about it, but he hated the thought of a government official coming to Destiny when they had so much going on. If Lisa died before the collapse, he would put her into the Jeep and take her to the coroner. Once the paperwork had been filed, he could bring her back home and conduct the service he had planned.

Why was everything happening now? Could he recruit a new engineer before it was too late? Or should they put their plans on hold? For a moment, he froze. Could he go through with everything? Covering up Grace's death was inconsequential compared to setting the trigger. What was the alternative? Even if Sonja moved in with him, they still faced continuous uncertainty. Could he keep her happy in Destiny? Or would she get bored and tired of waiting like Emma had?

The cart hit a rut in the road, jostling him out of his thoughts. Spencer turned on his headlights. A moment later, Randall appeared in the road. Thank goodness. He'd hoped to find him out here.

"What's going on?" His brother hopped in the cart.

Surrounded by only crops and shrubs, Spencer still kept his voice down. "It's Grace. I found her dead. Electrocuted."

A pause. "That's terrible." Randall's tone was a little flat.

The ugly thought came back, and Spencer had to ask, "Did you see Grace today? Or fight with her about something?"

"No. What are you implying?" Now Randall sounded tightly controlled.

Spencer sensed his brother had lied to him. But why? "If her death was an accident, then just tell me. I want to know what happened."

"You said it yourself. She was electrocuted, so it must have been an accident." Randall rubbed his hands on his head, a gesture Spencer hadn't seen since they were children.

A finger of fear stabbed at his gut. Randall only lied to him when he was in crisis mode. If his brother had accidentally killed Grace in a hot-tempered moment, that could have pushed him to the edge. "Are you feeling all right? This is a stressful time for both of us."

"I'm fine."

Spencer stared, searching for the truth, but the dusk light masked Randall's expression. "I'm just wondering if you should consider taking—"

"No meds! I'm fine. It must have been an accident, and I'm hurt that you would accuse me."

Was he wrong? Flooded with guilt, Spencer turned the cart around. "I'm sorry. I'm just rattled."

After a long moment, Randall asked, "Is she at the generator?"

"Yes. She was reconfiguring the setup, hoping to keep the batteries from overheating. I pushed her to get it done quickly."

"Don't blame yourself."

Spencer didn't know what to think or say.

"What's the plan?"

"We're going to bury her and tell everyone she had a family emergency." Spencer turned off the main road and headed for the creek.

"What about her car?" Randall asked.

"We'll say I drove her to the airport."

Randall seemed to relax at little. "Once we set everything in motion, none of this will matter."

Chapter 15

Thursday, May 9, 4:15 p.m.

McCullen stopped at the police department's investigations office, which had been moved out of the historic red-brick building they'd outgrown and into an office in the downtown mall. He hoped Rob Ramirez would be around. The detective was a friend, and they were on a bowling team together with two other patrol officers. It was McCullen's only social recreation. As an FBI agent, he avoided forming bonds. Too much of what he did and thought had to be kept to himself. After Emma dumped him, he'd been leery of getting emotionally involved too.

A middle-aged woman in civilian clothes greeted him and buzzed him in. He had to glance at her tag to remember her name. At a cluttered desk in the back corner of the space, Ramirez looked up.

"McCullen. I heard you caught the soggy corpse. Sorry about that. I'm swamped with a rash of car thefts, and Erickson is handling another rape."

"You know I like a challenge." He pulled up a chair. "I wanted to talk to you about a burglary or robbery that might have happened a few weeks ago."

"Connected to the homicide?"

"Yep, it's a weird one." McCullen glanced at his notes for the correct date. "A woman calling herself Charlotte Archer checked into the Four Corners Motel on Sunday, April 21st. Two days later, she was gone, and a rental car was left in front of room eight. The motel manager called Shasta Rentals, and they picked it up."

"Nobody reported anything to us."

"I know. There was nothing left in the motel room and supposedly nothing left in the car. But I questioned the kid who cleaned the vehicle, and he finally admitted he'd found burglary tools and a handgun."

Ramirez raised his eyebrows. "Would have been nice to know. What's the kid's name?"

"Jimmy Pearson."

"Never heard of him. He must not have been in trouble before."

"He's in high school, and he says he sold the gun to buy his mother medicine." McCullen reached for the evidence bag in his jacket. "But he kept the lock picks. I need to know who or what this woman robbed. Or tried to rob before she was killed."

"I'll check our records. We had a string of pizza robberies, but that was back in March." Ramirez turned to his monitor and keyed in the dates. "No burglaries or thefts reported on April 21 or 22, except for some vehicle break-ins around the railroad neighborhood."

Disappointed, McCullen asked, "Any assaults?"

Another moment. "No. Sorry." Ramirez tapped his desk. "Maybe someone caught her planning to rob them and killed her first."

"That's what I'm thinking. Would you run the name through your databases just to see?"

"Sure." The search took several minutes but produced nothing.

McCullen stood. He was on his own with this one. "If you hear anything that seems remotely connected, let me know."

Ramirez stood too. "We don't see many armed robberies committed by females. I wonder what the hell she was up to."

"I'm worried we may never know."

Back at the bureau, McCullen spotted an even bigger concern standing in the hallway outside their locked office. Luke Caldwell was a buff older man with angry eyebrows and a broad scowling face. Emma's father bellowed, "Where is my daughter? Why haven't you taken that damn community apart yet?"

Bracing for more, McCullen keyed in the code and gestured for Caldwell to follow him. "Let's keep this private."

"I want to talk to your boss."

Great idea. Gibson had made himself the contact person on Dallas' team, so let him deal with the victim's overbearing father. "I'll see if he's here." McCullen stepped into the main office and called out, hoping his boss hadn't left for the day.

Gibson came out of his cubicle, briefcase in hand. McCullen nodded at the big man in the lobby. "Mr. Caldwell would like to speak with you."

The three headed into the small space, which was less crowded than their interrogation room. As soon as he had their attention, Luke Caldwell blasted them. "What are you people doing? You know Emma is out there somewhere. What the hell is your plan?"

"We're making progress," Gibson replied calmly. "Please sit down."

"I don't want to sit. I don't want to be placated. I just drove a hundred and fifty miles because you won't return my phone calls!"

McCullen and Gibson stayed on their feet too. Caldwell was bigger than both of them.

His boss tried to take control. "We found her car Tuesday off Bear Mountain Road, so we have to consider that she might have been abducted by a stranger."

"Bullshit! That just confirms that she didn't run away. That she's still right there in Destiny."

Gibson kept his cool. "We have an investigation in place, and we hope to have a broader search warrant soon. Please be patient."

"It's been a week! That bastard has my daughter and grandson in some shitty basement, and if you can't go get them, I will." Caldwell's nostrils flared, and McCullen smelled coffee and bourbon on his breath.

"That would be a bad idea!" Gibson was loud now too. "You could endanger your daughter and yourself and jeopardize our investigation."

"What investigation? You're both right here. How the hell can you look for Emma if you don't leave the damn office?"

"Please sit down and I'll tell you!"

After a long moment, Caldwell perched on the edge of a chair, like a man ready to spring.

"We have another agent working the case," Gibson said. "And she thinks she'll locate your daughter very soon."

What the hell was he doing? That was too much information.

"Your agent is out at that crazy community?" Caldwell pressed.

"I can't tell you and you can't talk about it. Go home and let us do our job."

Caldwell stared at Gibson, then shifted his gaze to McCullen.

"Please. Go back to Sacramento," he pleaded. "We'll call you soon with an update, I promise." Caldwell lived in the capital, but his ex-wife, Emma's mother, was in San Francisco. They hadn't met her in person yet.

Caldwell stood. "I already checked into a motel, and I'm not going anywhere. If you don't find Emma in the next twenty-four hours, I'm going out there to raise holy hell."

Gibson tried to soothe him, but Caldwell kept threatening as he walked to the door. "I'll torture that son-of-a-bitch until he tells me where she is. I was in Vietnam—I know how to get information." Caldwell slammed out of the room.

"What a jerk." His boss shook his head. "We can't let him screw this up for us."

McCullen hesitated, then said what was on his mind. "You shouldn't have told him we have an agent in Destiny."

"I didn't exactly spell it out, and I didn't have much choice." Gibson grabbed his briefcase from the floor. "I couldn't let Caldwell go out there and start hurting people."

"I hope you didn't compromise Agent Dallas."

"I didn't. Why would Emma's father jeopardize this case?"

McCullen wasn't sure. "Maybe we should warn her."

"There's nothing to tell. Besides, Dallas said she's speeding up her plans and will go out tonight to locate the bunker. We may have a warrant tomorrow."

McCullen was jealous and irritated that Gibson had that information and he didn't. He was still part of the Eden team. "I'd like to be kept in the loop."

"I'll update you if anything significant happens." Gibson started to leave, then turned back. "Any progress on the floater?"

McCullen summed up what he knew about the case,

concluding with the missing gun.

"Was she shot?"

"No, but she had a head wound. Two newspapers will run a photo of the victim soon, and we'll see if anyone can identify her."

"Send the burglary tools to the bureau's lab and see if they can pull a print." Gibson sounded like a boss now.

McCullen bristled. "I planned to do that next."

"I know, but we have a lot riding on these two cases. They may be the biggest investigations we ever do." Gibson moved toward the door. "They could increase our funding, or maybe give us another agent."

"Once I've identified the victim, it'll be easier to pinpoint suspects. Don't worry, we'll solve them both." McCullen hoped he sounded more confident than he felt.

After Gibson left, McCullen went to his desk and searched CODIS for women with Sacramento addresses, hoping to spot a photo that matched Charlotte's license.

His personal cell phone rang, and he was surprised to see Kaitlin Tucker's name on the ID. Was she calling as a reporter or a friend? Reluctantly, he took the call. "Hey, Kaitlin. What's up?"

"You tell me. Do you have any leads on Emma Clayton's disappearance?"

She was calling as a reporter. "No, but the bureau is conducting a statewide search. We have her photo posted everywhere, including truck stops all along I-5."

"Good to know. Is Randall Clayton still a suspect?"

"We haven't ruled out anyone yet. You know I can't give you specifics about the case." That had been an issue in their short relationship.

"You know I have to ask." She paused. "What about the

dead woman in the pool? Any leads on her?"

"I already told you what I know. She was using the name Charlotte Archer, but it's phony, and we're still trying to identify her. Until we do, the investigation will be difficult."

"The motel manager said she'd been wounded in the head. Will you confirm that she was murdered?"

"I don't have the autopsy report yet, but we suspect foul play." He hated that expression.

Someone started talking in the background, but Kaitlin ignored them. "Is there any link between Emma Clayton and the murdered woman?"

It hadn't occurred to him. "We have no reason to believe that at this time. I have to get back to work, but I'll let you know if something breaks open." It was bullshit, and they both knew it, but Kaitlin didn't call him on it.

"Thanks, Caleb. I know you'll nail both."

Her confidence bolstered his, and he dug back into the files.

Chapter 16

Thursday, May 9, 7:15 p.m.

Dallas rounded the corner of the fourplex, and the sound of a door closing made her look up. Randall stood in front of her apartment, looking a little rattled. Dallas' heart skipped a beat. Had he been inside, snooping through her things? Or had he just left Raff's apartment instead? She started up the stairs as he came down, then stopped in the middle, blocking his path. How to play this? Sweet, but straightforward?

"Hey, Randall." Dallas smiled brightly. "Were you just in my apartment?"

He feigned surprise. "No, I was looking for Raff. Have you seen him?"

Liar. But she didn't call him on it. Conflict could get her kicked out. "No. I was at the community center trying to make a phone call."

"If you see him, tell him I need to talk." He stepped down, and she let him pass.

The prick. Dallas hurried upstairs and let herself in, noting the door was locked. She'd assumed he and Spencer had a key to the apartment, so she'd kept her non-Sonja phones and cash in a locked leather case. Good thing she'd taken her purse with her. Dallas headed straight to the bedroom to see if the case had been tampered with. Still on the shelf in the closet, it seemed untouched. Thank goodness!

She inspected the rest of the apartment to see if anything had been moved or fiddled with. Her laptop was still under the couch. But was it in the same place? It seemed farther back. Dallas turned it on, and the password dialogue box came up. Her shoulders relaxed. Randall hadn't accessed her files. But why had he come in at all? Did he suspect her? Or was he just a snoop?

She glanced out the window. He'd probably seen her coming along the path and knew to get out when he did. If he had even been inside. She had no proof. But the possibility that Randall was suspicious meant she had to step up her plan to find Emma.

Instinct told her an underground bunker was buried out there in the side of a hill. A secret bunker that most Destiny members didn't know about. If Emma Clayton and her baby were alive and captive on the property, they were likely in that bunker. She would go tonight.

She transferred her Kel-Tec from the secret compartment in her purse to a pocket inside her backpack, then threw in a flashlight, lock-pick, and camera. All the bureau needed to get a search warrant was photo evidence that the bunker existed and her claim that she'd heard a cry for help.

In case she encountered anyone, she had a story ready about stargazing away from the lights, but she decided to update her new contact anyway. From her laptop, she sent Gibson an email: *Leaving soon to search for the bunker. I should be in contact again by midnight or so.*

She remembered McCullen's request to keep him apprised of her actions, so she sent him the same message. He was still part of her team, and she really liked him. The memory of his mouth on hers distracted her for a moment and added to her heightened senses. She hoped they would have an opportunity to be alone together before she wrapped up this assignment and flew home. An after-the-fact hookup couldn't do any harm. And it would be her trump card if Trevor came around later and wanted to get back together. A one-night-stand confession would likely send him scurrying.

To kill time, she played chess online with a man in Singapore named Ian. He wasn't her regular favorite, and he beat her two games in a row, so she signed out. She had other things on her mind.

When the stars were finally bright against a dark sky, Dallas grabbed her pack, tucked her lucky cloth into her pocket, and headed out. Below her, Raff was coming up the path. *Oh crap.* She started to duck back inside, but he called out, "Hey, Sonja."

Reluctantly, she turned to face him. "Hey." She wanted to be friendly, in case he had information she needed. "Randall was looking for you earlier."

He shrugged. "Where are you headed?"

"Doing a little stargazing." She twisted sideways so he could see the small portable telescope attached to her pack. "What about you?"

"Just a dinner break. Probably frozen pizza. Care to join me?"

"Thanks, but I've eaten." She wondered why dinner was only a *break*. "Are you going back to work? That makes for a long day."

"Yeah, we've got a project we're working on, but I'm a night owl anyway, so it's cool." He reached the top of the stairs. "Stop by and have a beer when you get back if I'm around."

"Sounds good." Dallas smiled and hurried down the steps. What project were they working on? She'd have to pump Raff for more information when she had a chance. Right now, she had to locate Emma.

She strode to the end of the cul-de-sac and found the road that cut between the Clayton brothers' homes. Porch lights illuminated the front yards, but otherwise the houses were dark. It struck her as a little odd, but Randall and Spencer could have gone into town together. Once she was past the housing area, she clicked on the powerful flashlight that fit into the palm of her hand. A half-moon low in the sky cast a glimmer on the metal roofs of the storage buildings in the distance. Dallas kept up a good pace but didn't want to look like she was in a hurry.

As she neared the path that led to the creek, she heard a soft repetitive sound. She stopped and listened. Rhythmic and whispery. Familiar, yet unidentifiable. Instinctively, she slipped off her pack and dug out her small handgun. But the sound was not from any animal she could identify.

Feeling more secure with the weapon in hand, she started forward. The hill was just up ahead, and she felt more determined than ever to find Emma and get the hell out of this strange place.

The soft hum of voices drifted by on a gentle night breeze.

Dallas froze. Who was out there?

She turned toward the sound. It came from the area by the creek where the generator stood. Was Grace still at work in the dark? If so, who was she talking to?

Dallas spun and headed toward the creek. *It could be totally innocent,* she told herself. But after dark? That seemed suspicious. Spencer's push to have the generator ready by the next day, combined with Raff's mention of an IT project, had convinced her that something was going on. Something big and immediate. Something other than the kidnapping of Randall's wife.

Dallas moved quickly, sticking to the grass at the edge of the path so her footsteps wouldn't be heard. The voices had stopped, but the rhythmic sound continued. As she neared the slope to the creek, she clicked off her flashlight and slipped her gun into the back of her jeans. If they saw her, she didn't want to look like a federal agent coming at them with a weapon drawn.

As she came to the edge of the gentle descent, a soft light glowed below in the distance. About two hundred yards downstream from the generator, she guessed. The repetitive sound was louder now, and a second later, she identified it. Shovels digging a hole. Neurons fired all the way up her spine. Were they digging a grave to bury Emma? Why now, a week later? And what about the baby?

Slowly, Dallas made her way down the path, through the shrubs, until she came to the thicket of trees along the creek. The generator was there in the clearing, its metal casing catching the moonlight, but she saw no movement. The sound came from the right, and from here, she had to leave the path and make her way through the underbrush, which would be noisier. She took a gentle step to her left, and her foot landed on a twig. The noise seemed to crack open the night. Dallas froze.

The digging continued without pause, and she let out the breath she'd been holding. Painstakingly, she made her way to a large tree and sat down behind it to watch and wait. From her distance, she could tell one of the diggers was tall like Spencer, but the other one could have been Randall or Grace. Even with the glow of the lantern on the ground nearby, she couldn't see their faces. A long dark shape lay near their feet. A body? Her gut squeezed down tight. What the hell was going on?

Dallas pulled out the camera she'd packed. The telephoto lens would serve well, but without light, the pictures might be worthless. She'd have to prop it against something to stabilize it. But what if they heard the click? She put the camera in her lap, waiting for them to start talking again. She was close enough now to likely hear what they were saying.

After a long wait, Spencer's voice cut into the night. "I think it's deep enough."

The shoveling sound stopped.

"I don't know." The second voice was Randall's. "We don't want a coyote digging her up."

Her! Was it Emma? Why bury her here?

"They won't."

Dallas peered around the tree. The two men squatted at each end of the body and grunted as they lifted.

"Damn, she's heavy."

"Don't say that," Spencer chastised his brother. "I loved Grace."

The engineer! Had they killed her? But why?

The men shuffled toward the grave. Randall asked, "How do we do this without falling in?"

"I don't know. Maybe toss her a little, as disrespectful as that seems." Spencer choked with distress.

With an awkward heave, they let go of the body, and it fell with a thud into the hole.

Spencer made a funny noise that sounded like a sob.

Randall stepped over and patted his shoulder. "It was an accident. You weren't even there. Don't blame yourself."

"She might not be dead if I hadn't pushed her to fix the generator."

"But we have to be ready," Randall said. "It's not your fault she got careless."

Adrenaline already pumping, Dallas' shoulders tensed. Ready for what? She shifted to her knees, and a twig under her snapped.

The brothers both spun in her direction.

"What was that?" Randall's alarm was evident.

"I don't know."

Heart pounding, Dallas climbed to her feet. She couldn't be caught spying on them. No excuse would be believable. She took a few tentative steps, listening for their voices as she moved away.

"It must have been an animal," Spencer said.

"I don't think so."

Dallas kept moving, trying to follow the route she'd taken coming in. But the half-moon didn't provide much light, and she knew she was making too much noise.

"You start burying her, and I'll check it out." Randall's voice seemed fainter.

Dallas picked up speed as she gained distance, and once she hit the dirt path, she started to run. Her backpack bounced as she raced for the main road. She couldn't hear Randall behind her, but her heart pounded too loudly to hear anything else. When she reached the junction, she turned toward the community, abandoning her bunker-finding mission for now.

As she ran, she glanced over her shoulder. In the dark, she couldn't tell if Randall was back there. She thought she heard footsteps coming up the path from the creek. Dallas sprinted into a cornfield and lay on the ground between rows of young stalks. She faced toward the dirt road and peeked up after a few minutes, seeing a dark figure in the distance.

The man was still, except for his head, which scanned in every direction, looking for her.

Dallas lay flat again.

"Is anyone out there? There's no reason to hide," Randall called out, obviously trying to sound friendly.

Dallas kept motionless. After five minutes, she heard his footsteps moving away. She cautiously lifted her head and saw him jogging toward the creek. She lay down again and waited another five minutes. She figured it would take them at least twenty minutes to fill the grave, and she wanted to be home before they ventured back up to the road.

Dallas climbed to her feet and jogged toward the house lights in the distance. She had to report what she'd seen and heard. After that, she would find Raff and have a beer with him as a cover story. It was too risky to go out looking for the bunker again tonight.

Back in her apartment, she took her phone into her bathroom—in case the walls were thin—turned on the water, and called Agent Gibson, willing the call to go through. After eight rings, he finally picked up. "Gibson here. Everything all right, Dallas?"

"More or less. Sorry for the late call, but I had an interesting evening." She recounted the events, keeping the telling factual and low key.

"That is bizarre. We need to move in. I'll work on a search warrant tomorrow, but you'll probably have to come in and speak to the judge."

"I disagree, sir." Dallas plunged ahead. "I think I know where Emma is, and I hope to get proof soon. But something else is going on, and I need more time to figure it out."

"We can sort it out when we confiscate their computers

and cell phones."

"I don't think you'll get a warrant for anything but the gravesite. Not reporting an accidental death is a minor crime."

"I want to try." Gibson took on a tone. "This is my decision, and these men could be killers."

Dallas hadn't met Gibson, so she refused to be intimidated. "I know that, sir, but if I come into town to speak to a judge, it could blow my cover. And if we don't get a wide-ranging search warrant, we may never find Emma."

A long silence. "Okay. I'll give you another forty-eight hours. Send me a full report in the meantime."

"I'll get it all done."

Dallas grabbed a beer from the fridge and sat down at her laptop to write her report. She emailed it to Gibson, and at the last minute, sent a blind copy to McCullen. This had been his case, and if he was a good agent, he'd want to be kept informed.

Chapter 17

Thursday, May 9, 11:45 p.m.

Raff trudged up the steps, glanced over at Dallas' door, and wondered if she was still awake. Probably not. This community of anal, paranoid tree huggers followed the "early to bed, early to rise" bullshit. Yet Sonja was different. She had an edgy energy that didn't match the laid-back commune. Still, he was so tired from getting up at the crack of dawn he didn't think he had enough juice left to charm a hottie like Sonja.

But once inside, a restlessness kept him from settling down. The unit was nicer and newer than any place he'd ever lived in, but being out here in the middle of nowhere was depressing. He was used to being alone in his own space, but at least in Vegas he could go out and people-watch or chat up the neighborhood deli owner. As soon as he finished this job and collected the second half of his pay, he would scoot. The Destinites might want to spend their post-collapse life here in the sticks, but he would take his chances in the new chaotic world. Spencer's financial machinations would wreak havoc for sure, but they probably weren't destructive enough to cause the collapse of global society.

Randall's plans to blow up tech companies and internet hubs were far more serious, but harder to actually execute. Since Randall had paid him half the money upfront, Raff still planned to hack into the security at the Hudson Street building. But it wasn't his priority. Ideologically, he didn't want to help take the internet down, even for a short period, but he would get the codes if he could and earn his pay. He didn't really believe Randall and his followers could pull it off.

Raff grabbed a beer from the fridge, took off his shoes, and sat down at his laptop. It felt good to be back at his own machine—the only difference between work and play. He opened his private email account and scanned through the new edition of *Hacker News*. Silly stuff compared to what he had in mind.

He tapped into the proxy computer he'd taken over from an accounting firm in Israel, a bot Spencer didn't know about. From that IPS, he accessed the financial management company again, using David Cohen's login info and upgraded security status. The telecommuter's Hebrew name had caught his attention. Especially since Bentley & Eastman managed huge cash investments for Middle Eastern governments. Earlier, as he'd made millions disappear from the oil company's account—the first step in Spencer's cyber attack—Raff had started thinking about the deposits held by the governments of Lebanon and Syria. All that money and so little of it going to help people. Dirt-poor refugees like his grandmother, who lived in Gaza, and all those Syrian refugees who were starving in border camps.

Raff picked up his cell phone, wanting to speak to Noni, but knowing she had limited access to phone service. She'd been on his mind since he'd spoken to his mother, and late that afternoon, an idea had percolated. The cyber assault was so potentially devastating he'd dismissed it at first. Yet he'd kept coming back to it until he accepted that it was a righteous thing to do. The Middle East was a powder keg. Violent, misogynistic, backward, religious, and disruptive to global harmony. They were his people, all of them, Jews and Arabs alike, but he felt no connection to the region, except for his grandmother, and he was sick of the conflict and terrorism.

His hands paused on the keyboard. Once he set things in motion, he had no way to stop them. This mission was ten steps beyond the denial-of-service hacking he'd done. Or even his occasional selling of corporate information. This was serious shit. But what the hell—Spencer was about to unleash havoc on the world, so he might as well do his part to ensure that the future was more peaceful. That meant putting an end to the sectarian bullshit.

Shaking a little, he accessed the main fund held by the Syrian government. Seventeen seconds. Next he set up a hundred-million-dollar transfer to the account held by the Israeli company whose computer he was using as a proxy. Eventually, he would transfer it from there, but it might not even matter.

Raff clicked submit, and the cyber wheels started to churn. It had taken another count of seventeen. Thirty-four seconds in all. Could it really be that easy to start a war?

The next week would tell. The Syrian government might not even know the money was gone for a few days. Once Assad's officials discovered it, they would easily track the transfer to the Israeli proxy computer. Raff planned to keep moving the money until it ended up in a fund held by Israel's conservative government. The key issue was blame. Syria would quickly blame the Israeli government—which had been bombing missile shipments along their border—and wouldn't even try for a diplomatic solution. Assad would reach out to Iran instead, and the two countries would probably wage war on their centuries-old enemy.

Adrenaline surging, Raff stood and paced the apartment until his heartbeat quieted. He downed his beer, took a seat, and launched phase two. This time, he was looking for a proxy computer in Iran he could take over. Messing with Israeli money would be much more challenging, but he had to try. If successful, he would move funds into a global charity that aided Palestinian camps all over the Middle East. Maybe his grandmother would get some relief. Or maybe an Israeli missile would kill her first. Either way, it would be better than the life she lived now.

Jews, Arabs, Sunni, and Shia. They were all the same people, but couldn't stop bombing each other. They might as well wage all-out war and get it over with. He kind of hoped it would go nuclear. If no one in the region was left standing—including his grandmother—the world would be a better place. If Spencer was right and humans were doomed in the next couple of decades, there wasn't much to lose by trying.

A social networking site set up by Iranian college students proved to be vulnerable. Raff soon had full access to a computer in Tehran.

A knock on the door startled him. "Who is it?" Raff darkened his monitor and pushed to his feet.

"It's Sonja. Is it too late for a drink?"

Yes! Please let this be a booty call. His sexual encounters could be counted on one hand, but some chicks got off on geeks. Unfortunately, they never came back for more. *Remember to look her in the eyes,* he thought, closing his browser. Raff jumped up and hurried to the door.

"It's never too late." He held open the door, noting she'd

changed from the clothes she'd been wearing earlier when she'd gone out stargazing. *Too bad.* The baggy shirt she wore now probably wasn't meant to entice him.

On her way in, Sonja held out a microbrew with a weird label, and he took it. Cheap beer was fine with him, but he'd drink the good stuff if someone else bought it.

"How was the stargazing session?"

"Terrific. It's great being out here with no city lights. I saw Orion more clearly than ever."

He knew nothing about astronomy, so he smiled and moved on. "I was just thinking about how I miss the city and being able to run out for pizza late at night."

"Where are you from?"

"New York, originally, but I live in Vegas now." He was proud of both. "And you?"

"Phoenix. It's not Vegas, but you can find just about anything in the middle of the night, including a dentist."

Raff laughed. "So what the hell are you doing here?"

"Cooling off." She smiled and sat in the armchair.

Damn. He'd wanted to get close to her on the couch. He plopped down across from her. "Seriously. This is the middle of nowhere. Why Destiny?"

"My fiancé died."

"You told me that, but I mean, why here? Why not Maui or Vegas or someplace fun?" Wrong thing to say, he realized. Sonja was feeling lost and lonely, and he didn't want to blow his chance with her. "Are you really into the prepper thing?"

"Of course. I think the shit could hit the fan at any moment. North Korea is especially scary right now, and the jihadists never give up. Every major city is vulnerable to an attack of some kind."

"I know what you mean. I was ten when the towers were

hit. My dad was a stockbroker who died that day." Sometimes that line made girls soften toward him.

"I'm sorry. That was a crappy day for all of us." She pulled a fifth of vodka from her oversized bag. "Let's get drunk."

"Now you're talking." Raff stood. "I'll get some shot glasses."

After the first round, Sonja asked, "Why are you here, Raff? A young tech guy from the city in an isolated rural community?"

"I'm just doing a job for Spencer. I'll be gone in a week."

"What kind of job?" Sonja poured two more shots and gave him a sexy smile.

She was so pretty! "Just a tech job and not something I can talk about. Client confidentiality."

"Huh." She picked up her shot of vodka and gestured for him to do the same. "To the future, whatever it holds."

They belted down another round, and Raff felt it go directly to his head. The two slices of pizza he'd had for dinner were long gone from his belly.

* * *

Dallas was curious as hell. Destiny seemed to be preparing for a step back in time, so why had they hired a hacker for a short-term job? Some kind of cyber theft?

"What do you do for fun, Raff?" She grinned. "Besides vodka shots, I mean."

"I play chess and go to strip bars."

Chess? Excellent. "Do you have a board? Let's see what you've got."

"It's back home. But you're on. We'll play on screen." His

eyes lit up for the first time, and he grabbed his laptop from the desk.

Damn. She'd have to sit next to him on the couch. She preferred an old-fashioned board game, but she also played online. Her favorite competitor was a fourteen-year-old boy in Taiwan, but he hadn't been around lately. "Let's make this interesting. Every time someone loses a piece, they have to take a shot. In the end, the loser has to tell a secret."

"Any secret?"

"Just the one I want to know." She playfully punched his arm. "You're going down."

Dallas didn't know if she could beat him, but if he got buzzed enough he might tell her what she wanted to know anyway. "Excuse me for a minute."

She scooted to the bathroom, turned on the water, and vomited up the last two shots. She had to stay relatively sober to make this work, and she couldn't afford a hangover in the morning. Puking on cue had been her specialty as a child, and she'd used it to distract her bickering parents sometimes...and to get out of stupid school assignments.

She looked around for mouthwash and found a prescription bottle of Zoloft instead. Raff didn't seem like someone who took antidepressants—but then, who did? A dab of toothpaste would have to suffice. She didn't plan to kiss him anyway. He was *so* not her type.

Back in the living room, Raff had a chessboard displayed on screen. "Black or white?"

"Black. You can move first." *Let's get this over with.*

His first few moves were classic, but Dallas was setting up for a blockade. She soon captured his knight, and he groaned but cheerfully took a shot of vodka. After twenty minutes, he'd taken four more shots, and she'd had three.

Raff stared at the board longer and longer between moves and finally said, "I'm too drunk to do this."

"You concede?" Dallas had a good buzz, but she hadn't lost track of her mission. She never did.

"Yes. You win, but let's play again when we're sober." His words were so slurred she could barely understand him.

"You have to tell me a secret now." She squeezed his hand for effect. "I want to know what your job is. I'm fascinated by it."

"All I can say is I'm a hacker." He closed his eyes and leaned back on the couch.

Shit. He was going to pass out. "I knew that, so it's not a secret. Tell me more. It's only fair."

He mumbled something, but Dallas didn't understand. She leaned in. "What did you say?"

He mumbled again, then fell over on the couch, like a sleeping cow. She thought she heard "financial test." When she realized what that might mean, a shiver went up her spine.

"I'll let myself out." Dallas headed to the bathroom again and upchucked more vodka. It didn't change how buzzed she felt, but it would keep her functioning and make the morning more pleasant. Her taste and tolerance for alcohol was a genetic given, but her parents' overall worthlessness made her treat the stuff with some caution. It would be easy to fall into daily excessive drinking.

Dallas waited in the bathroom for ten minutes, entertaining herself with her cell phone. She wanted to contact her team, but her work phone was hidden back in her apartment, and there was no point in risking the use of her Sonja phone. She had to keep it clean in case creepy Randall kept snooping around. The report could wait. With any luck, she'd have real intel in a few minutes.

She moved quietly into the living room where Raff was still unconscious on the couch. His laptop was on the coffee table. Keeping an eye on Raff, she grabbed the computer and took a seat in the chair. She downsized the browser, leaving it open in case Raff woke up. She would say she was finishing their chess game.

Not a single folder showed on the desktop. No surprise. People with things to hide didn't leave their data on display. She opened the browser history tab and nothing displayed. He had either cleared it before he let her in or he had his computer programmed to keep it clear. She glanced over at Raff. Still out of it.

Determined to learn something, she tried to access his hard drive, but a dialog box came up, asking for a password. Knowing she was wasting her time, Dallas tried ten guesses—all geeky references to digital technology. No luck. Tech people used random letters and symbols for passwords, and they changed them often.

Raff started to snore. Instead of being reassuring, the sound unnerved her. Dallas quickly began opening programs, hoping their file histories might give her a clue. Nothing. The hacker was careful and paranoid. Even if she'd been sober and thinking at full capacity, this computer was beyond her skills. She thought about the computers in the data center in Spencer's house. Would they be as well-guarded? Those were the ones she really wanted to access.

Dallas reminded herself that her mission was to find Emma Clayton and her baby. The *financial test* was secondary. She couldn't blow her chance to save a woman's life by letting curiosity or ambition override her primary goal. She would report the information to Gibson and let him decide what to do with it. McCullen would get a copy of the report.

Dallas opened the browser again and left the chess game displaying. As she slipped out, she wondered if Raff had his computer programmed to record her snooping. If he did, would he tell Spencer—or worse, Randall—that she couldn't be trusted?

Chapter 18

Thursday, May 9, 5:45 p.m.

Luke Caldwell took the last pull from his thermos, grabbed his overnight bag, and walked into the motel. He planned to stay in this rundown little town until someone found his daughter, even if he had to do it himself. Emma and Tate had been missing for a week! As much as he loved his baby girl, a quiet anger kept bubbling to the surface. If only she'd followed his advice and had taken that job in Sacramento instead. If only she'd listened to him and not married Randall Clayton. The guy was such a smug, smooth manipulator. He'd been a politician, for chrissake, and seemed as slick and phony as a used-car salesman.

Luke also wanted to slap his hypochondriac ex-wife for asking Emma to stay with her and not telling him. He could have warned his little girl that leaving a control freak like Randall could be dangerous. Now his sweet baby grandson was gone, and he might never see him again.

"Did you want a room, sir?"

The clerk's impatience jerked Luke out of his thoughts. "Of course." He reached for his wallet. "I'd like to be on the end, if possible." He hated listening to other people's chit chat, noisy sex, and stupid TV shows.

"Sorry, those are taken." The guy didn't look concerned.

"I'll be here for a while. As soon as one opens up, I want

to change rooms."

"Do you want to pay for a week in advance? It's a better rate."

"No. If I stay a week, you can give me the rate then."

The clerk started to object, then closed his mouth.

"Where's a decent place to get a drink around here? Friendly but not too gay."

The girly-looking clerk rolled his eyes. "The Highland is three blocks down, and it's popular with hunters and outdoor sportsmen."

Luke was familiar with the place. Emma had been working there when the Claytons bought it. He didn't want to give the bastards any of his money.

A few minutes later, he dropped his bag on a ratty chair and turned on the TV. While he watched the news, he ate the second meatloaf sandwich he'd packed that morning. He could afford to eat out and stay in a nicer place, but why should he? This wasn't a vacation.

Around eight, he got thirsty and headed out, walking in the direction the clerk had pointed. The sun was low in the sky, and the noisy traffic had eased. For a moment, Luke enjoyed the fresh air with its perfect temperature and slight breeze. Then a sports car passed with loud thumping music and spoiled it. *Punk!*

He'd planned to find somewhere else to get a drink, but changed his mind and headed into The Highland. The tavern was his kind of place. Dark paneling, long accessible bar, big-screen TVs, and sports-themed pictures and signs. He moved past the half-empty tables. A good-looking blonde with plenty of cleavage was behind the counter. Luke eased onto a barstool and felt instantly better. The bartender came over and gave him a professional smile. "What are you drinking, sir?"

"Double Dewar's."

She reached behind her for the bottle and poured a generous drink. "That's twelve dollars."

"I'd like to run a tab."

"I'm sorry, but this is the first time I've seen you, so you need to pay for the first round." She flashed him another professional smile. "But there's a discount if you pay with cash."

Luke handed her a twenty and told her to keep the change. His first tip was always generous. She'd have to work for the next one. He downed the drink and ordered another. After that, her smile seemed more genuine. Two rounds later, she asked if he was new in town.

"I live in Sacramento." Luke hadn't talked about Emma's disappearance with anyone except the feds, but now it came rushing out. "My daughter and her baby disappeared a week ago. I'm here to find her."

"I saw the story on the news. It's such a tragedy. You're Mr. Caldwell?"

"Luke."

"Sadie." She leaned toward him, and for a moment all he could see was her cleavage. He realized she was still talking. "What makes you think she's still around here? Most people assume a sicko truck driver picked her up."

The implication that a serial killer had taken Emma enraged him. "Bullshit. Her husband has her locked up out there in that fucking prepper compound." He could hear his own voice and was surprised by how drunk he sounded.

The bartender's eyes widened. "You really think so?"

"Hell yeah. He's a control freak and she was leaving him." The pressure on his bladder was suddenly painful. As he slid off the stool, the room spun. *Whoa.* He needed to pace himself and stop ordering doubles. Maybe it was the altitude, but he felt woozier than he'd been in a long time. Weaving through the tables was tricky at first, but he'd had so much practice over a lifetime he managed just fine.

After he left the restroom, he stood in the dim hallway and tried not to sway as he reached for his cell phone. He hated the damn thing, but his girlfriend made him carry one. But that wasn't who he wanted to talk to. After three doubles, he always called his ex-wife. Sometimes just to hear her voice, to know that she was still alive. Sometimes he called to punish her for leaving him. Tonight he was worked up about Emma.

"What do you want, Luke?" His ex-wife sounded weary and impatient at the same time.

"I'm in Redding again. I'm not leaving without our daughter."

"Let the FBI handle it. You'll just make things worse."

"*I'll* make things worse? You're the one who asked Emma to leave that bastard and come stay with you." Luke's tongue felt thick, but he couldn't stop. "You didn't tell me or even warn her that it could be dangerous."

"Don't blame me, you drunken asshole. I didn't ask her to stay with me. She insisted."

"Bullshit. You made her feel obligated, like always."

"Fuck you! I have no control over Emma or her relationship with Randall. No one ever expected him to hurt her." His ex burst into sobs. "I'm worried that Emma and Tate are dead."

"Don't say that. Randall's probably just keeping 'em locked up. He thinks he'll get away with it because of the collapse they keep talking about."

"But that could be a lifetime!" She made no effort to

control her anguish.

"I'll find her myself if I have to torture that asshole to make him talk."

"Don't make things worse, you old fool. Let the FBI do its job."

"I don't have much confidence in this rinky-dink Redding crew."

She pulled in a long gulp of air. "Should we hire a private investigator?"

"What for? We know where she is. I'll search every inch of that property."

"What about hiring a search-and-rescue guy with a bloodhound?"

Luke knew there was a problem with the idea, but his brain was foggy. "I don't see how that will work. Randall will never let anyone on the property."

"Then how are you going to search?"

"I told you. I'll take him hostage. I'll force him—"

His ex-wife hung up before he could finish. *Bitch.*

Back on his barstool, he ordered a single and told Sadie to cut him off after one more.

She laughed. "I was going to ask for your car keys."

"I'm walking. The car is at the motel down the street." His voice still sounded sloshy in his own ears.

Sadie poured him another scotch that looked the same as all the doubles.

"Thanks."

He sipped this one, and Sadie leaned toward him over the bar. "You said you were here to find your daughter. Are you going out to Destiny?"

"If I have to." He remembered his talk with the agents earlier. "But the feds are working the case from the inside, and they asked me to wait."

"What do you mean?"

Luke realized he'd said too much. "Nothing. I'd better settle up and get going." He paid for the last three rounds and staggered out of the tavern.

Chapter 19

Friday, May 10, 3:07 a.m.

Randall woke from a nightmare of being buried alive. Sweating and dry-mouthed, he got up for a drink of water. He hadn't slept well since Emma's warm body had gone missing from his bed, but this was the worst night so far. Burying Grace had been bad enough, but hearing someone spying on them had unnerved him. Spencer thought he was paranoid, but Randall was sure he'd heard someone running away. It could've been Toby, that Blackwell boy he'd caught prowling around after dark before, but Randall didn't think so. This time he'd kept his suspicion about Sonja to himself. Still, Spencer had humored his concern, and they'd dug up Grace and reburied her a half mile away. By the end, they'd been numb with exhaustion.

As he climbed back into bed, his cell phone beeped on the nightstand, indicating a text. Curious, he looked at the message. It was from a man he knew only by his online name, Rebel2000: *I can't make the meeting. I hurt my back and I'm laid up. I can't even sleep, which is why I'm texting you now. Sorry.*

Randall cursed out loud, a long nasty outburst. What else could go wrong? Rebel's part of the mission was to set off an explosion in the Westin Building in Sacramento, which housed SAIX, an internet exchange center for Northern

California. Recruits from nine other cities—most in the U.S. but two in Europe—were gearing up for simultaneous attacks. His followers were just waiting for the green light. Randall expected most of the blasts to go off within an hour of each other, and he'd decided Monday morning would be best. Internet service in the U.S. and Europe would go down just as millions of people rushed into banks to withdraw money. The stock market would crash and business would grind to a halt.

But only if everyone did their job. Randall pressed call for Rebel's number, and the man answered, sounding surprised. "Randall?"

"You can't let me down. I need you to take care of business Monday morning." If he could wait that long. The stress was wearing on him.

"I would if I could, but I'm taking so much Oxy, I can't even think straight."

"It's only a backache. You'll be fine in a day or so."

"No, I'm seriously fucked up and need surgery. I'm telling you I can't do it. I've got the package ready and the employee security pass. Text me if you want to meet and pick them up. Sorry, man." Rebel hung up.

Stunned, Randall threw the phone. What a pussy Rebel turned out to be. Would his other recruits follow through? They damn well better. He'd committed a lot of time and money to getting them ready. But he couldn't find someone new in time to hit the SAIX. He'd have to do it himself. And that meant scoping out the building and picking up the security badge. *Shit.* He texted Rebel: *I'm on my way. Be there in 3 hours. Where do you want to meet?*

He made a thermos of coffee, grabbed his handgun and a

package of crackers, and headed for his vehicle. After he passed through the Destiny gates, he kept checking his rearview mirror for a few miles to see if anyone was tailing him. He suspected Agent McCullen, or maybe Sonja Barnes, might be watching to see where he went. No lights appeared. He checked again at the Highway 299 turnoff, then again when he neared the freeway. Once he was on I-5 headed south, he pulled off at the first opportunity, bought gas at an all-night station and watched for ten minutes. The only vehicle that came down the off ramp was a semi-truck.

Convinced he was clear, Randall got on the freeway and settled into the drive. He and Spencer had built and stored devices made from dynamite to blow the bridges when the time came. But that had been an easy task aimed at a middle-of-the-night destruction of property with no one hurt. Blowing out part of the Westin Building with people in it was a whole new level of action. A dread filled his stomach. Maybe Monday morning was too late, with too many people. A weekend with few people in the targets would be more humane. He wasn't a terrorist.

Visualizing the explosion made his heart pound. Could he really do this? When he'd conceived the plan, he'd counted on others to set the explosions. Not only did he lack the experience, he'd never been a violent man, except for fistfights in grade school when other kids made fun of his glasses and crooked teeth. Braces and laser surgery had eventually eliminated those problems, but the resentment had simmered. He'd gotten even with his tormentors, but in clever psychological ways, never with violence or vandalism.

Everything had changed now. Emma was in a suspended state, the world as he'd known it was doomed, and nine other futurists were ready to conduct their part of the mission. He had to suck it up and get his hands dirty. He'd done plenty of manual labor over the years in Destiny—building homes, farming the land, digging out the bunker. He wasn't the same white-collar suburbanite he'd been when he and Spencer had founded the community. He had to check in with his followers and see if they needed the attack to happen on a weekday for access. Maybe they didn't all have to happen at once. The SAIX was a critical part of the plan and he would make it happen, but he also had to live with whatever he did.

As he passed Santa Carmichael, the first rays of sun glinted on the horizon. The town stirred up a mixed bag of memories. His first marriage, which had gone to hell in four short years. The wonderful time as mayor when he'd finally done something that had made his father proud. Followed by his agonizing Congressional defeat and the stunning death of their parents in a murder-suicide. Everyone blamed it on his dad's early, aggressive dementia, but Randall had started to question everything and worried that the same violent fait awaited him. He pushed it all out of his mind. No living in the past. No thinking about his father. He'd suppressed it for years and now was not the time to dredge it up.

Hours later, as he neared the split in the freeway to head for Sacramento, his shoulders tensed. He had to meet with Rebel and pick up the security badge, but he wasn't sure about the bomb. He hated the idea of driving home with it in his truck. But the explosives he and Spencer had prepped were too big and bulky to carry into a building in a briefcase. He glanced at the text message from Rebel again. They were meeting at a covered picnic area in a park in Woodland, a town just outside of Sacramento.

Rebel wore a hooded sweatshirt and sunglasses and didn't

get out of his beat-up Saab. He handed Randall the security pass out the window and said, "The briefcase is on the floor of the backseat."

Randall glanced around the empty park, grabbed the case with the explosive, and hurried to his car. Flashes of Homeland Security agents rushing in to arrest him played in his mind, and his heart raced. He never thought he'd be in this situation, and his natural paranoia was kicking in. How did he know he could trust Rebel? Maybe his whole participation was a setup. In the early dawn, Randall didn't see any cars but theirs, and he forced himself to relax and drive away. One task down, one to go.

Twenty minutes later, he approached his target. The five-story Westin building had parking underground, but Randall found a spot on the street where he could watch the entrance. Employees swiped their cards in a security station outside the main double doors, but there were no guards. He glanced at the employee pass in his hands: Richard Salenka, a man about his age, but heavier, with close-set eyes and a disappearing chin. *Not good.* If anyone stopped him and looked closely at his photo ID, he'd be screwed.

As he crossed the street, the skin on his chest began to itch. *Oh no.* He hoped he wasn't breaking out in hives. That happened sometimes when he got overstressed, and it was miserable. All he had to do was use the badge to get into the building, find the network center on the second floor, and see what the security was like. He could handle it.

The reconnaissance went smoothly. Randall was pleased to discover the second-floor business only required employees to slide their badges through a wall-mounted security device. He walked past a few times and watched other employees. No need to risk getting caught today. Relieved, he bolted from the building and headed home.

Chapter 20

Back in Redding, Randall stopped at a market and picked up two romantic suspense paperbacks, a bar of dark chocolate, and a package of diapers. He hadn't been out to see his family yet that day, and he worried they might need something that wasn't stocked in the bunker. The books and candy would make Emma happy though. He wanted to win her back, so they could have sex again. Going without had ratcheted up his tension during this already stressful phase. He looked forward to a year from now when everything had settled into the new normal.

By the time he reached his house in Destiny, his eyelids were heavy and he could barely focus. After deliberating about where to keep it, he left the briefcase under the seat of his car. The explosive was small but unstable, so it seemed safer than carrying it in and out, and he probably wouldn't leave again until it was time. He went inside and slept for an hour, then loaded up a backpack with bottled water, baby food, and the things he'd bought for Emma. Still feeling groggy, Randall trotted over to his brother's garage to borrow the golf cart. He heard voices from Spencer's back deck. His brother was having lunch with Sonja. Randall didn't have time to be social, so he hopped in the cart and took off down the back road. They would see him driving away, but it didn't matter. Spencer would cover for him. They often visited the lockers to add or retrieve something from storage, and everyone in the community spent time in the greenhouses.

Today, Randall passed all the buildings without a glance, but he had to stop for a group of kids in the road.

He tried to appear casual, managing to smile at the young students, then spoke to Tina, their teacher. "Gorgeous day to be outside. What is your class up to?"

"We checked on the vegetable sprouts we started. The green beans were ready so we moved them into the planting beds."

"How are the tomatoes? I can't wait for the new crop."

"Coming along."

Randall nodded and moved on. Social niceties were almost impossible with the fate of the world on his mind and all the shit that was coming down later.

As he passed the turnoff to the creek, the memory of his argument with Grace surfaced. Oh man, that had gone from bad to worse. What a tragedy. Why did she have to be so bitchy? The whole accident could have been avoided. Now they had no engineer. The thought made him feel vulnerable. Were they really ready to be on their own?

Rounding the curve, he glanced back over his shoulder. No one was on the road behind him. Randall regretted bringing the cart. He would have to leave it parked out here, and if someone came along, they would wonder where the hell he was. *No one would come along*, he reassured himself. Sonja was with Spencer, the hacker never went outside, and the rest of the community was busy with their day jobs. Earlier, he'd spotted Sam, their main field hand, moving the irrigation wheels, a long tedious chore. So everyone was accounted for.

A few minutes later, Randall hurried up the hill, dreading

facing Emma as he dodged familiar shrubs and protruding rocks. Had it only been a week since he and Spencer had hiked up here, carrying the baby in a backpack and pulling Emma along between them, drugged and half-conscious? So much had happened since. He needed, more than ever, to be in control of events, but it felt like everything was spinning away from him.

A big boulder marked the entry. Behind it, a small downed tree still lay across the grass-covered trap door. Randall lifted the dead foliage aside and found the small handle. Once he began to pull, the counter-balance kicked in, and the heavy rectangular hatch opened with ease. Ducking down, he grabbed the railing and descended the stairs. A motion-sensor light came on to guide his steps.

Powered by an electric car battery, the bunker operated with minimal super-efficient lighting and a few small appliances. Plumbing, wiring, and supplying the bunker had taken a big chunk of their cash reserves, pushing them into buying The Highland as source of income. Excavating for the bunker, then burying it again with the mounds of earth they'd dug out, had been a huge job. Randall had run the backhoe until his hands went numb, and the repetitiveness of moving dirt to reshape the landscape made his mind go numb too. At the time, he and Spencer hadn't worried much about satellites spying on them. But the government had become much more aggressive in the last decade, and once they'd started planning the trigger, he'd become a little paranoid about eyes in the sky.

At the bottom of the stairs, the smell of wet earth filled his nostrils. Randall punched the numbers of his mother's birthday, backward, into the keypad. He changed the code every day to keep his wife from figuring it out. He braced himself and stepped inside—senses alert. The first time he'd visited Emma, she'd come at him with her fists and called him a bastard. He'd let her hit him a few times to get it out of her system, but he'd been married to Emma long enough to know she was still unpredictable.

As he stepped through the door, Emma rushed him. "Where the fuck have you been?" Her face contorted with rage.

"I had some important business to take care of this morning."

"What could be more important than your family?"

A little extra weight from the baby still clung to her hips, but the sight of his wife always aroused him. More exotic than beautiful, she commanded attention—a striking mix of Irish and Polynesian with platinum blonde hair, full breasts, and long legs. Damn, he missed her.

She shoved a palm against his shoulder. "Tate is running a fever. We need to take him to the ER."

Panic shot through Randall and he rushed to the corner where their baby lay in the middle of a large mattress. He knelt beside him. At five months, the boy still looked more like Emma, with chubby cheeks and hazel eyes. But he was a miracle. They'd tried for years before Emma finally got pregnant. Tender joy brought tears to Randall's eyes. He'd never loved anyone the way he did Tate. Yet when the baby was out of his sight for a while, he sometimes forgot about him.

The boy was asleep, but his breath seemed shallow and his cheeks were watermelon red. Randall touched his forehead. Quite warm. He turned to his wife. "No need to overreact. Babies run fevers all the time. I'll bring some Tylenol."

Emma's arms were crossed. "I gave him some from the first aid kit. It's not helping."

"Give him a cool sponge bath."

Emma punched him in the shoulder, and Randall fought the urge to hit her back. During all their arguments, he'd never done more than push her around.

"Tate shouldn't be here!" she shouted. "Take him back to the house. What if he gets sicker and needs to go to the hospital?"

She was right, but it was too much of a risk. They couldn't let anyone in the community see the baby. "You know Spencer has a lot of medical knowledge. I'll have him come out. Maybe Tate just needs antibiotics." Randall's panic eased. They could take care of this. In the near future, they might have to handle emergencies themselves. That's why Spencer had a wall full of medical texts.

Emma's shoulders slumped. "How long are you going to keep us here? We need fresh air and sunlight!"

"It's only for a few more days." He decided to tell her a partial truth, even though he'd promised Spencer he wouldn't. "We're going to test the financial system, which is near collapse." Randall stepped toward Emma and softened his voice. "It's what we want. To live here in peace, without the threat of annihilation hanging over us."

Her eyes grew wide. "You're finally going to trigger the financial meltdown?"

They had talked about this, but only in theoretical way. "It's just a test. But yes, we think the system will fail." The power grids were next, but Emma didn't need to know that.

"Of course the system will fail, but a collapse will take weeks," she argued. "If not months. And law enforcement will be one of the last government functions to shut down. When will you trust me enough to let me out?"

Randall reached for her hands, but she brushed him aside.

"It won't take weeks, I promise." *Should he tell her? She would find out soon enough anyway.* "I have a supplemental trigger in place. This meltdown won't just be financial."

Emma blanched. "What are you saying?"

"We're going to knock out network hubs and tech companies. The lack of internet will add to the chaos and accelerate the meltdown."

For a long moment, she was silent, and Randall watched her eyes run through a range of reactions. Finally, Emma said, "This is really happening, isn't it?"

Her acquiescence made him want her. "Yes. It's what we've prepared for. What we've dreamed of. A better life and a long-term future for humans."

"You don't have to keep me in here. I can stay in our home until the collapse takes effect." She reached out and stroked his crotch, sending a shiver of lust through his body. "Don't you miss sex with me?" she whispered.

Oh god, he wanted her. Right now. Right here in this secret underground place. Randall pulled her to him and kissed her mouth hard, his body pressing into her.

Emma jerked away. "Only if you let me out."

It was so tempting to bring her back into his bed. But too risky. Could he get past her resistance right now? He knew how to get her turned on in a few seconds.

"Don't even think about it."

Randall suppressed his frustration and willed himself to relax. "Be patient, Emma. It'll only be a few days. Everything will happen this weekend." He wanted so much to make her smile at him. He reached for the backpack, dug out the books and chocolate, and tried to hand them to her.

Emma knocked them to the floor. "Don't try to placate me. As long as I'm a prisoner, we are not a couple."

"Don't say prisoner. It's only a little while more."

Again, she was silent, her eyes calculating. "What exactly are you going to do?"

It occurred to him that if she knew about his plans, once he let her out, she would be complicit. Not that Emma would ever turn him into the authorities. She'd already proven that. "I have people in place who are prepared to set off explosives at tech companies in Silicon Valley and at internet hubs in New York, Seattle, London, and other major cities. All I have to do is send the email, and they go into action."

"Oh shit! I don't want anyone to get hurt."

"That's why we're doing it over the weekend. The buildings will be empty." Another lie, but she had to realize there could be collateral damage. Spencer had rejected the idea when Randall mentioned it long ago because of the possibility of harming someone. *Such hypocrisy!* The financial collapse would cause millions of people to starve.

"I'm sorry for keeping you here," he finally said. "I'll make it up to you in time." He tried to pull her in for a squeeze, but Emma turned away.

Tate woke and started to cry. His wife rushed to the baby, calling over her shoulder, "Just go! And bring more Tylenol, antibiotics, and rubbing alcohol."

Chapter 21

Friday, May 10, 10:45 a.m.

Spencer sat at his desk, opened his laptop, and logged into his blog. He'd been ignoring his online community for a few days, and he missed the social media support and stimulation. He also needed to recruit a new engineer to the community while he still could.

He responded to comments on his most recent blog and on his Google page, then started a new post. First he updated his followers about the progress on the generator and posted a picture of the lithium batteries, asking for suggestions on how to keep them from overheating. He was careful to post disclaimers about everything he shared publicly, knowing other futurists were thirsty for information and would try to replicate everything they did in Destiny.

Grace's voice tried to haunt him, but he kept shutting it down. He would mourn—and honor her—later, when the Emma crisis and the collapse was behind them. In the second half of his blog, he called for people with engineering backgrounds to contact him directly about joining the community, offering free housing and a part-time salary to the right candidate. He uploaded the post, hoping he wouldn't be inundated with opportunists.

His final task caused more unease. He crafted an email to Destiny members, explaining that Grace had been called away by a family emergency. He wrote that she'd taken the train late the night before and didn't know when she'd return. Spencer's mouse hovered over the send key. Would this cause anyone alarm, especially after Emma's disappearance? Grace had been estranged from her ex-husband and son, and she'd never talked about her parents or siblings. *It would be fine,* he told himself. The members were loyal and had no reason to jump to worst-case scenarios. As long as the feds didn't learn about Grace's sudden departure. Another woman gone, with her car left behind. *Damn.* They should have hidden Grace's car. No, they hadn't had time, and cars tended to surface eventually. The meltdown would start within the next forty-eight hours. Some elements were already happening. They just had to keep it together for a few more days.

Moments after he sent the email, Lisa's bell rang. Surprised, Spencer rushed to her room. She hadn't summoned him much lately, because the morphine made her sleep. But she was wide-eyed and signaling for him to raise the bed.

"Are you in pain?" He kissed her cheek, her skin cooler than it should be.

"No, honey. I feel better today, and I'd like to meet our new member while I'm awake."

Spencer swallowed the lump in his throat. This would be awkward, but he wanted Lisa's blessing. "I'll call Sonja and see if she's available. She'd like to meet you as well."

"You should have told me more about her."

They had talked about Sonja, but he still felt guilty. "I know. But you've been asleep a lot, and I wanted to get Sonja settled in quickly." Lisa knew he was working hard to recruit young people to Destiny.

"Call her now. My little revival won't last long."

Spencer reached for his phone, hoping Sonja wouldn't answer.

She did. "Hello, Spencer. I'm glad you called."

"Will you come to my house, please? My wife would like to meet you."

Only the slightest pause. "Sure. I'll be right over."

He turned to Lisa. "Sonja was an ideal applicant."

"Remember the last young woman who came out for an interview?" Lisa laughed, then started to cough. "When she mentioned hanging a crystal around my neck to heal my cancer, I thought you'd lost your mind."

Spencer smiled sheepishly. "Sometimes the kooks seem okay on paper."

"I hear Sonja is special...and very pretty."

Lisa knew Sonja was her potential replacement. Spencer tried to make peace with the whole scenario, but guilt tore at him. He should have waited. He shouldn't have let Randall pressure him into speeding up their plans.

"It's all right. Just don't forget me too quickly."

"Never." He pressed his face to hers, tears welling in his eyes.

The doorbell rang a moment later, and Spencer hurried to let Sonja in. He was tempted to coach her as they walked back, but he resisted. Sonja would handle this well. She was that kind of person, and he'd made a good choice.

After he introduced them, Lisa asked him to bring her some tea. Spencer obliged, curious about what Lisa would say to his would-be girlfriend.

* * *

Dallas smiled brightly and said charming things while part of her brain sent alarming messages. She felt like an exposed adulterer, even though she and Spencer had never kissed and her seduction of him was entirely staged. In addition, Lisa was challenging to focus on. The woman was so gaunt, she barely seemed human, as if the billowy pink nightgown was hiding a skeleton. Dallas had witnessed some horrible things, but this scenario had her nerves jangling.

"I'm glad you're here," Lisa's voice was a whisper. "Spencer will need a new wife soon."

Startled, Dallas struggled for the right response. "I barely know him. I just came here to be part of the community."

"But you and Spencer have a connection. I feel it."

What the hell was she supposed to say? "I feel it too. I think fate brought me here."

Lisa's tone changed, but it was subtle, because her voice was so weak. "As one of the survivors, you'll need to bear children. Can you?"

Dallas wasn't sure she'd heard correctly. "What do you mean by survivors?"

"After the apocalypse, whatever it turns out to be. Destiny members must repopulate."

They'd brought her in as a breeder. Nice. "I'll do my part."

"Good. Spencer always wanted children." After struggling to get the words out, Lisa closed her eyes.

"Are you okay?" *Dumb question.*

The gaunt woman didn't respond, but she was still breathing, a shallow ragged sound.

"It was nice to meet you." Dallas fled the room, desperate to escape the most uncomfortable conversation she'd ever had.

She met Spencer in the hall and was afraid to even

comment. "Lisa's asleep. I'll head back to my apartment."

"No. Stay for lunch. I want to get to know you."

"I need to wrap things up with a client, but I can be back here in half an hour." She wanted to update her team and reapply the pheromones. If she couldn't find the bunker tonight, she would need to get closer to Spencer and probe him for information. He was attractive, but not rough enough around the edges to generate real sexual chemistry for her. But she could fake her way through anything.

* * *

While Sonja was gone, Spencer grilled chicken and made a salad with lettuce from the greenhouse. Marissa had dropped off the vegetables the day before, as she did weekly. When lunch was ready, he left the front door open for Sonja, set a table outside on the patio, and checked on Lisa. She was sleeping peacefully. Her earlier conversation had been such a surprise. He woke each day now, wondering if he would find her gone.

As he walked back up the hall, Sonja breezed in, wearing a white tank top and a pair of shorts that looked like a skirt. She could have been a model for tennis clothing, but it was her face that held his attention. Wide cheekbones, brilliant blue eyes, and the most kissable lips he'd ever stared at. How could a man get this lucky twice in a lifetime?

"Let's go out to the patio. I made salad and grilled chicken. Will that work for you?" He stepped outside and Sonja followed.

"It's perfect. But honestly, I'll eat almost anything that's healthy."

"People with variable diets live longer." Without realizing

he was going to, Spencer kissed her cheek.

Sonja smiled. "This is so lovely here. I'll never get tired of seeing that gorgeous mountain."

"It really gives us a sense of place." Spencer joined her at the table.

"And the snow runoff produces the creek, which provides water and electricity. You've chosen an ideal location."

"We did our homework and looked for somewhere safe from storms, but we also got lucky. My late father knew the land owner."

They dug into the meal, and moments later, Sonja asked, "How is the generator coming? Grace seemed worried about it."

His gut tightened. *Why was she asking?* He took a moment to finish chewing. "The generator will be fine. Did you get my email this morning?"

"No. About what?"

"I must have forgotten to add you to my group list." He paused. "Grace had a family emergency and had to leave for a while. So we're looking for another engineer to join us." He tried to keep his voice light, but grief and guilt welled up. "You don't happen to know anyone with those skills who might be persuaded, do you?"

"Sorry, my friends are more the artistic type. I'm sure you'll find someone." She took a sip of wine. "There's no real rush, right?"

He wanted to tell her everything! Sonja had a magnetic pull that overwhelmed him at times. "With everything that's happening now, especially the European banks, the collapse could be imminent."

"But won't it be a slow process? Months or even years until the economy falls into a permanent recession?"

Spencer shook his head. Why didn't people realize this? "Once U.S. banks start to fail, people will panic and pull their money, and within days, the whole system will be crippled."

"That's faster than I imagined. But still, it's why I keep a portion of my estate in gold bars."

"You're smart. Even smarter to be here, where we'll be insulated from the worst effects."

She leaned toward him, and he wanted to press his mouth to hers. How could he crave her so badly with his dying wife thirty feet away?

"What do you think it will be like after? I mean for most people." Her eyes were troubled, and her compassion for others made him want her more.

"For the first few years, most people will manage to get by, even without heat or electricity. But food will become scarce, and whole regions will begin to starve. Resource wars will wipe out other large segments of the population." The food in his stomach seemed to congeal. Spencer put down his fork. "Maybe we shouldn't talk about this. It's too depressing."

"But large pockets of civilization will survive," she countered. "They'll form collectives like this one and become self-sustaining."

"You're right. The upside is that the collapse will reduce carbon emissions down to nearly nothing. Without factories, coal burners, or cars, we have a chance of keeping the earth's temperature inhabitable."

The sound of a motor caught their attention, and they both looked over at the road. Randall was taking the cart out. Spencer assumed he was going out to see Emma and the baby. "He's probably checking on the generator. More wine?" He wanted Sonja to stop watching his brother.

"No thanks. It's too early."

"What do you have planned for the day?"

"I thought I'd do some hiking. Explore the property."

He couldn't let her do that yet. "I have a better idea. Let's do some target practice."

Chapter 22

Friday, May 10, 7:30 a.m.

McCullen woke with a sense of urgency, something he didn't experience often. Not only was Emma missing—and likely held captive—he had a bizarre homicide to solve. Even though the victim had been dead for weeks, the burglary tools and gun she'd carried made him think something big might still be going down.

He rushed through a shower, then took McGoo out for a walk while coffee brewed. The black lab had come into his life as a rescue dog soon after Emma left him for Randall. The timing had been serendipitous, and the sweet animal had kept him from thinking dark thoughts on lonely nights. But now he wondered if bonding with McGoo had kept him from reaching out to people—or even dating. It was time. Jamie Dallas had stirred up feelings he hadn't experienced in years. Unluckily for him, she was only here for a short while, and he couldn't even have direct contact with her.

He stopped to let the dog pee on his favorite tree, then turned back. McGoo sensed his mood and started to run. McCullen laughed and jogged to keep up.

In the bureau, he checked his email messages, surprised to see one from Dallas. It had arrived just after midnight, and it had no message, just an attached report. McCullen read through it quickly, letting out a low whistle. The Claytons had secretly buried one of their members. Had her death really been an accident? Dallas seemed to think so.

He heard Gibson's heavy footsteps and looked up. His boss said, "You read the UC's report?"

"It's pretty weird. What did you advise her?"

"To ignore the illegal burial and find Emma Clayton if she can. I'm pulling her out in forty-eight hours either way."

"Why? That's not enough time."

"First a missing woman, then a dead woman. I think it's too dangerous for her to be there."

McCullen worried too, especially since his boss had leaked the intel to Mr. Caldwell. But he suspected Gibson had old-school ideas. "Are you pulling her because she's a woman? I mean, if it were me out at Destiny, wouldn't you leave me to finish the assignment?"

Gibson bristled, but took a moment to chew on it. "Maybe, but it's not just gender. You've got more experience."

"Dallas has more undercover experience that most agents ever get." McCullen had read reports. "On her last assignment, she infiltrated a group of eco-terrorists in Oregon and helped resolve a hostage/bomb situation."

"We'll see how it goes." Gibson shoved his hands in his pockets. "How's the homicide investigation?"

"Nothing new, but the victim's photo ran in the papers this morning, and I expect to get some calls."

"Let me know as soon as you have an ID."

"I will."

Gibson turned to leave.

McCullen wanted more. "What is Dallas doing today? Have you heard from her?"

"She's spending time with Spencer, then going back out

tonight to search for the bunker."

That seemed like such an overwhelming task. "I wonder if we could requisition a heat-seeking drone to fly over the property."

Gibson barely controlled his impatience. "It's fifty acres, and we're not exactly looking for terrorists."

McCullen tried not to feel stupid.

His boss continued, "Dallas sent an update this morning. Late last night, she cozied up to a Destiny member named Greg Rafferty. She found out he's a hacker who was hired to do a job, and he admitted something about a *financial test*. He was drunk at the time, and I can't find him in the database, so I don't have any intel I can act on."

"Why would a group of preppers need a hacker?" The idea disturbed him. So did the thought of Dallas drinking and making out with another man.

"I've been mulling that over. Maybe they need money and are planning a cyber theft."

"I wish we could get a search warrant for their computers, but we'd need real evidence to take to a judge."

"I know. Dallas is working on it."

His desk phone rang. "Agent McCullen here." Gibson walked away as he answered it.

"That picture in the paper this morning? I think I saw her a couple weeks ago." The caller was male and sounded middle-aged and rushed.

"What's your name, sir?" McCullen opened a digital note file.

"It doesn't matter. You wanted information and I'm giving it to you."

What did this guy have to hide? "Do you know who she is?"

"No. I just remember seeing her in the parking lot of the

Cascade Bank on Shasta View. She was in a Dodge Avenger, I think."

"What day and what time?"

"A Sunday night about three weeks ago. She was there when I stopped next door for a beer around nine, and I noticed the car was still there when I left a couple hours later. That's why I remember her."

Casing the bank to rob it? McCullen keyed in quick notes as he listened. "Where exactly was she parked?"

"On the north side near the back."

He knew the area, but he still needed the man's help. "Will you meet me there and show me where she was parked? I need to figure out what she was doing."

"I'm sorry, I can't." The witness hung up.

McCullen looked up the bank and street number to find the exact address, then left the building.

The quick drive across town reminded him of why he both loved and hated Redding. The air was crisp, trees were abundant, and the traffic was minimal. But the two cases he was working now made him painfully aware that his career and life in this quiet little town was normally so routine it depressed him.

As he approached the bank, he realized it was a new branch, retrofitted into what used to be a video store. Next to it on the right was The Highland, a restaurant and bar owned by the Clayton brothers. Emma had been the manager when they'd bought it, only months after he'd started dating her. After she dumped him, McCullen had avoided the place for years, then eventually started eating occasional dinners there.

As he parked and climbed out of his car, the pungent

smell of fried onions drifted over, causing an avalanche of memories. Late dinners and flirting with Emma, rounds of beer in the tavern with Carson, a friend who'd been killed in a hunting accident—and the night Emma had told him she was seeing someone else.

After a moment, he realized he was staring at the place, its cedar-shingled exterior dark and uninviting. He shook it off. That was the past. Right now he had a homicide to solve. He pivoted and walked into the small bank next door. One teller was behind a tall curved counter, and another woman occupied a corner desk. He headed for the corner. "I'm Agent McCullen with the FBI. Do you have a moment?"

"Sandy Warsaw. I'm the branch manager." She stood and shook his hand. "How can I help you?" The redhead seemed too young to be a bank manager, but this wasn't much of a bank.

McCullen showed her Charlotte's driver license photo. "Have you seen this woman?"

The manager gave it some thought. "No. Why?"

"She was spotted outside the bank about three weeks ago. I'd like to see your security video for the 21st and 22nd of April."

"What is this about?"

"She's a homicide victim, and I'm trying to identify her." He also needed to ask some specific questions. "Can we talk in private?"

Ms. Warsaw led him into a back room about the size of a walk-in closet. They sat at a small table that smelled like sweaty dollar bills.

"We have reason to believe this woman may have been planning, or involved in, a robbery."

"This bank?" The manager's voice tightened into a

squeak.

"Possibly. A witness says he saw her parked in your lot on the evening of April 21st or 22nd. We want to know if she came into the bank, or if she had an account here."

Warsaw shook her head. "I'm sure she's not a customer, but you can ask our teller if she saw her come in."

"Have you had anything unusual happen in the bank in the last month?"

She let out a little snort. "We're as boring as a cornfield in Kansas."

He suppressed a smile. "Any suspicious characters hanging around?"

"Nope."

Frustrated, McCullen pushed to his feet and handed her a card with his email. "Please send a copy of the video footage to me this afternoon. Thanks for your time."

Before leaving, he showed the photo to the teller, asked the same questions, and got the same answers. It puzzled him that Charlotte Archer had never been inside the bank. You couldn't scope out a security system from the parking lot.

Outside, he walked around to the back of the property on the north side of the building, where the witness had said the victim's car was parked. In one direction, he was staring at the brick wall of the bank. In the other, was the back entrance to The Highland. Had Charlotte been casing the bank or the bar?

Chapter 23

Friday, May 10, 1:46 p.m.

Randall bumped along the road, alternately worrying about his son Tate's fever and his SAIX mission. Even though Rebel had given him an explosive with a timer to leave in the Westin Building, he wanted to put together another device as a backup. He and Spencer had dynamite, blasting caps, and fuse wire in one of the storage lockers, as part of their preparation, in case they ever needed explosive for mining or dam building. They had used dynamite to shatter a huge boulder when they were building the underground bunker years ago, so he had some experience with it. This time, he might use it to shut down a local technology company that was rapidly becoming a go-to browser and cloud-storage center for internet companies. DigiSpace hadn't been on his original list of targets, but now that he was directly involved, it was a viable communication center to hit.

As Randall neared the cluster of houses, he noticed his brother and Sonja were no longer on the back patio. Where was Spencer? He hoped he hadn't gone into town. Tate needed antibiotics, and Spencer was the one who knew which kind and how much. Randall parked the cart next to Spencer's house and hurried to the front door. He pounded once, then turned the knob. Spencer kept his home open so community members could help care for Lisa, only locking a few rooms for privacy.

Randall stepped inside and called out, trying to sound more casual than he felt. He heard voices in Spencer's study and started across the living room. His brother came up the hallway carrying a semiautomatic handgun. Behind him, Sonja shouldered a Bushmaster rifle. *What the hell?*

"I'm going to teach Sonja how to shoot." Spencer grinned, looking ridiculously happy.

What was he thinking? Randall tried to keep his voice calm. "I need your help with something important." He turned to Sonja, who looked sexy in her little skirt and weaponry. "Will you please excuse us? Spencer and I have things to attend to."

His brother's jaw tightened, and Randall thought he saw a flash of anger in Sonja's eyes as well. But she gave him a charming look of disappointment.

She touched Spencer's shoulder. "Should I put this back in the gun safe?"

"I'll take it." Randall stepped forward, and she handed over the rifle.

She smiled at him but he ignored it. Sonja headed for the front. "I'll see you later."

They both waited until she'd closed the door.

"What is this about?" Spencer still looked annoyed.

"Tate has a fever of a hundred and two. Emma has been giving him Tylenol, but she says it's not helping."

"Oh hell. Why now?" Spencer turned toward the hall. "Let's put these weapons away and round up some amoxicillin."

Randall followed. "I'm glad you think antibiotics will be enough. Emma wants to take him to the ER."

Spencer stopped at his bedroom and gave Randall a look.

"We can't exactly do that now, can we?"

Randall felt the blame, as always. A spark tossed carelessly on his tinderbox of stress. "You helped me kidnap her! And if we're serious about triggering a meltdown, we need to accept that we're on our own and deal with whatever comes up."

"You're right. We can handle this. Babies get fevers all the time." Spencer grabbed the rifle from him and put it in the gun safe. The handgun he shoved under a pillow. "I'll get amoxicillin from the medicine closet in Lisa's room and meet you in a minute."

With everything happening, Randall had forgotten that Lisa was even in the house. She'd been incapacitated for so long, and with Sonja hanging around, it seemed as if Lisa was already gone. On his way out, he glanced in her room, but she had her eyes closed.

The sunshine had given way to a high layer of clouds, and Randall was relieved. Somehow, the bright glare had made him feel exposed. What he needed to accomplish in the next few days was better served by shadows. Randall waited in the cart on the passenger's side, and Spencer joined him a few minutes later.

For a minute, they didn't speak, and Randall worried that his brother was angry. Finally, Spencer said, "Lisa met Sonja this morning. She approves of our relationship."

"That's a little odd." Randall wanted to ask how long Lisa would live, but Spencer had stopped speculating months ago.

"I think Lisa might only have a few days." Spencer's voice was careful. "Even though I'm ready to move on, I wish she would hold out until we get through the transition period."

"That would be best. We've got enough going on." Randall didn't even want to think about calling the coroner or holding a service for Lisa. "Should you take her to the hospice center?"

"No! I promised Lisa she would die at home."

"We'll deal with it."

The storage lockers were on the right, and Randall decided to get out. "Stop here. I don't think we should both go to the bunker. Someone might come looking for us. I'll go into the main storage locker, then head back."

Spencer chuckled. "You just don't want to see Emma while she's still mad." The golf cart came to a halt.

"Can you blame me?" Randall reached for his backpack. "Thanks for taking care of Tate. Your medical study will pay off for all of us."

"I'll be back soon. Even with Raff's help, there's still plenty left to do for the financial attack."

A surge of fear washed over Randall. Could he keep Destiny going after the collapse if something happened to Spencer? Of course he could. He had to stop underestimating himself. Randall hopped out. It was time to start making another explosive.

Chapter 24

Friday, May 10, late afternoon, Damascus

Hakim Chehab's cell phone rang, and he glanced at the ID: *Bentley & Eastman.* A ripple of concern gripped him. Why would the asset management firm call him directly? He gave a traditional Arab greeting, but spoke in English. "Welcome, welcome. This is Hakim Chehab."

"Praise Allah. May your day be full of light. I am Raja Haddad, assistant director of the London Division of Bentley & Eastman Investments. I'm concerned that I have troubling news."

He knew it! The tone and greeting had not fooled him. "What has happened?"

A pause, then the man responded in a near whisper. "A hundred million dollars was transferred out of the Syrian Central Authority account."

A spasm shot through his chest. "What do you mean *transferred*?"

"It was moved to an account in the International Bank of Israel. Did you authorize that transfer?"

Israel! The infidels! He finally found his voice. "Of course I didn't! Who made the transfer? And whose account has the money?"

The director cleared his throat. "We're still trying to track that down. We think your account was hacked."

No! They had safeguards! "Get it back." His voice was a growl.

"The money has been moved several times already, but we're doing our best."

"Unacceptable! You will replace it with your own profits." Hakim hung up and threw his phone against the wall. Thoughts and emotions roiled, churning in a rage that he could barely contain. Outside his office window, traffic flowed and life went on as usual. *A hundred million!* His cousin, the Syrian president, had to be informed. Would Bashar punish him for it?

His assistant tentatively peered through the door. "Can I be of assistance?"

"No!"

His face disappeared. Trembling, Hakim called Bashar al-Assad on his direct line. If the Israeli government was behind the theft, it could not go unchallenged. Israel had been bombing missile shipments inside their borders for months. If they had not been dealing with an internal insurgency, they would have retaliated already. Their ally, Hassan Rohani of Iran, would be informed, and the Arab nations would unite to destroy their enemy.

Assad answered, "Praise Allah. I am blessed by the sound of your voice, Hakim."

"Thank you, but I do not have good news. On the other hand, this loss might reunite Syrians against a common enemy."

Chapter 25

Friday, May 10, 4:15 p.m.

Back at the bureau, McCullen listened to his voicemail. Two more people had called about Charlotte's photo. The first was a woman who believed the dead victim was her daughter, Rebecca Roswell, who'd been missing for three years. He returned her call and discovered the daughter would have only been nineteen—but the victim looked at least thirty. He took the information and asked her to bring in something of her daughter's for a DNA comparison. The grieving mother seemed relieved to have something to do.

The second message was from a man who claimed the dead woman was Abby Smith, a girl he'd gone to high school with in Sacramento. That seemed more likely. He returned the call, but got no answer, so he did a quick online search for Abby Smith. In minutes, he found one with a Facebook page who lived in Eureka and looked somewhat like Charlotte's fuzzy driver's license photo. But she had posted on her page recently, and none of her friends or family seemed concerned she was missing, so he crossed her off too.

Both tipsters were local, and McCullen wondered why no one from Sacramento had called. The photo had supposedly run in the *Bee* that morning as well. He called his contact at the newspaper and discovered Charlotte's picture hadn't run yet because of a "glitch." The sports editor promised to get it on the website ASAP and into the print version in the morning. Irritated by the delay, he opened the criminal database and started comparing Charlotte's photo to women with a history of financial crimes. He'd already run a comparison to bank robbery convicts and suspects. After an hour, his eyeballs ached and he glanced at the time. It was after six. He would run home and grab some dinner, then stop at The Highland to show Charlotte's photo around to the evening crew. His earlier stop had been a waste of time because it was midafternoon, so few employees and even fewer customers were present.

The point of going home for dinner was to spend a few minutes with McGoo, who tended to get nervous and start chewing things when he was gone for long periods. While his soup heated, McCullen played tug-of-war with the dog and kept one eye on the news. Even though he wanted a transfer to a bigger FBI office, he worried that a promotion would mean giving up his pet. Important cases would mean longer hours and more travel, neither of which would work out with the dog. The one time he'd taken him to a boarding facility, McGoo had lost weight and chewed off patches of his fur. How did other agents keep from getting lonely? The job was already a marriage killer.

Dusk fell as he drove back into town and parked at The Highland. The lot was full, and the employees wouldn't appreciate being questioned during their busy time. But it had to be done.

He entered the restaurant side of the building. It was closest to the bank, and the manager would more likely be over there. The bar staff was smaller, and he remembered Emma commenting that it mostly ran itself. From the lobby, he flagged down the manager, introduced himself, and showed her Charlotte's photo. "She might have come in or been sitting in the parking lot next door about three weeks ago."

"Sorry, I've never seen her." The manager's dark hair was pulled back so tight it looked painful.

"Have you had any sign of someone trying to break into the place?"

She blinked. "Not that I'm aware of. Is this woman a criminal?"

"That's what I'm trying to find out." McCullen looked around at the busy staff. "I'd like to hang out in the kitchen until I've shown this photo to everyone on duty."

"Your timing is really bad. We're pretty busy here."

"Is your full staff on tonight?"

"Almost."

"Then my timing is great."

She sighed and walked him through a swinging door into a narrow galley, where the smell of hot grease hung in the air, and employees squeezed by each other in constant motion.

"I really don't think anyone here would have seen the woman if she sat in the parking lot next door." The manager checked her watch.

"What about smokers going out back for a break?"

"Maybe. Talk to Jessie, the line cook, and Sabrina, the tall skinny server."

Someone complained about being out of fried shrimp, and the manager excused herself.

McCullen stepped up to the stainless-steel counter separating the cooks from the servers. "Who's Jessie?"

A thin-faced man looked up from the grill. "Who wants to

know?"

"Agent McCullen, FBI." He held out Charlotte's photo. "Have you seen this woman hanging around?"

"I don't think so. But then, I don't see customers."

"She could have been watching from the parking lot next door. You might have seen her when you were out back taking a break."

"I didn't see her." His tone was unconcerned and his eyes impatient.

Over the next forty minutes, McCullen questioned everyone who came into the kitchen, including the dishwasher. No one had seen the woman who called herself Charlotte Archer. When he spotted the manager again, he called her over. "Can we step into your office for a minute?" The noise in the galley was overwhelming, and he didn't understand how anyone could concentrate.

The office was tiny and crowded, and McCullen didn't bother to sit. "I need to know if the business keeps cash on the premises."

"We do, but it's in a safe. The owners encourage people to pay cash by giving a discount."

Maybe he should alert the IRS. "When is the cash deposited?"

"Typically on Monday."

"So Sunday night, after a busy weekend, would be a good time to rob the place?"

She nodded. "We do a lot of cash business, but no one knows the combination except the owners."

Did Charlotte know about the safe? Is that why she'd chosen The Highland? "Who opens the safe for the Monday deposit?"

"Usually Randall Clayton. But Emma used to make the

deposits when she was managing."

"When did she give up the position?"

"About six months into her pregnancy, but she was planning to come back." The manager's eyes clouded. "You haven't found Emma, have you?"

"No." Frustrated, McCullen kept digging. "Do you recall anything unusual that might have happened about three weeks ago?"

She didn't even pretend to think about it. "No."

"What about Sunday, April 21st?"

This time, the manager glanced at the wall calendar above the desk. "Not really. But I think that was the last time I saw Emma. She stopped in that night to talk about coming back to work and how the transition would go."

A strange thought hit him. "She was taking her job back from you?"

The manager's mouth tightened. "Yes, but I knew from the beginning her leave of absence was temporary."

"Did you resent giving up your responsibilities?"

"No." She shook her head, defiant now. "We planned to share the manager position, and I was going to pick up some server shifts. I looked forward to making tips again."

McCullen let it go. It seemed unlikely this woman had killed Emma and her baby over a high-stress, low-paying restaurant job. He wasn't technically investigating her disappearance anyway. But his instincts told him Charlotte probably knew the Claytons and might have a reason to target them. Which meant Randall—with his short fuse—could be guilty of both crimes.

Chapter 26

Friday, May 10, 7:30 p.m.

After hours in the data center pulling together batches with thousands of email addresses, Spencer needed a break. He'd stayed up late the night before tweaking the phony fraud alert and he thought it was time for Raff to see it. He turned to the hacker. "I'm sending a test of the fraud alert to your proxy email account. Tell me if you think it's ready."

He sent one to himself at a remote address and studied the communication. It looked perfect to him.

"The logo isn't quite right." Raff tapped his own monitor. "The blue is a little dark, and I think they've updated it recently. But I'm not sure what is different."

"Shit." Spencer cursed himself for not checking. He opened the FDIC's site and studied the logo. He didn't see the difference between their logo and his.

Raff lumbered to his feet and came over. After a moment, he yawned and said, "It's the space between the symbol and the inside of the letter C."

Spencer stared and quickly spotted the discrepancy. "I don't know if I can fix it."

"Don't worry. No one but an expert will know." Raff shrugged and went back to his computer.

Deciding the hacker was right, Spencer continued setting up email batches. He'd written code to facilitate the process, but it still took time. Sending out too many at once would cause them to land in spam folders, and it might alert one of the various email providers.

"I just moved a shitload of money out of Standford Oil's account," Raff said casually. "So technically, we've launched our first strike."

An electrical charge coupled with an unexpected wave of worry washed over him. Everything would get really bad before life on earth got better. It might even take ten or twenty years for things to improve. "When will we see the effect?"

"By Tuesday, we should see news reports that gas prices are skyrocketing. By the end of the week, we'll hear that a refinery is scheduled to close."

It was the beginning of a new carbon era. Spencer wanted to celebrate, to raise a drink in toast. But he wanted to share that moment with his brother, who hadn't been around much lately. He assumed he was spending time with Emma and Tate. "Let's grab some sandwiches and a beer from the kitchen."

"Now you're talking."

Halfway through his meal, Spencer's cell phone buzzed. A text from Randall. *Tate's fever is worse & he's vomiting. Emma is freaking out. I think we have to take him to the ER.*

No! Spencer texted back. *Bring him to me. If you take him, you'll be arrested.* He had no intention of taking the baby to the hospital unless it became necessary. He would put little Tate on a saline/amoxicillin IV, and the boy would be fine.

Raff asked, "Everything okay?" They stood at the bar counter, eating off paper towels.

"Mostly." Spencer took a long pull of beer. The trigger

was already set and things were in motion. They had to get through the transition. It was just a matter of stalling long enough for the chaos to begin and law enforcement to be too distracted with looting and shooting to focus on a missing woman and her baby.

He wrapped his sandwich and put it in the fridge. He wanted Raff to go back to the data center so he could prep for the baby. Eventually, he might need Marissa, their nurse, to come over and help monitor Tate, but he hoped that wouldn't be necessary. "Let's go back to work."

"Five minutes won't make a lick of difference in this grand scheme, but you're the boss." Raff, talking with his mouth full, grabbed his beer and headed for the computers.

Spencer followed, sat at his station for five minutes, then excused himself. He didn't owe Raff any explanations, and he hoped the hacker would leave the compound as soon as his job was done.

While he grabbed an IV stand out of the medical closet, he wondered about bringing Tate's crib over from Randall's home. But he didn't want any Destiny members to witness it, so for the moment, he moved a small daybed for Tate into Lisa's room. Marissa would be over in the morning to help with Lisa, and he'd have to either hide the baby for a while or tell the nurse something about Tate's presence. But he didn't want to think about that yet.

Lisa woke and questioned what he was doing, then drifted off while he tried to explain. He moved an end table near the IV stand, injected antibiotics into a saline bag, and located liquid anti-nausea medicine. He could do this. In the post meltdown world, they would have to take care of themselves anyway. Access to a lab for blood work would have been helpful though.

The front door banged open, and moments later Randall rushed into the room, carrying the baby. Spencer held up his hand to remind his brother that Lisa was resting.

"What is this?" Randall gestured at the daybed and IV, his voice a harsh whisper. "I thought you were taking him to the ER."

"Not yet." Spencer took the cranky baby from his arms and laid him down. "Only as a last resort."

"We can't let my son die. Emma will never forgive me."

"He'll be fine. I'll do everything they would at the hospital."

Randall grabbed his shoulder, his eyes wild. "You're not a doctor."

Spencer hated to be reminded of that. "I'm not a kidnapper either, but that's the position we're in!" His voice was too loud, and he glanced over at his wife. She mumbled something but didn't wake up. He turned back to his brother. "If we take Tate to the ER, we'll have to make up a name and a story about whose kid he is. Otherwise, they'll call the FBI. This is a small town and everyone knows Emma and Tate disappeared."

"We can tell them he's the baby of a new member. Maybe Sonja's. She seems bonded to you. She'll go along."

Spencer considered it, but didn't want Sonja involved. "Let's give this a chance." He rubbed Tate's hand with antiseptic and inserted the IV. The baby wailed. Randall hovered, but kept quiet. Spencer took the boy's temperature: 103. "I'll cool him off with cold compresses. While I'm doing that, you need to go into town for blueberries, so I can make a fever elixir." Sometimes, herbal remedies were the most effective.

Chapter 27

Friday, May 10, 9:35 p.m.

Randall stopped at Safeway, picked up the fresh berries, and felt nervous about checking out. Would the clerk know who he was? He hadn't come into town much since they'd confined Emma, because he didn't want people looking at him with suspicion. *Fuck 'em*, he thought. Once he'd left politics, he'd sworn to never concern himself with other people's opinions. He strode to the counter, made brief small talk with the clerk, and decided he was done hiding.

Back on the road, he headed for The Highland. They'd bought the business as a source of income, and it had done well. Once they'd started talking about causing a meltdown someday, they'd put the bar on the market. It had taken months, but a buyer had finally come forward. The deal was in progress, and they hoped to sign papers next week and get their money out before the collapse. Afterward, restaurants would probably struggle and close. He might as well pick up the day's cash and have one last drink in the place.

The crowded parking lot was always a good sign. Randall entered through the back door of the kitchen, knowing it was good to keep the employees on their toes with unexpected visits. The galley was bustling with energy but running smoothly, and he couldn't find anything to correct. He pulled the big bills from the safe and hustled into the bar where the pace and lighting were more low-key. He didn't understand why Emma wanted to go back to managing the restaurant. He'd tried to convince her Tate needed her at home. But all that would be a pointless argument soon.

He stood at the end of the bar, happy to see Sadie was working. His friend glanced over and smiled. "Hey, Randy."

"Hey, Sadie. What's new?"

She brought him a Coors Light without asking. "Mom's getting married again, but I'm not going to the wedding, so, not much." She took out an order pad. "Are you eating?"

"No, just the beer. I was in town and thought I would say hello."

Her expression changed to concern. "Have you heard anything about Emma and Tate?

He worked up some disgust. "No, and I don't think the FBI is doing much to find them."

"Emma's father was in here last night."

Something in her tone caught his attention. "What did he have to say?"

"He said the feds have someone working the case from the inside."

Randall's heart skipped a beat. "What does that mean?" He was pretty sure he knew.

"I asked him and he jumped up and left. He was shitfaced, so I'm not sure you can take anything he said seriously."

"He's a jackass." Icy tendrils of panic crawled through his veins, but Randall didn't let it show. He would sit here, drink his beer, and think it through. His first thought, of course, was Sonja. She'd come out of nowhere and charmed his brother into shortcutting the screening process. *Crap.* But having an undercover agent inside the community wasn't even the worst-case scenario. *Working it from the inside* could mean the feds had surveillance on their phones and email accounts, which could land them in prison.

Sadie leaned toward him and whispered, "What do you think happened, Randy? Was Emma abducted by some psycho or did she run off? Women do that sometimes, you know."

The question annoyed him. "I hate thinking about it."

Sadie squeezed his hand. "It must be hell not knowing."

"It is." Randall took another long drink, then pushed the half-full bottle back at her. "I have to get going. Say hi to your mom for me."

"Yeah, like that'll happen." Sadie laughed.

Randall left her a tip and hurried outside to his truck. He had to warn Spencer. He started to send a text, then changed his mind. What if the feds had surveillance on him? They needed new phones ASAP. But shit, he couldn't buy one tonight. Their email could be at risk too. He'd been cautious about contacting his associates only through online chats, but they would have to create new personal accounts now. Fortunately, Spencer had several secure email addresses he could use to send the financial triggers. The FBI couldn't possibly know about them all.

But they may have sent Sonja. *Fuck!* He hadn't trusted her from the start.

Would Spencer take him seriously this time or call him paranoid again? Maybe he would dig a little deeper into Sonja's background or search her apartment again before telling his brother they couldn't trust her.

Randall climbed in his truck. His headache was merciless now, and his chest itched to the point of a burn. He unbuttoned his shirt and spotted two red welts. Hives. He'd have to start taking antihistamine and wished he'd finished his beer. He wanted desperately to speed up the trigger, but Spencer's digital attack could take days. The physical assault had to wait for the right moment. He hoped his body wouldn't betray him in the meantime.

Once he hit the main road out of town, he pressed the gas, tension mounting. Halfway home to Destiny, a dark thought possessed him. What would he do if he discovered Sonja was a federal agent? That would depend on how much she knew. *She couldn't have learned much yet,* Randall told himself. She'd only been in the community for a few days. He remembered the noises they'd heard when they buried Grace. If that had been Sonja spying, she had probably reported it.

Maybe it was time to make Sonja disappear too.

Chapter 28

Friday, May 10, 11:15 p.m.

Dallas checked the time in the corner of her screen. Was it still too early? Dressed and ready for another attempt at finding the bunker, she was too hyper to stare at the computer any longer. She'd planned to wait until after she heard Raff come up the stairs and settle in, but he was obviously working late. She'd also considered sleeping for a few hours, then going out in the middle of the night, but the thought had made her laugh. Sleep? Hah! She wanted to find Emma ASAP—if she was still alive—and call in her team to search the place. These freaks were up to something besides kidnapping, and instinct told her it was going down soon.

She plugged her computer into the TV, found a Zumba workout, and peeled off her shirt. The upbeat salsa music was just what she needed. When she hit the point where she would need a shower, Dallas shut it down and texted her team: *Going out to locate the bunker. I should be back in 4–5 hours.*

At the most, she thought. She knew the approximate location, but finding the access or documenting the proof that someone was inside would be the challenge. Dallas checked her gear one more time: flashlight, lock-pick, handgun, water bottle, and camera. Her Sonja phone was in an outside pocket of the backpack, and her lucky cloth was in her front jeans' pocket. At the last minute, she grabbed her work phone and tucked it into a pocket inside the backpack. She might not have reception out on the hill, but if she found Emma, she had to try to contact her FBI team immediately.

She stepped outside and waited, scanning the area. No movement on the streets of the cul-de-sac. At the end, Spencer's house lights were on, as were the lights in the data center. She would have to be careful how she accessed the back road. Hurrying down the steps was louder than she would have liked, but now that she was on the move, she wanted to clear the neighborhood quickly.

Dallas jogged toward the brothers' side-by-side homes, then veered left and headed for the garden behind Randall's. His house was dark and his vehicle was gone, so she wasn't worried about him seeing her. Once she hit the soft edge between the grass and the soil, she turned right and jogged along one of the many paths that crisscrossed the property. This one led from the community building to the dirt road behind Spencer's house. A low sound caught her attention. Was that a car engine? She turned back toward the houses, but the night was dark and the sound was gone.

Senses heightened, Dallas kept her pace casual. She hoped to seem like a restless athlete taking a slow jog before bed. She didn't want to raise any suspicion from Spencer, should he look out his back window and catch her movement. Her black clothes and small backpack were hard to see in the dark, and she felt relatively safe. Once she hit the dirt road, she relaxed a little, but still didn't turn on her flashlight. She wouldn't use it until it was time to leave the main path and begin searching the hilly terrain.

Ten minutes later, she sensed the ground subtly rising under her feet and realized it was time to venture off the road. She stopped and flicked on her flashlight. In the sudden absence of her footsteps, the night was eerily quiet. Except for a hushed sound. Breathing? Dallas spun around. Under a cloudy moonless sky, the landscape was black. Nerves humming, she waited and watched. Nothing moved, except a gentle breeze, carrying cool night air with the scent of fir trees and corn stalks.

Dallas turned back to her task and shone her light at shoulder level. The hill rose off to her right—the same spot Spencer had glanced at when she mentioned an underground bunker. She bet the structure was nestled into the hill and that the brothers had used the sloped terrain to minimize the excavation. The next part of her search would be tedious, checking behind every rock for something that looked like an entry and peeking into every clump of shrubs for a latch of some kind. Dallas got to work.

* * *

Randall heard Sonja's footsteps pause and nearly stumbled as he tried to stop quickly. He pulled in a breath, squatted down, and held as still as he could. It was no easy task. Adrenaline had been pinging his nerves since he'd left the tavern. When he'd pulled through the Destiny gate at nearly midnight and spotted a slim dark figure running toward his back yard, his heart had thundered like a racehorse. He'd cut his lights and engine, rolled slowly into the driveway, and grabbed his 9mm from under the seat. Leaving his truck door ajar, he'd followed the figure on foot as she set off down the back road.

Where the hell did Sonja think she was going at midnight? Dressed in black and wearing a small backpack?

Someone—maybe Spencer—had mentioned she was into astronomy, but the cloud cover was too heavy for stargazing. She was up to something, for sure. He'd suspected she was looking for Grace's grave, but Sonja had jogged past the turnoff to the generator and didn't stop until she reached bunker hill, as they privately called it. Now she was searching the ground at the halfway point in the slope. *Shit!* She was only about twenty feet from the opening to where Emma was.

She had to be a federal agent sent here to find his wife!

Randall worried that Sonja could hear his heart pounding in his chest, but she hadn't looked back since that first stop. He'd been right about her from the beginning. And his brother had called him paranoid. It would be the last time. Could he text Spencer without making any noise? Did he even have his phone, or had he left it on the seat of his truck? Randall patted his pants pockets and didn't find it. Instead, he slipped his gun into his right hand. The act was physically comforting, giving him the control he needed. Yet psychologically, he'd crossed a line into new territory. He and his brother had made many critical decisions in the last week, but this one might be irreversible.

A bright light with a narrow beam clicked on, and the dark figure moved forward, scanning back and forth. How did she even know the bunker was in this area? Had Spencer stupidly told her? Had lust and loneliness rotted his brother's brain? Even though the Emma situation was his own fault, Randall resented Spencer for making it worse. What the hell were they supposed to do with Sonja? If that was even her name.

Should he confront her? Then what? Kick her out of the community and hope for the best? She would be back with a search warrant in twenty-four hours, and he would be in jail shortly after. *Could he kill her and be done with it?* Only if it was necessary to save the mission. But even if he eliminated her, other federal agents would come looking when she didn't check in. One option seemed prudent and palatable. Put her in the bunker with Emma and wait for the meltdown. When they finally released her, the world as she knew it would be gone, and she might decide to stay and make the most of her situation. They certainly needed more babymakers. She might run, but by then, it wouldn't matter. What was left of law enforcement would have their hands full keeping government offices protected. They wouldn't have time to worry about a harmless, isolated community.

Randall moved toward her slowly, watched her search for the entry, and plotted his attack. Sneaking up on her might be impossible. He could approach her in a friendly manner, then pull the gun. What if she was armed? Did undercover agents carry weapons? Fear snaked through his bowels. She was probably a trained fighter, and he hadn't been in a physical confrontation since fifth grade. This would not go well. Should he just shoot her in the back? Randall brought up his weapon. His hands shook, his chest itched, and he thought he might be sick.

Her light stopped moving, and Sonja dropped to her knees next to a big boulder. She'd found the entry. Was this the right time to rush her? No. He wanted her inside the bunker. He might as well let Sonja go down the stairs on her own, then knock her out and drag her inside.

* * *

In the dark, the black U-shaped latch was nearly impossible

to pick out against the green grass, but Dallas expected it to be there and didn't give up. She had spotted a fresh footprint in the dirt about ten yards back, and behind the giant boulder seemed like an obvious place to put the entry. Even in broad daylight, you could lift the trap door without being seen from the curve in the road. She pulled the decaying tree limb out of the way and squatted a foot or so from the handle. After a hard tug, the trap door lifted on its own.

Musty cool air rose from the opening. Dallas leaned over the hole, listening for sounds of activity, but heard nothing. It was midnight, so Emma and her baby could be sleeping. *If* they were down there. Her gut told her they were. Randall didn't act like a man who might never see his family again. Dallas scanned the narrow cavity with her flashlight and spotted an interior door. If she could just make contact, she could call in backup, and maybe a Redding police SWAT team could come out and force the entry. She slipped the flashlight into her pocket and moved into position over the ladder.

Hanging onto an interior strap, Dallas planted a foot on the second rung, then grabbed the edge of the ladder with her free hand. It was an awkward transition, and she wondered how they'd carried Emma down. She had to have been unconscious. Maybe Spencer, being the bigger one, had strapped Emma to his back. Dallas climbed down the ladder, hating the feeling of being underground. So unnatural. If a meltdown ever did happen, she would rather die than live underground for any length of time.

At the bottom, she used her flashlight to examine the door. Made of steel with a keypad entry. Dallas pushed the handle, then pounded on the door. "Emma, are you in there?"

For a moment, there was no response. Dallas started to bang again, but a female voice called back. "Who are you?"

"FBI. I'm here to help." Dallas slipped off her backpack to dig out her cell phone. She probably couldn't get service, but she had to try. First she reached for her weapon.

Suddenly, a massive weight landed on her back, knocking her to the ground. Her head smashed against the door, and for a moment she blacked out. When her brain was functioning again, she tried to push off the ground, but her arms were weak, her lungs burned, and a funny noise dribbled out her mouth. She'd had the wind knocked out of her.

A faint clicking sound caught her attention, and the door next to her swung open, slamming into her. Dallas rolled on her side and struggled to reach her weapon, which she'd dropped when she hit the floor. Weak and winded, she felt as if she were underwater. Someone grabbed her hair and dragged her through the opening. She kicked at his legs just as her hand found the Kel-Tec. She swung the gun up, but Randall knocked it away before she could pull the trigger. *Fuck!*

A foot smashed into her head, and shocking pain waves clouded her thoughts. She tried to reach her backpack, but Randall stomped on her hand, snatched the pack and gun, and ran from the dark room. The door slammed shut behind him.

Chapter 29

Fuck! Fuck! Fuck! The slam of the door sent a wave of panic through her body. Dallas sat up. She wanted to rub her head, but her right hand hurt too.

"Who are you?" The captive woman had stood there silently while Randall assaulted her.

"Sonja Barnes." Dallas instinctively stuck with her alias. "Are you Emma Clayton?"

"Yes. I'm sorry Randall kicked you. Are you all right?"

"Mostly." Dallas looked around, but the room was lit only by a small lantern in Emma's hand. Dallas guessed the size to be about forty-by-twenty. "Where's your baby?"

"Tate has a fever, so Spencer took him to the hospital."

Dallas tried to work out the logistics, then shut down the thought. The baby didn't matter right now. She had to get out of this underground prison. Head throbbing, she pushed off the concrete and examined the door. Also made of metal, the handle was locked in place. A keypad to the left was the only means of exit.

She turned to Emma. "Any idea what the code might be?" A pointless question.

"No. Randall keeps changing it."

"Have you tried to get out?"

"I've tried a few codes, but the door is locked and I'm underground. What else could I do?"

So Emma wasn't the self-reliant type. Dallas tried to remember what she'd seen of the mechanism on the outside before she was attacked. Another keypad, also to the left. The door locked every time it closed. They clearly hadn't wanted just anyone to come and go freely from the bunker. But why was Emma here? Dallas had to know. "What happened? Why is your husband imprisoning you?"

The pretty woman turned on another lamp. Dallas guessed it was battery powered.

"I was leaving to go stay with my mother." She bit down on her lower lip. "But I think they have something planned. Something that might have prevented me from getting back."

A jolt shot up Dallas' neck. "Tell me everything you know."

Emma chewed her lip, struggling with what she should say.

Dallas wanted to slap her. "If you're working with Randall and Spencer to commit crimes, I'll leave you here when I go."

"No!" Emma looked alert for the first time. "I didn't know anything about their plans until after they kidnapped me."

"What are they up to? I need specifics."

"I don't know details. I just know that Spencer is trying to trigger a financial collapse, and Randall..." She hesitated for a long moment. "I think his followers might blow up some internet buildings."

"Good fucking god." Rage and frustration made her head hurt worse. "Why? What do they have to gain?"

"Nothing personally." Emma sounded defensive. "They want to stop global warming before it wipes out humanity."

Dallas tried to process their egomaniacal thinking. "So they trigger a metaphorical flood, and Destiny gets to be

Noah's ark? The sole survivors that repopulate the earth?"

"Something like that." Now Emma looked ashamed.

Too stunned to respond, Dallas tried to form a plan. The concrete walls were impossible to get through. She had to find a weakness in the door. She glanced at Emma. "Are there tools down here? A screwdriver maybe?"

"Of course. We're preppers."

"Get 'em."

Emma walked toward a freestanding cabinet on wheels. "They're in here." She dragged the unit toward Dallas.

The walls started to close in, and her thumping heart grew loud in her ears. How had Emma stayed so calm down here? Was she medicated? Dallas didn't ask. She had to get the hell out, access one of her spare phones, and let her team know what the crazies had planned. She yanked open the top drawer and found everything a do-it-yourselfer could want. A giant screwdriver caught her eye. She grabbed it and headed for the door.

Oh shit. It swung outward, so the hinges were on the other side. Removing the door wasn't an option. Rage welled, and Dallas fought the urge to smash the screwdriver into the keypad. She would try a few codes first.

Emma stood behind her, and Dallas asked, "What is Randall's birthday?"

"August first, 1972. But it's not that."

A Leo, and ten years older than his wife. Dallas keyed in the numbers. No luck, but she had to start with the obvious. People tended to make passwords easy to remember. "Keep giving me dates. Your birthday, your anniversary, your son's birthday."

"You're wasting your time. I've tried all those."

Dallas spent twenty minutes on it anyway, then picked

up the screwdriver. What if she disabled the keypad? Would the door open...or would it lock permanently? She pressed the tip of the tool between the metal edge of the keypad and the concrete wall and gently pried. The mechanism didn't budge. She might not be able to access the wires without dislocating them. *Fuck!*

She fought to stay calm. There had to be another way out. A second exit—of course. Preppers were thorough and paranoid types. They likely hadn't built a bunker with only one access point.

Heart pounding, she spun around. "We have to find the other exit."

"There isn't one." Emma shook her head, looking a little dazed.

"I'm going to tear this place apart looking for it. Give me the lantern."

Emma handed it over, then went to a shelf in the kitchen for another. Dallas followed her, eyeing everything. Calling it a kitchen was too generous, but the space did have a countertop, cupboards, and a sink. They had plumbing!

"Where does the water go?"

"I don't know. The bunker was already here when I married Randall."

"Where does the ventilation come from?"

Emma pointed at a three-inch vent near the ceiling. "Oxygen is pumped in through that opening."

Three inches was no help. Dallas yanked open a cabinet and started pulling food items down to the counter. "Help me look for a larger opening!"

Emma joined the search, but they found nothing in the kitchen. Dallas ran to another freestanding structure with floor-to-ceiling shelves and drawers. She looked around and didn't see a movable chair. Just a bed, a couch, and a table covered with paperbacks, chocolate, lotion, and other female stuff. Stacks of plastic crates lined the back wall. Dallas wondered what was in them. What did people pack for the end of the world? She hoped to go out in a blaze of glory, or even a sudden, stupid death, but not cowering in a cave, fighting over the last can of tuna.

"I need something to stand on," she snapped at Emma. "Help me clear the crap off this table."

"We have fold-up chairs." Emma dug one out from between two plastic crates. "What are you gonna do?"

"I'm still looking for a vent. So should you."

Dallas climbed on the metal chair and pulled blankets and reference books from the top shelves, letting them fall to the floor. No vent. She made her way down the shelves to the drawers at the bottom, which were filled with medical supplies, batteries, and packages of dried fruit.

The walls were uninterrupted concrete everywhere.

Except for a back corner, which was screened off by plastic panels. Dallas rushed over.

"That's the composting toilet," Emma called, following her.

Dallas opened the makeshift door. The toilet was tall with a solid white base, and the smell was milder than she'd expected. But the appliance was not her concern. The large vent behind it, covered with a slotted grate, made her heart leap with joy.

"Help me move this thing!" With no plumbing attached—only an electrical plug —the toilet was portable.

The damn thing weighed a ton, and even with both pulling, it moved inches at a time, and they had to stop twice. When they had a foot of clearance from the wall, Dallas stepped in and examined the screws on the vent. Phillips head. She rushed back for the correct tool and quickly removed the four screws. Stale warm air trickled out the opening.

Just big enough for an average person to fit through, the tunnel was lined with dense wet earth. The brothers had probably intended the vent to provide a flow of oxygen as well as function as a means of escape. Dallas turned to Emma. "Get some flashlights." Randall had taken all of her gear, and it pissed her off all over again. Had he found the FBI cell phone hidden in a compartment inside the backpack? If she didn't check in by morning, her team would come looking.

If Spencer's financial malware was already on its way into cyberspace, the bureau needed to focus on a public communication effort. More important, they had to pinpoint Randall's targets for destruction. She had to get out of here fast and warn them.

Emma handed her a small light that would strap around her head, like a miner would wear. *Very handy.* Dallas pulled it on. "Do you know where this tunnel comes out?"

"No, but based on the direction, it's probably near the creek."

Dallas had thought the same thing. As much as she wanted to climb in the tunnel and crawl like crazy to daylight, her job was to rescue Emma. "You first." Dallas pulled the metal chair into place.

Emma chewed her lip. "You should go. I'm afraid I'll freeze up and block us both."

Relieved, Dallas stepped up on the chair, climbed into the vent, and started crawling. Small rocks cut into her hands and knees, and in places cold water ran down the walls and puddled in the tunnel. The hand Randall had stomped earlier ached from the weight of her upper body, and her head throbbed where she'd been kicked. None of that mattered. After a few minutes, the vent curved right and began a gentle downward slope. She stopped and called back, "Are you with me, Emma?"

"Yes." The voice behind her came through gritted teeth.

The air was suddenly warmer. Dallas picked up her pace, ignoring the pain flooding her body. In a moment, she could smell fresh air. Another hundred feet, and she emerged, landing in dense brush that she had to claw her way out of. She could hear the creek nearby. Thank goodness. She would follow the waterway to the generator, then make her way back to Destiny from there.

Behind her, Emma cried out. Dallas turned to see her fall on her face. But she was fine, and they were outside, free of the bunker. Now they just had to steer clear of the Clayton brothers. Dallas instinctively reached for her weapon—which she no longer had.

L.J. Sellers

Chapter 30

Randall raced back to the cul-de-sac, his thoughts spinning as quickly as his feet. He'd just kidnapped a federal agent, and now they had to put everything into action immediately. Spencer would be furious, but they were both far too committed to stop. The carefully orchestrated meltdown they'd planned spun more out of control every moment, and the stress was making Randall itchy and ill. This had happened to him on the campaign trail too. Near the end of his last election he'd been covered with hives and vomited daily.

As he neared Spencer's house, he slowed to a walk to catch his breath. He needed to appear confident, in control. He knocked on his brother's back door, not wanting to be seen out front. In the middle of the night, it was best not to barge in. They all kept weapons handy.

After a long wait, Spencer came to the door. The skin under his eyes sagged, his hair was tousled, and he had what looked like mucus on his shoulder. Randall remembered that Spencer was taking care of Tate. "How's my boy?"

"A little cooler now and sleeping." Spencer stepped back to let Randall in. "You need to stay with him for a while and give me a break."

"We have another issue." Randall headed for the fridge and pulled out a couple of beers. He downed half of one, ignoring Spencer's folded arms and bracing stare. Finally, he plunged in. "Sonja Barnes is an FBI agent."

"What? Why do you say that?"

"I followed her out to the bunker tonight. She was looking for Emma." Randall pulled off her backpack and set it on the counter. "She carries a gun."

"Oh no. Where is she? What did you do?" Panic made Spencer's voice sound unnatural.

"I put her in the bunker. I didn't know what else to do."

"You locked a federal agent in the bunker?" Spencer rubbed his temples and made an odd moaning noise. He looked up, eyes blazing. "Why didn't you talk to me? We could have just made her leave."

"She found Emma. It was too late!" Randall hesitated, then lowered his voice. "Was I supposed to kill her?"

"No! Christ. Don't even say that." Spencer began to pace. "Did you restrain her?"

"I didn't have the chance." Randall wondered if he'd made a mistake. "I just locked her in, like we did with Emma."

"So what's the plan?" His brother's harsh mocking tone made Randall cringe.

"We speed up everything. Send out all the financial emails and crash the banking websites." Randall figured it was time to ease Spencer into the whole truth. "I think Raff should target communication companies as well. We need to shut down the internet. Unless we create total chaos, this FBI agent could still make trouble for us."

Spencer was silent for a long moment, then a look of weary resignation settled in. "How did you know Sonja was a plant? What made you follow her?"

Randall told him about the conversation he'd had with Sadie in the tavern. "But if you remember, I warned you the first day she was here."

Spencer's eyes went wide. "Did you get her cell phone?"

"She had two. One in an outside pocket of the backpack and one zipped inside."

Spencer riffled the pack for the hidden phone and began reading her messages. "I'll send a text to her contact, telling them everything is fine."

"Great idea. We should keep sending them for a while. Maybe eventually, we'll say she plans to join us and won't be back to work."

"That's brilliant."

Randall loved hearing it. Spencer so rarely praised him.

His brother glanced at the clock. "I have to get back to the data center, and you'd better look in on Tate."

"What do you think about my idea to crash the internet?"

"I don't know. Does it fit our mission?"

"Yes! Our goal is to cut carbon production so drastically that we halt global warming." Randall was feeling more upbeat. It was about time they finally took charge. "You're targeting oil companies with financial paralysis, so shutting down the internet just speeds everything up."

"But Raff is too busy with the financial attack. He doesn't have time to hack into a bunch of tech companies with tight cyber security."

"Maybe I do." The hacker's voice came out of nowhere as he crossed the dining area. "But not right away." Raff met Randall's eyes. "Are you still planning to blow up internet hubs?"

Spencer spun toward him. "What? You have explosives set?"

"Not set. Just a few people ready to make it happen."

"No violence!" Spencer stomped and clenched his fists.

"We agreed that no one would be directly hurt."

"Fucking semantics," Raff said. "Everyone is going to suffer. You can't create a new world without breaking the old one."

"No explosives!" Spencer yelled. "We're not terrorists."

"You can't stop me," Randall argued. "All I have to do is send one group email."

"Listen to reason! It isn't necessary. We've already got Standford Oil's finances frozen. By Monday the company will be rationing gas, and by Friday it will shut down refineries. And that's just one element. Don't do it." Spencer pleaded with him. "Just go take care of your baby. Raff and I can finish this."

Randall was done arguing. He needed to check on Tate, but after that he would head to his place and load the second explosive into his truck. Halfway to Sacramento, he'd send the email that would put his team into action. Even if everyone else failed in their mission, he wanted to shut down the capital city. He owed the state that for rejecting him.

Chapter 31

Raff was pumped to the max. He was sedentary by nature, didn't even watch sports because it was too intense for him. But this was wild. Sonja was an FBI agent and the wacko brothers had kidnapped her. His usually methodical mind raced from one thought to another. His instinct was to bolt. Pack his shit, jump in his car, and get the hell out of this freaky little pseudo-paradise. The feds would eventually show up to find their girl, and he didn't intend to be here.

But if this crazy-ass scheme the brothers had cooked up even half worked, who knew what would happen? Especially if Randall and his little group succeeded in blowing up internet hubs. That would keep the feds busy! And if thousands, or millions, of people charged into their banks on Monday demanding all their money, riots might break out when the banks ran out of cash. That would keep law enforcement busy too. If the brothers kept sending texts and emails from Sonja's devices for a while, they might buy themselves enough time to get away with it. Crazy-smart motherfuckers!

Raff decided to finish the job Spencer had paid him for, stir up a little more shit in the Muslim wasteland, and hang around for a day or so to see what happened. This was too fucking awesome to walk away from just yet.

First he told Spencer he needed a break and headed back

to his apartment to pack everything but his toothbrush. In the dark, he quietly carried both bags to his car. Ideally, he planned to sanitize the room of his DNA before he left, but he wanted to be ready to make a speedy exit. He put popcorn in the microwave and downed a beer while he waited for it. The stink of sweat rose from his armpits, and he regretted packing his deodorant. He used a paper towel to wipe his pits, grabbed his bag of popcorn, and started down the stairs. He remembered Sonja downing vodka shots and kicking his ass at chess. She'd been pumping him for information! He liked her even more. Too bad she was a fed—and locked in a bunker. He wondered if he should do anything about that. Nah. She could take care of herself.

Back in the data center, he grunted at Spencer, then took his spot in front of a monitor. The only way to ensure a full-fledged war in the Middle East was to piss off the clerics who ruled Iran. The night before, with the help of a hacker friend in Tel Aviv, he'd finally found and taken over a group of proxy computers in Israel. He had hoped to access banking information through them, but he didn't have time now. So he began an assault on one of the Iranian government's websites. Once he modified the standard "server slowdown" bot-code to target the specific URL, the proxy computers would start sending hundreds of access requests every minute, overloading the site's server and shutting it down. No real harm would be done, but Iran's cyber specialists— probably former hackers—would trace the attack to the Israeli proxy servers. Combined with the theft of Syria's money, the cyber assault from Israel might push the hard-line Iranian clerics to their limit. They could launch a first strike before the day was over. The world would soon learn whether Iran really had nuclear missile capabilities.

Raff worked quickly to set up the code. There was so much he still wanted to manipulate. And so little time.

* * *

Spencer sat in front of the monitor and couldn't see straight for a moment. Excitement, fear, and anguish made blood rush to his head and his eyes blur. The thing he kept coming back to was that Sonja was a federal agent. She had played him like a patsy and it hurt. Loneliness had made him vulnerable, and it shamed him. But he had to get past it. Right now, they had to keep pushing the system until it toppled. Someone had to be willing to think long-term. He and Randall had known for years it was the right thing to do, and circumstances had finally forced them to act.

It was time. Spencer queued up the first batch of emails and hit send. Not letting himself stop and process what it meant, he kept going, releasing batch after batch. Some recipients would start taking money out of ATMs immediately. Others wouldn't even open their email until Monday morning. The effect might have been better if he had waited until Sunday night like he'd planned, but he had to act now or his head would implode.

After a while, Raff said, "He's right about the DNS root servers. I'm gonna see if I can get access to 60 Hudson Street's security."

"No. Let's just finish this financial assault. Maybe step it up if we can."

"Oh, we can." Raff grinned, like a bully about to punch someone.

Spencer wished he could have set the trigger without

enlisting the help of someone who didn't understand or respect their cause. "I don't want to do any physical damage or hurt anyone. We're just trying to shut down the social and financial engines that are driving us to extinction. We want people to get back to basics and thrive."

Raff laughed, a nasty sound. "You're delusional. People will be hurt. They'll lose their jobs and their homes. They'll starve."

The argument unnerved him because he knew it was true. "But not for long. People will regroup and farm the land. They'll build collectives and start sustainable businesses."

"What about the takers, the crazies, and the jihadists?" Raff shook his head. "In a suddenly chaotic world, evildoers will take advantage."

"There are more good people than bad. Society will rebuild."

"You're not worried about Islamic extremists taking advantage of the chaos and lax security in the United States?"

Oh shit. They hadn't even thought about that. "The airlines will shut down for lack of fuel. The terrorists won't be able to come here."

"They're already here." Raff rolled his chair over and clapped Spencer on the shoulder. "But don't worry, the sleeper cells will be distracted by the war in the Middle East."

At first Spencer didn't react to the common phrase, but Raff's tone was so confident and sly, he began to fill with dread. "What war in the Middle East? Are you talking about the conflict in Syria?"

"I'm talking about the mother of all holy wars. As long as we're starting over and determining a new future, I'd like a world with fewer Islamic assholes blowing things up."

Panic ripped through Spencer. "What are you saying?"

Raff grinned again. "I shifted some money around and may have started a war between Israel and Syria."

For a moment, Spencer was too stunned to speak, then outrage enveloped him. "Put the money back! Right fucking now. You have to undo this."

"I couldn't put it back even if I wanted to. They tightened their security—but a little too late."

"Then we have to contact them. You have to stop this."

"Good luck with that." Raff turned back to his computer. "I have more buttons to push."

Oh dear god. He'd unleashed a monster. Spencer's mind went blank as rage took over. He lunged forward, grabbed Raff by the shirt, and yanked him out of his chair. "Get out of my sight! And off my property!"

Raff straightened his glasses and chuckled. "It won't change anything. I can hack portals from anywhere." He pointed a finger. "You started this. I'm just making it a real transformation instead of your half-assed effort."

Spencer wanted to pound his smug face with a fist. But Raff would just hit him back, and a fistfight wouldn't stop the hacker from doing whatever else he had planned. Was it already too late?

"Excuse me." Spencer walked out of the room, then ran down the hall to get his handgun. He had to stop Raff from doing more damage. Iran and Israel had nuclear weapons, and millions of innocents could die in a single blast.

He grabbed his Glock and ran into the hallway, then heard Lisa call to him from her bedroom. He didn't have time for her right now. He stuck his head in and said, "I'll be right back, sweetheart."

Spencer strode across the living room and into the data center.

Raff glanced up as he came in. "Whoa! Don't shoot me. We can talk about this."

They were beyond negotiation. He pointed the weapon at Raff's head. "Put both hands on the desk. Now!"

The hacker did as instructed. Spencer turned the gun around in his hand and stepped forward. With Raff watching him intently, he smashed the butt down on the hacker's right fingers.

Raff shrieked in pain. "What the fuck!" He pulled his crippled hand to his chest.

"Put out your other hand."

"No!"

Spencer pressed the gun to Raff's head, surprised at how calm he felt. "Your hands or your life. Choose."

Whimpering, Raff put his other hand on the desk. Spencer smashed those fingers too.

"When I'm finished with my work here, I'll set your broken fingers and give you some pain meds. For right now, get out of my sight."

"You're crazy!" Raff called over his shoulder as he shuffled from the room.

Spencer tucked the gun into the back of his pants and went to see Lisa. He wasn't worried about Raff. Even if he left Destiny, he wasn't likely to tell the authorities anything.

He stepped into her room, smiling and trying to seem calm. Every conversation could be her last, and he wanted her death to be peaceful. Spencer glanced at little Tate. He was sleeping easily, but Lisa looked troubled.

"Spencer, you have to stop this." Her voice was weak, but he sensed her intensity.

Did she know? "What do you mean?"

"The trigger. Don't do it. It's not right." Her breath was so ragged, each word came in a little puff.

She must have overheard him and Randall talking. "You know we have to shut down the industrial complex. Humans won't survive global warming."

"Some people will. It doesn't have to be you...and your brother."

But he wanted it to be him and Randall. They had prepared for it. They deserved to survive. "Why shouldn't it be us?"

"Because you're a good man, and the suffering you cause will haunt you."

She was right, and for a second he hated her for it. "Everything is already in motion."

"You can stop it. I beg you."

Lisa grabbed his hand and squeezed. Crushing guilt and grief overwhelmed him. For a moment he couldn't think. If not for Emma and Sonja's captivity, couldn't they just go back to the way it was? Or start over somewhere else?

Lisa's dying eyes locked onto him, and Spencer tried to weigh his options...and obligations. He had to talk to Randall. Hopefully his brother would be rational. He'd gone to Sonja's apartment to gather up her things and eliminate any evidence that she'd been there. Spencer would confront him when he came back.

"It's probably too late," he finally said, "but I'll try.

Chapter 32

Dallas ran along the back of the fields, glancing down the rows of corn, watching for movement on the road in the distance. Behind her, Emma struggled to keep up. Dallas was torn. She wanted to stay with Emma because that was her original mission, to find and rescue the kidnap victim. But so much more was at stake now, and the sooner she notified the bureau the better. She might also be better off without Emma in tow if she encountered someone.

She turned to Emma, who was breathing hard. "I'm going ahead. I need to contact the bureau right away. When you get close to the community, just sit down and wait for me to come back."

"What's going to happen to Randall?"

Why did she still care? "I don't know." Dallas adopted a more commanding tone. "Get close to the houses, but stay out of sight and wait for me. Or another agent."

Dallas took off, running at full pace. She had to get to her apartment and access a phone or a computer. She would try the computer first, because the satellite internet was more reliable than the phone service. She also needed a weapon, feeling naked without her gun. She knew where Spencer kept his weapons and could probably access one. Should she grab a rifle on the way or make contact first? She couldn't decide. She wished she knew where Randall was. He'd probably gone straight to Spencer to tell him she was an agent. They were either on their way out to the bunker to kill her or working feverishly to put their plans in place. Which meant Spencer was likely in the data center with Raff. But where would Randall be? She couldn't predict.

Contact first, she decided. She was too outnumbered and outgunned in the community to stop this doomsday plot on her own. She glanced toward the road again. She hadn't seen or heard any movement in the dark. At least they didn't know she'd escaped yet.

The field ended, and she started down a path toward the main storage lockers. Were there weapons in there? Dallas shut off the light still strapped to her head and slowed her pace. She didn't want to attract any attention. Jogging up to the first building, she groaned in disappointment. It had a keypad like the one in the bunker. *Shit.* She tried the pushdown handle anyway. Locked.

A smaller storage building nearby was also locked. From here, she might be visible to anyone looking out their window or wandering around the community. In the middle of the night, most of the members were likely asleep, but the ones she feared were not. Dallas stopped in her tracks. Were other Destiny people involved in the plot? Not knowing, she couldn't trust anyone. To get to her apartment, she had to cross the open space behind the brothers' homes. She considered crawling to keep out of sight, then rejected it. She was in a hurry—and dressed in black.

Dallas ran like the wind toward the safety of the community center, then pressed herself against the side while she caught her breath. She was almost there. She rounded the corner and took off down the path, glancing left to see if Randall's vehicle was still in his driveway. The sight of his truck gave her mixed emotions. He hadn't left yet to blow up something, and that was good, but his continued presence was a risk to her life. The footpath to the apartment complex ran behind several houses, but their interior lights were off. Unless Randall had notified everyone to watch out for her, she would make it.

As she sprinted, a stupid thought popped into her head. Had she locked her apartment when she left? Did she still have her key? Dallas stopped behind a tree and checked her front pocket. The key was still there. She slipped her hand into her other pocket and rubbed her lucky cloth. Now she was ready.

Dallas bolted past the homes and headed for the stairs leading up to her unit. As she neared, she sensed movement in the road. Dallas spun and saw Raff shuffling toward her.

"Help me." His voice was a sob, and he held his hands against his stomach.

Dallas tensed. The hacker was definitely part of their scheme. Did he have a gun?

"The bastard broke my fingers," he whined.

Dallas didn't know what to think. "Who?"

"Spencer. You have to drive me to the ER." He was trying not to cry.

"I can't right now."

She spun and charged up the stairs. Key still in hand, she stuck it into the deadbolt and turned. As she pushed the door open and stepped inside, she realized she hadn't heard a click. Maybe she'd left it unlocked. As she started to reach for a light, something hard and heavy smashed into the back of her head. She staggered forward, fighting to think through the pain. In a blind rage, she grabbed the first thing she saw and swung around with it gripped in both hands. The metal laptop smashed into Randall's neck and ear as he charged her again.

He cried out but raised his arm to strike another blow. He held a large handgun, she realized. Dallas ducked to the side as it came toward her head. When she'd regained her footing, she punch-kicked his knee, knocking him sideways. He staggered and went down on one knee, still gripping the weapon. She needed her fucking gun! Did the bastard have it on him? She moved in for a kick to his throat and heard a sound behind her.

Dallas spun back. Just as she caught sight of Emma's blond hair, the woman smashed her temple with a fist-sized rock. Her world went dark as she collapsed.

Dallas lapsed in and out of consciousness as they restrained her wrists, ankles, and mouth with her own duct tape. At one point she heard Emma ask, "Are we going to kill her?"

She thought she heard Randall say, "No, she can bear children."

Blood trickled down her face, and Dallas kept her eyes closed. They might as well think she was out of it.

"I'm heading out to destroy an internet hub," Randall said, his voice excited. "Come with me. It'll be exhilarating."

"I want to see Tate in the hospital." Emma moved toward the door.

Randall followed. "He's at Spencer's and he's getting better."

"I need to see my baby."

Randall grabbed his wife by the shoulders. "But you'll come with me after that? I need you, Emma. Let's start this new era together."

She paused, then said, "All right."

The couple kissed and walked out.

Dallas wanted to punch Emma in the face. The stupid twat. Why the hell didn't she run when she had the chance? She deserved whatever happened to her.

Dallas focused on the duct tape across her mouth. It was a short piece and hadn't stuck well. If she could work it loose and get herself over to a spare cell phone, she might be able to make a call.

Chapter 33

McCullen woke in the middle of the night and couldn't go back to sleep. He'd been awake off and on, hoping to hear from Dallas again. Her last text had come around eleven when she'd said she was going out to search for the bunker. It had been less than four hours, but he was worried.

He climbed out of bed, went straight to his laptop, and sent an email to Dallas and Gibson: *What is the update? Where are you?*

His boss was probably sleeping. Gibson was a late-night drinker, and their quiet little office in Redding didn't usually call for after-hours work.

McGoo padded into the room and nudged him with her head.

"All right. We'll go out for a minute." He pulled on jeans and shoes and took the dog out for a brisk walk. Preoccupied with Dallas' safety, he kept imagining scenarios out at the compound. Dallas finding Emma, then being discovered, shot, and dumped in the woods. Randall shooting both women and burying them in a giant compost bin.

McCullen jogged home and forced himself to shake it off. Dallas was an experienced undercover agent, and the Clayton brothers had no history of violence. He would hear from her any minute.

At home he made himself a PBJ and tried to figure out

what to do next. Going back to sleep wasn't an option. His cell phone rang, and he scrambled to find it. A frantic search finally located it on his bedroom dresser. "Agent McCullen."

"Sorry, it's so late, but I'm calling about the picture of the woman in the newspaper that's supposed to go out in a few hours. I'm on the printing crew, and I just saw it. Her name is Tamara Slaney." The man was calm and articulate. Not one of the crazies who liked to call for attention.

"Hold on a sec." McCullen rushed to his briefcase and searched for a pen. He grabbed his casebook, asked for the spelling, and wrote down the name. "Who are you and how do you Tamara?"

"Darrell Finley. I worked with her at Sterling Real Estate a few years ago."

"In Sacramento?"

"Yes."

"Do you know what happened to her?"

"What do you mean? She's dead, right?" His voice caught.

"She is. I'm sorry." McCullen started over. "Do you know where she went or what she did after you worked with her?"

"Not really. A lot of people left the business during the recession."

"What else do you know about her?"

"Only that my ex-boss saw her a few months ago and said she'd fallen on hard times."

That might explain why she'd planned a robbery. "Do you know her family? Or someone I should contact?"

"Her husband's name is Carter Slaney." The tipster hung up.

Knowing who the victim was gave him a shot of optimism. If he could link her to the Claytons, he'd have a reason to go out to Destiny. He jumped up and dressed for work.

The bureau was empty at two-thirty in the morning, but McCullen made a pot of coffee anyway. He would need it. He wanted to contact Dallas, but if she was in a tight situation, getting a call from a federal office could jeopardize her life. Why hadn't they heard from her? At his desk he called Gibson and left a message, asking for an update. They had an agent in the field who could be in trouble, and his boss needed to be aware, no matter what time it was.

After a quick search of the white pages, he found Carter Slaney, called him, and left a message. He probably wouldn't hear from him until the morning, but McCullen felt compelled to keep moving forward. He knew the murder victim had been involved in something, and he needed to know ASAP.

He began an online search for Tamara Slaney. An old real estate page came up first, followed by several civil court cases in which she'd been sued for unpaid bills. He ran her name in the criminal database and came up empty, then looked for her in the missing persons file. Another dead end.

How had Charlotte/Tamara arrived in Redding? If, in fact, she still lived in Sacramento. The woman had rented a car here in town, but unless she lived here, she'd likely taken a bus. Or a flight. Or hitchhiked.

He called the Greyhound depot and got lucky. The night clerk reported that Charlotte Archer had purchased a ticket for a trip from Sacramento to Redding on Sunday morning, April 21st. McCullen rubbed his tired eyes. Why would someone go out of town to commit a robbery? So no one would recognize her? Or had she targeted The Highland for a reason? He needed to call the DMV later and see if Slaney had her own car.

His phone rang and jarred him out of his thoughts. "Agent McCullen."

"This is Carter Slaney. Why did you call me in the middle of the night?"

"Do you know Tamara Slaney?"

"She's my ex-wife. Why?"

"I'm sorry, but she's dead. She was murdered in Redding a few weeks ago."

A long silence. "I'm sorry to hear that." He measured his words carefully.

Had her ex followed and killed her? "When was the last time you saw her?"

"A year ago. I didn't know she'd moved to Redding."

"I don't think she did. Do you have any idea who would want to kill her?"

The man made an odd sound. "Any of her ex-husbands might want to, but I assure you I did not."

"How many ex-husbands did she have?"

"Two others that I know of."

"You were her last?"

"Unless she got married again this year."

A glimmer of an idea took shape. "Do you know the names of her previous husbands?"

"The first was Jake Wilson, a college sweetheart. They lasted two years. The second was Randall Clayton, who was once mayor of Santa Carmichael. I think they lasted four."

Randall Clayton? That was interesting! McCullen thanked him and hung up, then processed the new intel. Tamara had come to Redding to rob her ex-husband's business and had been murdered instead. Had Randall caught her in the act, then followed her to the motel to keep their confrontation away from his business? It was time to talk to the bastard again.

As he stood, Gibson returned his call, his voice gruff.

"McCullen, you need to back off. I just heard from Dallas. She found the bunker and it's empty. She's starting to think Emma Clayton isn't on the property."

A little stunned, McCullen was silent. Why hadn't Dallas texted him too? Something wasn't right. Finally, he said, "I need to go out to Destiny to question Randall Clayton about my homicide victim."

"Seriously? Why?"

"The victim is his ex-wife, and I think she tried to rob The Highland."

"I'll be damned." Gibson paused.

McCullen could visualize him rubbing his chin. He started to give more detail, but his boss cut him off.

"Don't go out there yet. Give Dallas the weekend to see what she can find—even if she can't locate Emma."

"This homicide is my investigation. I have to be able to question the main suspect."

"He's not going to tell you anything. Let Dallas do her job while you question everyone else."

McCullen worked to control his anger. "But if I bring Randall in for questioning, that will give Dallas an opportunity to snoop around his place."

"I'll talk to her and see what she says. But I think you'll compromise her investigation if you stir up new shit for Randall right now."

McCullen disagreed but he kept his mouth shut. "Keep me informed." He hung up before his boss could say anything else.

Now what? Who else could he question besides Randall Clayton? Typically, he would talk to the suspect's family and friends, but they all lived in Destiny. Maybe someone here in town knew Tamara Slaney. Who would claim the body? The thought reminded him that he hadn't heard from the medical examiner. McCullen checked his mail cubby to see if the printed report had been delivered late the day before, and it had.

He tore open the large manila envelope and read through the findings. In short, the victim had experienced a subdural hematoma, caused by a blow to the head, but the water in her lungs indicated she was still alive when she was submerged. She had definitely been murdered. The report gave no indication of what she'd been struck with, and he was still waiting to hear from the lab about the lamp he'd sent in. He'd have to track down her last address and question the people who had known Tamara before she took a bus to Redding to commit a crime.

Restless, he went out for a walk around the block. He needed to question Randall Clayton and search his car and home. The bastard had made two women disappear within a space of weeks, and they had to hold him accountable. McCullen spun and headed back to his office. At his desk, he downloaded and printed the first picture he found online— Randall and Emma's marriage photo—then headed out to the motel where Tamara had been killed. It was one of the few places that would be open and have someone on duty he could question. If he learned anything, he would write a search warrant and take it to a judge. If not, he'd head out to Destiny to bring Randall in for questioning. His boss wasn't always right.

The night clerk at the Four Corners Motel took a quick glance at the photo. "Sure, I've seen him. Everyone knows Randall Clayton. He ran for Congress, then moved here to become a prepper. A nutjob, if you ask me."

L.J. Sellers

McCullen resisted comment. "Have you seen him at the motel in the last month?"

"No. Why?"

"I need to ask everyone on staff."

"I'm the only one here now, but the weekend maid will show up around nine this morning."

"Call me when she gets in." He handed him a business card. "I also need the names and contact information of every guest who was in the motel when the victim was here."

"That could take a few hours."

McCullen wanted the information as soon as it was ready, but he also planned to pick up his suspect before he did anything else. "I'll be back for it."

His sense of urgency had been escalating all night, and he wanted Randall Clayton in custody as soon as possible. If Randall learned through the local grapevine that he was suspected in his ex-wife's death, he might flee or go into deep hiding. With fifty acres and long-term supplies, he might never be seen again.

Chapter 34

Randall's heart worked overtime, and his brain felt supercharged, like he'd just done a line of coke. Emma was back with him, he and Spencer had set the trigger, and now he was about to destroy a major network hub. That damn FBI agent had proved to be a major pain, but he'd handled her too. A burst of laughter shot out of him. God, it was good to be alive and finally making things happen. He grabbed his wife's hand as they left Sonja's apartment.

"What now?" she asked.

"I need to talk to Raff, the hacker we hired. Then we hit the road. The explosives are already in the back of the truck." He started for the stairs, then noticed the lights were on in Raff's apartment. He strode next door and pounded.

After a long moment, Raff yelled from inside, "Open it yourself!"

Was he drunk? Randall yanked open the door and stepped in. Emma stayed behind him in the doorframe. Raff sat on the couch with his laptop nearby. His eyes were puffy, and his flabby face distorted with pain.

Randall ignored Raff's personal issues. "Did you get the code to the New York network exchange?"

"No, and I can't."

"Why not? I need it now! And I paid you for it."

The hacker held out swollen hands. "Your brother broke

my fucking fingers!"

"What?" Confused, Randall stepped in for a closer look. "Spencer did that? Why, for god's sake?" His brother was not a violent man.

"Because he's a psychopath control freak. He wants to end civilization, but only in a gentle way. Fucking hypocrite."

Randall tried to fill in the blanks. Raff must have been plotting something horrible if Spencer had attacked him to stop it. "What the hell were you trying to do?"

"You amateurs needed help, so I started a war." Raff rocked forward in pain. "Do you have any Vicodin? Or Oxy? I need something."

A jolt squeezed his chest, but he couldn't tell if it was fear or excitement. "You started a war? Which countries?" If the conflict went nuclear, he was glad they'd built the bunker.

"Israel and Syria. And Iran...and maybe other Arab nations." Raff let out a pained grunt.

"But why?" Randall thought he knew.

"*You're* worried about global warming and the human species. *I'm* worried about Islamic extremists and dirty bombs. And U.S. soldiers getting their legs blown off because most Muslims can't get along with anyone, including each other." The speech seemed to exhaust him, and he lay down on the couch. "So let 'em blow each other to hell."

"That's harsh." Randall's thoughts raced. Did a single hacker really have the ability to start World War Three? If Israel was threatened, America would get involved. He didn't want that on his conscience, but it was out of his control. And it could only help their cause. "We have a nurse who can help with your hands. Her name's Marissa, and she's in the yellow house across the street." Randall turned to go.

"Open me a beer before you leave. Please!"

Randall wanted to ignore him but took a moment to honor his request. On his way out, he wondered if he needed to talk to Spencer. Had his brother had a change of heart?

Emma grabbed his arm before they reached the stairs. "Do you really think he started a war? Should we check the news?"

Randall kept moving. "We don't have time. We need to hit the network centers this morning, so the shutdown happens all at once. As soon as we're on the road, I'll send an email to signal the others."

"I have to check on Tate and take a shower first." Emma hurried down the steps behind him. "I couldn't get clean in that tiny bathtub."

"See the baby, then get in the truck. Your shower can wait a couple of hours." He grabbed her hand and started to run. "Remember, we have a federal agent tied up on this property, so the sooner we distract her buddies, the better."

Inside Spencer's house, Emma ran down the hall to see the baby, and Randall headed into the data center. His brother stood, staring out the window into the darkness.

Worried, Randall called out softly, "Spencer?" When his brother turned, Randall asked, "Are you all right?"

Spencer opened his mouth to speak, then paused. Finally, he said. "I don't want to go through with this."

Oh shit. Randall knew he had to tread carefully. "It's too late. You sent the emails. Raff fucked with the Middle East. It's happening."

"I only sent half the emails, and we can notify the banks to send out a correction." Spencer's voice had a dazed tone. "I'll make Raff undo everything he did. Or make him tell me how to do it. I shouldn't have hurt him so badly."

"What about Sonja? Or whatever her name really is? How do we put her back?"

"I don't know." Spencer scowled. "That's what I'm trying to figure out."

"If we stop the collapse, we either have to kill her or let her go. And if we let her go, we'll both end up in prison." Randall started to think Sonja should die. He wished he'd shot her out on the hill. It would be harder up close.

"We may have another option," Spencer said. "Maybe we could give her some drugs to mess up her memory."

Randall lost his patience. "That's not realistic. She escaped the bunker, but Emma and I subdued her again. Now she's duct-taped in her apartment. We have to deal with her and keep moving forward."

Spencer lunged toward him. "I won't let you harm her! This is out of control!"

Randall quickly held up his hands in supplication. "Deal with her your way, but be smart. I'm not going to prison." He stepped toward the door. "I have something important to do."

"No explosions! I don't want anyone to get hurt."

"It's the weekend. No one will be in the buildings." *A straight-out lie.* His instructions to his conspirators were to minimize the number of people killed, but they knew there would be casualties. Randall strode out.

He felt Spencer coming after him and spun back around. "Don't try to stop me."

Spencer lunged at him again, and Randall shoved him back as hard as he could. His brother stumbled and landed on a chair. Randall bolted through the door and yelled, "Emma! Let's go!"

She rushed up the hallway into the living room, looking

irritated. Randall grabbed her hand and pulled her toward the front door. He glanced back, but Spencer hadn't followed him.

As they hurried next door, Randall tried to think of what else he would need. He had one of his guns. Did he need another? If things went badly, he'd rather take his own life than go to prison. He was also prepared to shoot a security guard if he had to. Once he sent the email and unleashed the rest of the team, he had to do everything he could to fulfill his end.

Inside his house, he picked up an extra handgun, several bottles of water, and the ten thousand in cash from the safe—just in case things didn't go according to plan and they had to run for it. Emma used the bathroom and stuffed a few things in an overnight bag. They stepped out the front door into the night, and it occurred to him that it might be the last time he saw his beloved Destiny. He hoped not.

"We're making a better future," he declared. He and Emma headed for the truck.

Chapter 35

Getting the duct tape off her mouth took longer than Dallas had anticipated. It was still rolled into a wad across her bottom teeth and her lips felt raw, but she could at least make noise now and speak to some degree. A dispatcher might not understand what she was saying, but they might be able to trace the call.

Dallas had considered kicking the wall between her and Raff's apartment to attract his attention, then changed her mind. She'd heard Randall go next door to talk to him, so the creepy hacker was probably working with the deviant brothers and wouldn't likely help her. He might even try to harm her. She was feeling lucky to be alive. With all the weapons the Claytons kept around, she couldn't believe Randall hadn't shot her. Apparently he wasn't a cold-blooded killer—just a psychopath who wanted to keep her around as a breeder.

The house was dark except for a lamp next to the couch, but she could see light in the bedroom. Ankles and wrists bound, head pounding from the rock assault, she flopped her way across the living room carpet, feeling like a clumsy seal. Weary of it, she tried standing and hopping but soon fell on her face. It hurt her nose, but at least she didn't smash her head again. Exhausted and aching, she finally reached the composite floor in the hallway, and the slick surface made the short trip to the bedroom a little easier.

Her suitcase was open on the bed. Randall had apparently been searching her things when she interrupted him. Dallas glanced at the dresser where she'd put her spare cell phone in the middle drawer. It looked undisturbed. Thank god. Dallas maneuvered onto her knees, grabbed the narrow handle with her teeth, and pulled. The drawer moved an inch. She tried again, yanking this time. Another three inches. It took four more pulls to move the drawer past the hinges so it could drop to the floor. She rested for a moment, teeth aching. All those childhood fillings had ground against the metal handle and sent chills down her spine.

The only garment in the drawer was a pair of yoga pants, which she pulled out with her teeth, exposing the phone. Once she had it activated, she could use voice commands to call 911, but how the hell was she supposed to turn the damn thing on? One way or another, she had to make it happen.

She leaned over and used her chin to press the edge of the phone with the switch against the side of the drawer. Nothing happened on the first five tries, but finally the familiar light of the home screen came on. Dallas gave it a moment to fully engage, then used her chin again to press the genie button. "Call 911," she mumbled through the wadded tape.

The phone didn't respond, so she tried again, speaking more slowly. She still sounded a bit garbled, but the beautiful sound of a call going through filled the silent room.

"What is your emergency?" a chipper female voice asked.

"Kidnapped. Call FBI." She had to keep it simple to be understood.

"Did you say kidnapped?"

"Yes. Call FBI. Agent Dallas."

"Call the FBI in Dallas Texas? Where are you now?"

"Redding. I'm Agent Dallas." The damn duct tape got in the way of her tongue and made her sound ridiculous.

"I'm having trouble understanding you. Can you tell me where you are?"

"Outside Redding. Destiny."

She heard the front door open and footsteps come her way. "Send help now!"

Dallas sat back on her heels so she could face whoever had come to assault her. Spencer walked into the room, carrying her weapon. His face was inscrutable. *Oh shit.* Dallas tried to show no fear, but her heart ached for all the things she hadn't done with her life yet.

"I see you called for help." Spencer reached down and hung up on the dispatcher. "There's no need for that now."

He stared at her for a long moment, and Dallas struggled to get up. She wouldn't beg for her life or even try to bargain, but she would ram him if he gave her a chance.

"I'll be right back," he finally said.

She tried again to stand. Just as she made it, he came back carrying a steak knife.

"Sit down on the bed. I'm going to cut you loose."

Why would he? This couldn't be good. She complied, leery but relieved, as he removed the rest of the duct tape from her mouth.

He talked as he sawed through the tape, his voice flat as if he were in shock. "I had nothing to do with Emma's abduction or yours. I just learned of Randall's criminal activities minutes ago. I'm freeing you so you can go after him. I think he plans to set off an explosion."

Dallas watched his face, which gave nothing away. She didn't believe a word of it, except the part about blowing something up. Spencer had clearly turned on his brother, playing the good guy to save himself from prosecution. She would work with that. "Emma said you had plans to cause a financial collapse. Tell me the details, so our people can stop it."

"I don't know what else Randall had planned." He started on the tape around her ankles.

"Can you guess? If you want immunity, you have to help the bureau stop this."

"He mentioned something about a run on the banks, but he destroyed the computers before he left. And I think Randall has followers out there that he'll contact now, if he hasn't already. They might be planning multiple explosions." Spencer handed over her gun, then slipped off her backpack and gave it to her.

Relief washed over Dallas. She checked the chamber, but the gun was no longer loaded. "What are the targets?"

"I really don't know. I had no part in planning any of this."

"Is Raff involved? Does he know?" Dallas gestured at the dividing wall.

"No. I hired him to set up networks, maybe join the community if he liked it here."

Lying ratface. She kept the thought to herself, needing his cooperation. But first she had to call her team. "Will you sit down and write out a statement with everything you know?" Dallas looked around. Did she have any paper? She found a small tablet in her suitcase and handed it to him.

"I'm sorry things worked out this way. I really liked you." Spencer gave her a sad smile.

Dallas tried not to roll her eyes. "Excuse me." She waved at him to leave. He didn't act like someone who'd make a run for it.

Spencer walked out, and Dallas called McCullen. She thought he might be quicker to respond at four-thirty in the morning than Gibson. McCullen picked up immediately. "Dallas. What's happening?"

"Randall Clayton just left the property, and Emma has gone along with him. I think they plan to blow up something connected to internet infrastructure. I'm going after him."

McCullen sucked in a quick breath. "I may have spotted his truck a few minutes ago. I was on my way out to Destiny, but I'll turn around right now."

She was curious about why he'd been headed her way, but now was not the time. "There may be other targets, so I need to call Gibson. Stay on Randall and update me with your location in a few minutes."

Searching for her car keys, she called her team leader, and he finally picked up. "What's going on?" he asked, his voice scratchy. "Did you find our missing woman?"

"Yes, and she's no longer a victim. She's working with her husband to set off an explosion, but I don't know where yet."

"Holy shit!" Something loud thunked in the background. "Give me a second."

She found her keys and took a long drink of water while Gibson got himself situated.

Still sounding breathless, he asked, "What are they driving?"

"Dark blue Ford truck, early 2000 model."

"What do we know about the target?"

"Emma referred to them as 'internet buildings,' so that could be tech companies or places where servers are housed." Dallas grabbed her laptop and headed for the door. "The plan is to cause a financial and social meltdown, so they could hit government buildings too."

"You're saying *they*. How many people? How many targets?"

"I don't know."

"I'll get the whole bureau on this. We need immediate access to Randall Clayton's cell phone and email account."

Dallas pounded down the stairs. "They've also got a financial scheme cooking that is supposed to cause a run on the banks. We need to notify all the financial departments. I wish I knew more."

"You may have mitigated the worst of it. Good work."

Not really. She'd been captured and detained twice, and the suspects had given her most of the information. "I'm going after Randall. I may be able to reason with him if I can get him or Emma on the phone."

"I'll get a crisis team from the Sacramento office to make contact and be on standby."

"We need a team out here at the compound too—tech experts who can examine damaged computers." Dallas unlocked her rental car. "I'll call again when I'm on the road."

She thought about the impending confrontation with Randall and wished she had her sniper gear. She remembered Spencer's gun safe and sprinted for his house. It wouldn't be the same as her Remington, but the Bushmaster would do in a pinch.

Chapter 36

McCullen braked to a near stop and made a wide U-turn in the road. The truck he'd seen going the other way in the dark hadn't really registered, except as a local farmer or hunter. He'd expected to arrive at Destiny while everyone slept and knock quietly on Dallas' door first to make sure she was all right. If she hadn't been there, he would have called for backup, rousted Randall out of bed, and hauled him into the bureau for questioning. Encountering the suspect on the road had not been on his mind. Now Randall had a five- or seven-minute lead.

Punching the gas, McCullen pushed his sedan to seventy. Even in the dark, he knew the road well and could handle the speed. Where was Randall headed? Without knowing the target, the bureau would waste time and manpower trying to cover every potential—and could still miss the mark.

His thoughts turned to Emma. What had happened with her? He wanted to believe Randall had forced her to go along, but Dallas had indicated Emma was a willing partner. In fact, Dallas had sounded pissed off about it. Had she rescued Emma only to have the victim rejoin the man who'd abducted her? Law enforcement saw that kind of behavior all the time. McCullen thought back to his relationship with Emma. She'd been rather passive-aggressive at times. But she'd been fun too—and very sexual. It saddened him to think of her going to prison.

A wild thought popped into his head. What about Tate? If Emma and Randall were both incarcerated—or dead—the system would have to find a guardian. McCullen decided it was time to request a DNA test for himself and the baby. He'd been thinking about it for months.

A year and a half earlier, he'd stopped at The Highland for a drink after a long day. Emma had joined him at the bar, flirting outrageously. They'd gotten drunk together and arranged to meet at a motel a few blocks away. After an hour of crazy monkey sex that required two trips to the shower, he'd sobered up and sent her home. He'd never regretted the sex—the best he'd ever had—but cheating with another man's wife had left him ashamed. He'd stopped going into The Highland again. Then months later, he'd heard Emma was pregnant.

He'd tried not to think about it, but in the back of his mind he'd known it was his kid. Randall and Emma had been married for years without producing any children. McCullen had even entertained the idea that Emma had slept with him just to get pregnant. Was it true? Was Tate his kid and about to come into his life on a permanent basis?

Unsettled by all of it, McCullen put his coffee back in the holder and watched the dark road ahead. He didn't see any tail lights, but he knew the turnoff to Highway 299 was coming up. Randall had probably made the turn already, and McCullen didn't want to miss it. He also had to call Dallas again and update her on their location. He put in his earpiece and hit callback. He didn't use the cell phone much in the car and had never mastered voice commands.

"Dallas here. I'm on the road now. Where are you?"

"Near the 299 junction, trying to decide if I should head east or west."

"Randall is likely to stick to back roads if he thinks we're following him." In the background, he heard her car engine wind up to full speed.

"Can you think of any reason he would head north?" McCullen hoped she'd learned something about their plans.

"Not unless he decides to skip the planned attack and run for it."

McCullen didn't think he would. "I'll turn right and head toward Deschutes Road. I think Randall will avoid the city and head south until he can hit I-5 somewhere." He pushed his speed, hoping to catch up to the truck. What if Randall went the other direction and eluded him?

A huge deer came out of nowhere and bounded into the road. "Shit!" McCullen slammed the brakes and swerved right, missing the creature by an inch. He shot off the pavement into a shallow ditch, riding slanted on the slope until it flattened out.

"McCullen, are you okay?"

"I nearly hit a deer and ended up in the ditch, but I'll be back on the road in a minute." *Damn.* The misadventure had set him back, giving Randall a wider lead.

After a minute, Dallas said, "Spencer blamed it all on Randall. The abductions, the financial hacking, everything. He even told me to go after him."

"That's cold. Maybe Randall knew and decided to make a run for it. Maybe you should head north."

"No, I heard Emma and Randall. He's determined to be disruptive. I think he has an inferiority complex."

McCullen agreed. Randall had grown up with a brother who was taller, better looking, and more of a leader. Living in that shadow must have warped him a little. "Are you headed my way?"

"Yes. I'm going to call Randall and see if I can engage him, figure out where he's going before the crisis team takes over."

"Good luck. He's a crafty bastard."

"So is Emma. That bitch hit me on the head with a rock, and I've still got a major headache." Dallas' voice was charged with energy.

"But you're okay?"

"I'm fine. I've got Spencer's rifle, and I'm an excellent shot. Given a chance, I'll take Randall out rather than let him set off an explosion in public."

McCullen liked her more all the time. Too bad he hadn't met Dallas five years ago instead of Emma. "I'm out for now, so I can watch the road. Stay in touch." He clicked off his phone and gave the sedan more gas. He needed eyes on Randall ASAP.

The image of Emma striking Dallas unnerved him. But Emma had hit him once when she'd thought he lied to her. He hadn't lied, and the blow to his upper arm had surprised him. How violent was Emma? She was on her way with Randall to blow up a building. It was early Saturday morning, and the building might be empty, but it was still coldly criminal. He was feeling lucky she'd left him when she did.

His cell phone rang and he glanced at the number. A Quantico area code. He tapped his earpiece to answer. "McCullen here."

"Gerry Sanders in the crime lab. I found a partial print on the lamp you submitted, but it's not showing in the database."

"Still, that's good news. Anything else?"

"Luminol revealed a blood smear, but I haven't been able to extract enough from the smooth surface for testing. Sorry."

"Thanks for calling." McCullen kept his eyes on the road. He would deal with this information later.

* * *

Dallas raced down the narrow road, glad there was no traffic. The near total darkness was unnerving, but she'd taken high-speed driver training at Quantico without killing any fake citizens, so she would be all right. As long as a deer didn't wander into *her* path. They didn't worry about such creatures in the desert. Around Phoenix, you were more likely to run over a snake or a rat.

She pushed her speed, pleased to be driving an Audi, and eased up only for the sweeping curve where Emma's car had gone off the road. Had Emma ever really been a victim? She'd seemed pretty happy to get out of the bunker at the time. Dallas shook it off. Emma didn't matter now. She had to talk to Randall. She picked up her Sonja phone, glad she was compulsive about creating contacts. "Call Randall Clayton."

He was egotistical—or curious—enough to pick up. "Sonja, you are hard to keep down. What do you want?" An edge of panic made him sound amused.

"Just wondering where you're headed. Emma told me you planned to hit internet buildings. Does that mean tech companies or network server locations?"

He made a startled sound. "Why should I tell you?"

"It's not too late to give up before you get caught."

He laughed, a phony sound. "I'm not going to get caught, so unless you're in a car right behind me, you're wasting your time."

"I am in a car right behind you."

A sharp intake of breath, followed by a pause. "You're lying. No one is back there. I've been watching."

"No, *we're* watching. Before you do anything stupid, you should know that Spencer blamed you for everything. He said he tried to stop you, then he cut me free and sent me after you."

"Bullshit! My brother would never turn on me. You're trying to drive a wedge between us."

Now Dallas laughed. "Too late for that. Spencer already opened up a chasm." She tried to push him into a mistake. "Still headed to the capital?"

"Nice try. Now fuck off." He hung up.

His abruptness made her think she'd guessed correctly. But what did he plan to target in Sacramento? The capitol building itself? Dallas wondered how long it would take the bureau to get a chopper in the sky over this area. Even in the dark, a chopper could pick up Randall's truck and track its movements. But pulling people out of bed and putting them into the right gear and location took time. Gibson's job was to prompt the FBI director to execute warrantless phone and email searches, and that would take a series of phone calls and maybe as long as an hour. Companies and buildings around California could start to blow up at any minute. Or maybe Randall's reach was even wider. How many conspirators did he have?

Dallas pressed the gas, hitting ninety, determined to catch up.

Chapter 37

Gibson's hands shook as he called the cell phone of his supervisor in the Sacramento office. Tempted as he was to make a direct call to the main office in Washington D.C., the bureau was a chain-of-command entity, and this was how it had to be done. He just hoped following protocol didn't take too long.

After four rings, a tense female voice picked up. "This is Kerry Meyers. How can I help you?"

"Special Agent Gibson, FBI field office, Redding California. We have a national security situation."

"Give me the details." She didn't miss a beat.

"Randall and Emma Clayton are in a truck with an explosive, headed for an unknown target, likely in Northern California. More terrorists are probably involved. We don't know who they are or what their targets are. We need to access Randall Clayton's phone and email records immediately to determine who he's working with."

"Let me get online with the D.C. office." The special agent in charge fumbled something, trying to access what sounded like a keyboard. "How do you know this?"

"We had an undercover agent in a local survivalist community looking for a missing woman. She found a lot more than that."

"Spell the suspect's name and give me every contact

detail you have for him."

Gibson gave her the intel, then added, "Our agent in the field thinks the targets are tech companies and internet hubs. Can we get the National Guard out to protect Silicon Valley?"

"That will be up to the director."

"There's more."

"I'm listening." Her voice had a little catch.

"There's a cyber attack hitting the banking system that could wreak havoc on Monday."

"That's not our department. Call the FDIC, or maybe the Federal Reserve."

"Should you call Homeland Security?"

"Again, that will be up to the director. The administration has made it clear that terrorism is our jurisdiction. I'm sure the bureau will put SWAT units and hostage-rescue teams in the air shortly."

"I have two agents pursuing Clayton . They may have visual contact. Please ask the tactical units to be careful."

"Once our chopper team has picked up his vehicle, get your people out of there."

"Will do."

"What are Clayton and his group trying to accomplish?"

"If I find out, I'll get back to you." Gibson hung up and pulled on his pants. He wasn't making another call in his underwear or without coffee.

Chapter 38

Randall had planned to cut through town over to the freeway, but with an FBI agent on his tail, he decided to stick to the side roads for a while. After a short stretch on 299, he turned south on Deschutes. His legs trembled as he drove, and he worried about wrecking the truck and blowing themselves up. The hives on his chest itched so badly he wanted to tear off his skin.

Had Spencer really turned on him? Was it over? Sonja was certainly on his case. If he had one fed after him, more would be coming. It was starting to sink in that even if the trigger plans were successful—and they still could be—he and Emma would likely be arrested and jailed. Randall couldn't accept that. He could come to terms with the idea that the new world he'd helped create would go on without him, but he wouldn't let them put him in a cell. He was prepared to die for his cause.

"That was the FBI agent, right?" Emma's hands were gripped tightly together. "She got loose and is following us?"

"Unfortunately." He decided not to tell her about Spencer's betrayal.

"What are we going to do?"

Randall was still deciding. It was hard to think and concentrate on the road while driving seventy miles an hour in the dark. "We have three options. We can stop the whole thing by calling off the other futurists and letting them arrest us. That means prison for me, but probably not for you. We can say I forced you to come with me." He glanced over to see her reaction, but she kept her face averted.

"Or we can make a run for it. I have contacts in Oregon who will take us in. We can change our appearance, get new IDs, and start over."

"What about Tate? We'd have to go back for him eventually." Emma's eyes watered with distress.

"Or Spencer could bring him to us." *Not if Spencer was in jail,* Randall thought. The state would take custody of Tate as soon as they became fugitives, but Emma didn't need to know that.

"What's the third option?" she asked.

"We go for it. Set the explosion at the exchange center, and let the others set theirs. We can try to run after that, but we'll likely be killed by federal agents. I won't let them take me alive."

"Oh fuck." Emma choked back a sob. "It wasn't supposed to be like this. Your followers were supposed to set the explosives, and I never thought you would really go through with it."

His hands tensed on the steering wheel. How could she doubt his nerve? Besides, this was her fault. "You started the whole thing by packing your bags to leave Destiny. Now deal with it."

"My mother was sick. It was just temporary."

"Your mother is a hypochondriac, and you usually ignore her. This time I thought you were leaving me."

"What difference does it make now? We have to make a plan!"

"What do you want to do?"

She grabbed his shoulder, so he would look at her. "Let's call it off and make a run for it. I want a fresh start."

Randall was torn. "There's another option. We can let the other explosions happen, but skip our part. The financial triggers have been set, so the meltdown is happening anyway." He didn't know if he should tell her about the war Raff might have started. "All we have to do is get out of the state, then start gathering supplies again."

"Do we have the money for that?"

"I have cash with me. We can stop at ATMs along the way and take out the limit at each one."

"This is freaking me out! I don't want to die or go to jail." Emma nervously rubbed her legs. "But you're right about letting your followers go through with their attacks. The more diversions the cops have, the less likely they are to come after us."

Randall noticed a sign for the 44 turnoff. He would take the exit heading east, then go north on a back road like Oak Run and disappear.

The phone in his lap rang again, startling him. He looked at the ID: Agent McCullen. What the hell? Was he still looking for Emma? The thought almost made him laugh. He decided to let the asshole know that Emma was with him, that she'd chosen him again. "What can I do for you?"

"Put me on speaker. I want to talk to Emma."

Shit. How much did he know? "I don't think so. She's made her choice."

"I don't think you know your wife very well."

Randall could hear an engine in the background. Was McCullen in a vehicle? "What are you talking about?"

"Put me on speaker, and I'll tell you some things about Emma that you might want to know before you make a major life decision. But I want to hear her voice first."

Randall glanced at his wife.

"Who is it?" she asked.

The knot in Randall's stomach tightened. He knew better than to trust what law enforcement said. They often lied to accomplish their goals. But he wanted to watch Emma's reaction to what McCullen had to say. Her face would tell him the truth. Randall clicked over to speaker. "Make it quick."

"Hey, Emma. How are you?" The agent's tone was mocking.

"Caleb? What do you want?" Emma sounded worried.

"Does your husband know what happened on April 21st?"

Randall glanced at his wife. Her eyes were wide with fear.

"Hang up," she hissed. "He's just trying to mess with us."

Emma's obvious distress caused a wave of nausea to roll over him. "What is this about?"

McCullen's voice came at him again. "Did you know your ex-wife is dead, Randall? They pulled her out of the pool at the Four Corners Motel. She'd been conked on the head."

Confusion overwhelmed him. Tamara was dead? Killed in Redding? "When did this happen? Why didn't anyone tell me?"

McCullen's voice through the speaker was matter-of-fact. "Tamara died about three weeks ago. Right before her death, she was seen in the parking lot next to The Highland. Emma was in the restaurant that night."

"So what are you saying?" Randall eased up on the gas. He was having trouble concentrating, and he didn't want to miss his turn.

"Tamara came here to rob your restaurant. Emma saw her casing the place, followed her to the motel, and killed her.

Didn't you, Emma?"

"No! Why would I do that?" Emma was shouting, her fists clenched.

"I'm still working on motive," McCullen said, with forced cheerfulness. "But I think Tamara might have known that Tate wasn't Randall's kid."

It hit him like a blow to the chest. "What the fuck do you mean?" Randall screamed at the phone, but stared at his wife.

"She slept with me about nine months before he was born."

Another body blow, followed by brain freeze. Randall heard Emma protesting and McCullen sneering, but it all sounded distant and he couldn't focus on either.

McCullen had one more blow. "I also found Emma's fingerprints on the murder weapon."

"That's impossible!" Emma shrieked. "I wiped—" She caught herself but it was too late.

The dark road in front of Randall curved left and he pressed the accelerator.

"Slow down!" Emma gripped the strap above her door.

Randall ignored her. The exit came up but he flew through the intersection. He wasn't making a run for it with a woman he couldn't trust. A whore and a killer. Disgust filled the holes in his belly eaten by anger.

"Randall, please—"

"Shut up! I need to think."

Ten minutes later, he changed his mind again. He would blow up something today, but not the network building in Sacramento. It was too far away, and the feds would have too much time to stop him. What was nearby? What could he plow into that would wreak havoc?

DigiSpace, the internet company just outside of Redding.

He would turn back and drive like a madman into the building. The impact would set off both explosives in the truck.

He and Emma would die. And that was fine with him.

Chapter 39

Emma struggled to stop crying. How had all this happened? The last three weeks had been a nightmare! Until recently, her life had been fine—or mostly fine, except for boredom and dealing with Randall's control issue. Then she'd spotted Randall's ex-wife spying on the restaurant, and everything had gone to shit. Now they were speeding down the highway in the dark with FBI agents chasing them, and Randall was freaking out and talking about blowing them up.

Panicked, Emma tried to smooth things over. "I didn't hook up with Caleb. He's lying to distract you and gain an edge. Cops do that."

"Yeah? After years of trying, why did you suddenly get pregnant?"

"It happens." The way Randall looked at her sent shivers down her neck. She'd always known he was a little sociopathic—it was part of the attraction—but he looked murderous. She'd recently discovered that anyone could become that way. "You have to let this go! We're in a lot of trouble and have to be smart."

"What about Tamara? Tell me what happened!" He grabbed her hair and pulled her toward him. "Tell me everything, or I swear I'll run us into the next big tree."

Emma hated what had happened, and she would never tell him everything. But as she started to explain, that night came back to her in graphic detail.

She'd gone out the back of the restaurant to sneak a cigarette. She'd quit smoking years ago to make Randall happy, but she smoked every once in a while when the stress of the restaurant got to her.

She was staring at the bank next door, not really noticing it, but thinking of something else, when she realized there was a car parked in the back of the lot. Very unusual for the bank at night. The vehicle wasn't familiar, but the woman in it seemed like someone she knew. The dark and the distance kept her from being sure, but later, when the restaurant had closed, Emma grabbed her purse and went out to check. The car and the woman were still there. Curious, worried, and a little pissed, she headed over. The woman started the car and backed up, but not before Emma realized it was Tamara, Randall's ex-wife. What the hell was she doing in Redding, spying on their business?

Emma hurried to her own vehicle and quickly pulled out of the parking lot, following the Dodge Avenger. Tamara drove a half mile to the Four Corners Motel. Emma pulled in just in time to see her going into a room near the end. Was Tamara here to cause trouble for Randall? Or mess with her marriage?

She decided to find out. Nervous, but determined, Emma knocked on the door. The room was silent. Finally, she called out, "It's Emma Clayton. I want to talk to you."

From inside Tamara told her to go away.

"If you don't tell me what you're up to, I'll call the police and report that you were casing the restaurant." Emma kept her voice low, not wanting to wake up anyone.

The door opened, and Tamara gestured for her to come

inside. Emma noticed that the years had not been kind to Randall's ex. Her hair was fried from bad bleaching products, her eyelids had gone saggy, and the corners of her mouth were turning down. But she was still curvy and blond, and older men would find her attractive.

The motel room smelled nasty, like sweat or dog hair, and Emma wanted to get the encounter over with. "What are doing in Redding? What do you want?"

"It's none of your business. I'm leaving tomorrow, so don't worry about it." Tamara sounded as if she'd been drinking, but her tone was casual.

"Why were you watching the restaurant? Are you spying on me? Or were you planning something?"

Tamara suddenly lashed out. "I need money. Randall spent all of mine buying that goddamn piece of property and all those fucking prepper supplies."

"You were going to rob us?"

"That bastard owes me. Give me ten grand and I'll go away and you'll never see me again."

"Are you crazy?" Emma wanted to walk out, but she didn't trust this woman. "I'm tempted to call the police."

"I'm tempted to tell Randall that baby isn't his."

A knife to her stomach. "You bitch. What do you know?"

"I know that Randall is sterile. We tried to have kids too, and there's nothing wrong with my goods. I've been pregnant twice. Just not with Randall."

Fear gripped Emma and made her feel on fire. "That doesn't mean anything. Just leave us the hell alone."

They both tried to keep their voices down, so they didn't end up with the manager pounding on the door.

Tamara repeated her demand. "Give me ten grand or I'll tell Randall you cheated on him and that Tate is not his kid.

I'm pretty sure I know who you cheated with too. This is a small town, and I lived here, remember?" She spat the words out in a harsh whisper.

Emma's thoughts came rapidly, crashing into each other and making her pulse race. Randall would divorce her and fire her from the restaurant. She'd be a homeless, jobless single mother, and everyone would eventually know the truth. Even if she stole the money from The Highland to pay this nasty bitch, Tamara might come back for more.

The woman stepped toward her, menacing. "I'll give you until noon tomorrow to get the money." Tamara turned to open the door.

Rage and panic took over. She had to stop this woman now. Emma looked around and saw a lamp with a heavy base. She grabbed it from the nightstand and swung at Tamara's head. With a peculiar grunt, the woman collapsed on the floor.

For a moment, relief slowed her racing heart. Her secret was safe. But now what? Emma scrambled to think it through. She had to be smart. Had she touched anything but the lamp? No. It was late and probably no one had seen her outside the room. Even if they had, the motel guests would pack up and leave tomorrow or the next day. She just had to buy some time. But what the hell could she do with the body?

Emma remembered the motel had a pool. One that was covered for the winter. She could drag the body into the pool. First she had to get a towel and stop the woman's head from bleeding into the carpet, then she had to wipe down the lamp base and put it back. She could do this. When it was over, she would forget about it. Tamara was a blackmailer. She couldn't feel guilty about her death.

Yet she had. Mostly she'd worried about being caught. She'd worried about Randall finding out about Tate. She'd started to resent her life and her husband. Then her mother had called with yet another illness, and Emma had decided to take Tate and leave. To get away from the bad memories and make a fresh start. She'd hoped that getting away from Randall would also help her bond better with her baby. But that wasn't going to happen now.

So she didn't tell Randall about wanting to leave...or the truth about Tate's paternity. She had to convince him to head north, maybe ditch the truck and steal a car so they could lose the feds and run for it. They could still have a life. Or could they? Emma was sick with uncertainty. What about Tate? Would Caleb claim him? She was torn. Maybe she didn't want a life on the run. Maybe she didn't deserve to live.

Chapter 40

Dallas pushed her speed, glanced at the dashboard clock, and racked her brain for Randall's likely target. The location of the other buildings worried her too. It could take hours for agents to connect with multiple service providers, access Randall's emails and texts, and read though the data. If Randall and his conspirators had been careful, the real target names might not even be there.

Could she talk him into calling it off? She'd failed in her last attempt. Maybe she should just let a crisis negotiator handle it. But it could be another twenty minutes before a specialist was woken from sleep, informed, and into position. There was also no guarantee Randall would take a negotiator's call. She had to try again. Dallas pushed redial and held her breath.

Randall answered on the third ring. "What now, Sonja? Oh wait, that's not your real name. You lie and sneak and trick people. But then, all women do."

His bitterness surprised her. He'd been almost exhilarated when they'd talked a few minutes ago. "I'm sorry I lied about my name and my purpose. Emma's father wanted us to find her. You can understand that."

"He's an alcoholic asshole."

This was getting nowhere. "Randall, you need to call this off before it goes too far. You haven't done anything wrong yet. Emma's obviously not going to testify against you, and nothing's been destroyed. We can work out a plea deal."

He laughed, the bitterness deepening. "Let's not forget the assault on a federal officer. Besides, there is so much more going on that you don't even know."

"Tell me. I think I've earned it. What can it hurt now?" Dallas had to ease off the gas as a farm truck appeared in the road ahead of her. She honked and flew around him.

"It's too late to stop anything." Randall's voice had a catch in it, and she heard Emma crying in the background. *What the hell had happened?*

"It's not too late. Call off your conspirators! We can work out a deal."

"We're not turning ourselves in, and our little bombing spree is nothing compared to what's going to happen in the Middle East."

The words made her skin tingle. "What do you mean?"

"Raff took it upon himself to start a war between Israel and Syria."

Adrenaline rushed into her gut, and she tightened her grip on the wheel. "What exactly did he do? Tell me!"

"I don't know, but I'm sure it's financial, and I'm sure it's too late to stop it. The world is about to change in a very big way. See ya."

The bastard hung up. Dallas glanced at the road ahead and noticed a glow on the horizon but no taillights ahead of her. Would she ever catch up? Had they made a turn? She wished McCullen would check in, but she had to call Gibson again. She would have preferred to call the bureau's director in Washington, but she didn't have him in her phone.

A voice command put her through. "Gibson, we have another problem. There's a hacker named Greg Rafferty out at Destiny. He supposedly tried to start a war between Israel and Syria by moving money around. We should get the secretary of state involved right away."

"Are you serious? What the heck is in the water out there?"

She could tell Gibson was in his car too, and their connection wasn't good.

"They have a collective end-of-times mentality." Dallas switched back to her immediate concern. "Do we have a chopper in the air yet?"

"I don't know. I've made the calls and that's all I can do. I don't command any real resources here in Redding."

"Has McCullen checked in?"

"No. Do you have eyes on anyone?"

"Not yet. I'm worried I missed a turn."

"Where do you think Randall is heading?"

"Possibly Sacramento. We need to pinpoint tech companies or network hubs in that area."

"I'll get people on it, and we'll send out SWAT teams. Any other ideas?"

"Randall is unpredictable. Something personal happened between him and his wife. He might even be suicidal."

"Shit. That's the worst."

"I know." Dallas hesitated. "I think his other conspirators might be targeting communication centers. Like Google and Yahoo and other Silicon Valley businesses. What better way to disrupt everything than to take down the internet?"

"We'll get protection for them as well. First I'll call the secretary of state. Keep me posted."

Dallas clicked off, noticing a sign for a junction with Deschutes Road. Had they taken it? Why hadn't McCullen contacted her? She clicked on the dashboard GPS and saw that a right turn would take her south. She took the exit, hoping Randall had too.

Her phone rang again, and she touched her earpiece. "It's Dallas."

"McCullen here. I think I have him in sight now. We passed the 44 junction, so we're still heading south."

"I hope you're on Deschutes Road."

"We are. Where do we think he's going?"

"I think he was headed for Sacramento, but he must know he'll never make it. He seems to be having a personal meltdown."

"I just gave him bad news about his wife."

That might not have been the best idea. "Can you get close enough for a shot at his tires?"

"I'm trying."

"We could use a little daylight." The stress of racing in the dark was wearing on her, like a physical pressure. She was also fighting exhaustion from being up all night, and her head ached from the two blows.

"Oh shit!" McCullen shouted. "He just passed me going the other way."

The sound of squealing brakes vibrated in her ear. Dallas hit her brakes as well. "He must be headed for a new target. Something close." She braked again, looking for a place to turn around or lie in wait for him.

"I think I know," McCullen said. "There's an internet company just outside of Redding off Rancho Road."

"I just passed that turn. I'll head back and get there before he does." She spun the Audi into a fast U-turn, crunching in the gravel along the side. Hitting the gas again, she sped back the way she'd come. "Give me a marker for the road I turn on."

"It's Kenzie Way. There's a mechanic shop on the corner—a white building. Turn right. Kenzie Way is about half a mile long, and the internet company, Digi-something, is at the end."

"On my way."

Her heart pounded as she tried to visualize how this would play out. She would park her car off the road near the target and stand ready with the rifle. What she did next would depend on how Randall approached.

The sky began to lighten, and she could see occasional buildings and homes along the highway. Thank goodness. It wasn't enough daylight for a clean long-distance shot, but all she had to do was stop the damn truck. If Randall got out with an explosive in his hands—or taped to his chest—she'd take him out.

"McCullen, you still there?"

"Yep. What's your location?"

"I just passed a dairy."

"You've got another three miles. Should I stay online with you?"

"No, I have to run through some scenarios."

"I'll be right behind Randall and will back you up. He's not getting away. Good luck."

Dallas raced along the rural road, not feeling any more familiar with it this time. The hardest part of undercover work was not knowing the geographical area. At least McCullen was there to give her some guidance.

She pushed hard, her forearms tense from gripping the wheel, and her right hand bruised from Randall's stomping. The three miles seemed to take forever. Finally, the white mechanic shop glowed in the distance. She took her foot off the gas, but waited to brake until the last minute. Headlights came at her in the distance. The locals were starting to move around.

Squealing around a corner, she passed several homes and businesses, hoping that none would be in danger. They weren't even sure where Randall was going. Dallas had a flash of doubt. What if he was headed back to Destiny? To destroy his creation—and maybe the brother who had turned on him? FBI agents were converging on Redding now, but they were coming up I-5 from Sacramento and San Francisco. Gibson was probably still at the bureau making calls. She hoped he'd enlisted the Redding Police to secure the evidence and suspects still at Destiny.

What if Randall was headed into town? Dallas' gut was in turmoil about turning off the road to wait. McCullen had better be right.

The DigiSpace building was now visible in the distance. Halides illuminated the parking lot, and a few lights were on inside the building. Long and low, the single-story business was tucked into a clearing of Douglas firs. Two cars were in the parking lot, so she had to assume people were in the building, despite the early hour. They could be a janitor crew and needed protection.

Dallas slowed and looked for a place to wait. She spotted a rise in the terrain off to the right. A home was perched at the top of the hill, but halfway up was a flat spot, a parking area. She took the driveway, cruising up to the gravel turnout, then backed in so she'd be facing Randall as he came down the road.

Engine off, she tucked her phone in her pocket, grabbed the rifle, and climbed from the car. The house at the top had no lights on, and she was grateful. The last thing she needed was a gun-toting homeowner coming down to give her shit for being on his property.

Tapping her earpiece, she called McCullen. "I'm in place. Do you have eyes on the suspect?"

"I think so. There's a vehicle in the distance moving fast. It's only a mile or so from Kenzie Road."

"Let me know if it turns." Dallas took several long slow breaths, then prepped as best as she could. She opened the barrel of the rifle and checked for rounds. Fully loaded. She noted the wind—a gentle breeze from the north. She wished she had her own weapon, but at least this one had a scope. Without a tripod or adequate lighting, this wasn't ideal sniper work, but she would do her best. She reached in her pocket for her lucky cloth, held it to her nose, and inhaled deeply. A quiet calm settled over her. She could do this.

"He's turning!" McCullen's voice rang in her ear.

Dallas brought the rifle up and sighted on a fixed spot on the road. If Randall came in slow, like he was going to park, she'd wait for him to get out of the truck. If he came in fast like a suicidal nut trying to ram the building, she would stop him before he reached the spot. She would put her first shot into his head if she could. After that, she'd aim for the tires to slow down or derail the vehicle. Her right hand ached, her head still hurt, and she worried she would miss.

She heard the truck engine roaring toward her and brought up the rifle. Dallas emptied her mind and relaxed her shoulders, as ready as she could be under the circumstances.

An engine started across the road in someone's yard, a faint sound she barely heard over the roar of the truck bearing down. Across the way, headlights came on and eased toward the road. *Shit! Stay out of the way,* she silently pleaded.

The oncoming truck gained speed. Randall wasn't

slowing down to park and get out. Dallas put her eye to the scope.

The neighbor's car slammed to a stop just as the blue truck screamed past. Randall's face came into her sight.

Dallas pulled the trigger.

The blast shattered the night, followed by the quick sound of breaking glass. The truck slowed slightly as Dallas took aim at the front tire. She fired again. And missed the tire, hearing the bullet plink into the truck's metal body. She aimed at the back tire as the truck flew past , still traveling around sixty.

The popping sound was music to her ears. She took three more shots, blowing out the other back tire and putting two rounds through the back window of the truck's cab—in case Randall was still in control. The vehicle slowed and careened off the road, ramming into the four-foot building sign on the edge of the property. The impact slowed the truck down again, but it didn't stop until it rolled into a car in front of the building. Dallas braced for an explosion.

The dawn was silent.

She lowered the rifle and ran toward the collision. Randall might not be dead. She had to keep him from setting off his device, whatever it was. As she neared, she saw no movement from the truck. She heard McCullen's car roaring up the road behind her and heaved a sigh of relief.

Emma climbed from the passenger's side, her face dazed and bloody.

"Get away from the truck and on the ground!" Dallas had no cuffs and no way to detain her, but McCullen would be here in a moment.

She moved around to the driver's side, keeping her distance. They needed a bomb unit before anyone got near the vehicle. Randall was slumped over the wheel. She raised her rifle and peered through the scope. Her first bullet had hit its mark, and the bomber's face was demolished. She had to think of him that way and remind herself that she'd saved the people in the building.

But it wasn't time to celebrate. More bombers were headed to targets, and only Randall knew who and what they were. She needed his cell phone right now. Dallas sucked in a breath and jogged over to the truck. She gently pulled the driver's side open. The coppery scent of blood mingled with hot metal and radiator smells. She ignored Randall's body and visually searched for his cell phone. She spotted the briefcase on the seat beside him. The explosive?

McCullen's voice came from a hundred feet behind her. "Get away from the truck! It could blow."

She knew that. Randall had been on the phone right before he crashed. It had to be here somewhere. Yet it wasn't on the dashboard or floor. She reached between his legs and found the device. Dallas grabbed it and got the hell away.

McCullen ran to her and gave her a quick squeeze. "Good work, Dallas."

Pounding footsteps made them both look up. Emma sprinted toward the tree-covered hillside. McCullen sighed. "I have to arrest her for murder." He bolted after her.

Dallas shook off her surprise, found her last contact with Agent Gibson, and hit callback. "I have Randall Clayton's phone and I'm looking at his last text message. He sent a *go* message to nine people. Should I read you the numbers?"

Gibson hesitated. "I'll put you in contact with Special Agent Kerry Meyers in Sacramento. Give her the information directly. I'll text her and let her know to take your call."

Dallas waited to the count of sixty, hoping against odds

that they were not too late. She felt shell-shocked, as if she'd just missed being in a fatal accident. The lack of sleep hit her full-on too. She trembled as she made the call.

A woman picked up. "Special Agent Kerry Meyers."

"Agent Jamie Dallas. I have a list of the terrorists' phone numbers. Two of them are in Europe."

"Give them to me."

Dallas read through the list, speaking slowly. They had no room for error. If these were all cell phones, law enforcement would be able to pinpoint their locations and hopefully arrest the perps before they set off explosions.

The bombers had a ten- or fifteen-minute head start. Dallas worried that they were too late, but she'd done everything she could.

Chapter 41

Hakim Chehab glanced at the clock on his computer. On any other Saturday afternoon, he would be golfing or sipping tea with his lovely wife. Not today. He'd been on the phone for hours—with President Assad, the asset management company that had lost a hundred million of Syria's money, and briefly with President Rohani of Iran. On this afternoon, he found himself in the stressful position of brokering talks that could escalate into a war with Israel.

In theory, they all wanted it. The Jews had no place in their region, and their destruction would honor Allah and allow the Palestinians to go home. Yet, they all dreaded the conflict. The United States would back Israel, and the Muslim casualties would be horrendous. He didn't want those deaths on his conscience. In his heart, he believed they could conquer their age-old enemy. In his head, he wasn't nearly as sure.

His cell phone rang, and he glanced at the ID. The name was blocked but the call came from America. Curious he answered. "Greetings. I am Hakim Chehab, minister of foreign affairs. I hope you are well this evening."

"This is John Altman, U.S. Secretary of State. Thank you for taking my call."

Why was the American diplomat calling him? Bashar was not giving up his leadership and would not succumb to outside pressure. "You are welcome. How can I assist you?"

"You can stop making plans for war with Israel." Altman gave him a moment to process the information, then added, "Whatever Syrian money has been taken or is unaccounted for is the work of a hacker. The Israeli government was not involved."

Relief, then anger threatened his composure. Hakim prayed for guidance. "How do I trust this? You're Israel's ally."

"We have the hacker in custody, and we're certain. We also have experts trying to locate the money. I'm happy to speak to President Assad in person, if he wishes."

"I will pass the information along. Thank you for your call."

For a moment, Hakim weighed his choices. If he kept this to himself, they had an opportunity to wage war with their enemy and reunite Syrians. Yet he remembered his initial relief at the news. He would call his cousin and tell him that Israel was not the thief. This would be the president's decision.

Chapter 42

Sunday, May 12, 8:52 a.m.

Dallas took a seat in the conference room at the Redding bureau. Gibson was already at the table, and McCullen sat down as she did. She'd stayed at his place the night before—after a long day of debriefings and interrogations—and they'd driven in together that morning. As much as she would have enjoyed a sexual romp with him, it hadn't happened. They had both been exhausted. And McCullen had been depressed about arresting his ex-girlfriend and learning her fingerprint matched a murder weapon. Not to mention discovering she was a sociopath.

"Good morning." Gibson pushed a box of pastries toward her. "I owe you a nice breakfast, but this is the best I could do on short notice. The Washington bureau is going to call in a few minutes."

Dallas thanked him, took a small muffin to be polite, and sipped her coffee. Still drained, she looked forward to napping on the plane later that afternoon. She needed some time off, but the Redding/Shasta area no longer appealed to her. She was thinking about a trip to Flagstaff after she checked in with her boss in Phoenix. Or maybe Maui. She hadn't taken a real vacation in years.

"Your work on this case was commendable," Gibson added.

"Thank you." She disagreed, but she was smart enough never to argue with praise. "Have you heard any updates?"

"I questioned Emma Clayton last night about Tamara Slaney's death, and she claims it was self-defense. She wants us to drop the charges in exchange for her testimony against Spencer Clayton." Gibson glanced at McCullen, who sadly shook his head.

Dallas nearly choked on her disgust. She couldn't believe she'd risked her life to save a scheming self-centered killer. She felt sorry for McCullen, who'd wasted years pining for Emma. "At least Spencer Clayton had the decency to let me go and tell me about the situation in the Middle East." *Why was she defending him?* "But I hope he goes to prison. Did the tech people recover anything from his damaged computers?"

Gibson nodded. "They did indeed. He sent millions of fraudulent FDIC emails over a period of twenty-four hours. The DOJ is threatening him with treason charges as well. He'll probably take a plea deal for financial crimes to avoid the treason trial."

"Did he trigger a run on cash machines?" Dallas wanted to know. As of late the night before, they hadn't heard an update, but the main effect of the financial trigger wouldn't have happened until Monday morning, so the FDIC had all day to send out corrective emails and run public announcements.

"I haven't heard." Gibson didn't look worried either.

The conference phone in the center of the table rang and grabbed their attention.

Gibson clicked a button, and a voice said, "This is Robert Palmer, director of the FBI."

Gibson looked startled, then cleared his throat and introduced himself. "Thanks for calling, sir." Gibson finally lost his grumpy look. He introduced Dallas and McCullen, then leaned back in his chair. "We hope you have good news for us."

"I do. But first, let me congratulate all of you for the excellent work you did. You prevented hundreds of deaths from potential explosions and saved the economy millions of lost dollars. You're all in line for promotions and a presidential award."

Dallas was pleased she'd get a raise, but she planned to stick to undercover work. She was impatient to know the outcome. "Did any of the bombs go off?"

"A network exchange site in Reston, Virginia experienced an explosion, but only two people were in the building, and they only suffered minor injuries. Internet service in the region was disabled for thousands, but it'll be repaired soon. With the help of the British MI6, we were able to intercept all the others before they reached their targets." Palmer excused himself for a moment.

In the short break, Dallas met McCullen's eyes and smiled. He'd done a great job with both cases, and she hated seeing him so down.

The FBI director came back on. "I also wanted to tell you that we have seven of the perpetrators in custody. One was killed in an attempt to stop him, and the one female bomber is still at large. But we know who she is, and we will find her."

Dallas felt relief—and her first real sense of accomplishment. "What about Middle East diplomatic relations? Did we manage to avert a war?"

Palmer paused. "My understanding is that the situation is stable, but talks are still going on with Iran."

"What about the money?" Dallas didn't know the full extent of what Raff had done.

"Some has been recovered, but millions are still missing. The hacker hasn't spoken a word since we moved him from the hospital to a federal detention center."

"Why was he in the hospital?" McCullen asked.

Gibson cut in. "Spencer Clayton broke his hands so he couldn't do any more damage online."

The thought made her laugh. McCullen smiled too.

"That's all I can tell you," Palmer said. "And it's all the time I have too. Thanks again for your excellent service."

Later in the airport, Dallas checked her personal emails. Trevor had contacted her again, asking when he would see her. She started to delete it, then changed her mind. She'd been gone less than a week, she hadn't cheated on him, and he was a good guy. Maybe she'd invite him to visit Flagstaff with her and see how it went. She hit reply and texted: *I'll be home soon. Call me tomorrow and we'll have lunch.*

That would make her shrink happy… for a while.

L.J. Sellers is an award-winning journalist and the author of the bestselling **Detective Jackson mystery/thriller series:**

> The Sex Club
> Secrets to Die For
> Thrilled to Death
> Passions of the Dead
> Dying for Justice
> Liars, Cheaters & Thieves
> Rules of Crime
> Crimes of Memory
> Deadly Bonds

Agent Dallas novels:
> The Trigger
> The Target

Standalone thrillers:
> The Baby Thief
> The Gauntlet Assassin
> The Lethal Effect

When not plotting murders, L.J. enjoys performing standup comedy, cycling, social networking, and attending mystery conferences. She's also been known to jump out of airplanes.

Thanks for reading my novel. If you enjoyed it, please leave a review or rating online. Find out more about my work at ljsellers.com, where you can sign up to hear about new releases. —L.J.

Made in United States
Orlando, FL
21 August 2022